The Temptation of a Gentleman

(THE JORDANS BOOK 2)

Jess Michaels
writing as
Jenna Petersen

THE TEMPTATION OF A GENTLEMAN

(The Jordans Book 2)
Copyright © Jesse Petersen, 2011

ISBN-13: 978-1501004414
ISBN-10: 1501004417

All rights reserved. This book or any portion thereof may not be reproduced or used in any manner whatsoever without the express written permission of the publisher except for the use of brief quotations in a book review.

For more information, contact Jess Michaels
www.AuthorJessMichaels.com
PO Box 814, Cortaro, AZ 85652-0814

To contact the author:
Email: Jess@AuthorJessMichaels.com
Twitter www.twitter.com/JessMichaelsbks
Facebook: www.facebook.com/JessMichaelsBks

Jess Michaels raffles a FREE Kindle or Amazon gift certificate EVERY month to members of her newsletter, so sign up on her website:
http://www.authorjessmichaels.com/join-the-jess-michaels-newsletter/

If you have loved and accepted me, I thank you.

And most especially Michael, who loves and accepts me in every way.

CHAPTER ONE

London, 1815

"Get your mind out of the game and into the parlor, Woodbury," Noah Jordan admonished himself as he paced the sitting room of the Ives family.

He groaned. Impossible. He had been trying to focus on the impending arrival of the woman he was courting, but his errant thoughts continually drifted to the letter in his pocket.

He fingered the parchment restlessly before he took a seat near the fire, but he didn't need to withdraw the envelope to know each and every word that was written inside. They were imprinted on his brain. His former employer, Lord Golding wanted him back in the field. To play the spy just one last time.

It was an opportunity Noah had immediately grasped. After being removed from active duty one year before, he'd been increasingly consumed by ennui. Duty required he participate in the boring practices of the *ton*. One of which was finding a proper wife. Just the thought made him grimace. Courting was boring as hell. He shuttered to think what marriage would be like. Night after night with the same woman, only escaping to play a hand of cards or discreetly visit a mistress.

He groaned inwardly.

He forced his frown into an awkward smile when the door opened and Lady Charlotte Ives entered. As always, she was the epitome of grace and classic beauty. Every golden lock was in place and her gown matched the blue of her eyes to perfection.

Despite all that, she did very little to make his blood burn.

He rose to place a perfunctory kiss on her perfumed hand. "Good afternoon, Lady Charlotte."

"Good afternoon, Lord Woodbury," she replied as she took her place on the settee.

He flinched at the sound of his father's title coming from her lips. Despite the old man's death six months before, Woodbury still seemed to belong to him. Noah had always been more comfortable with the title Lockhart. But those carefree days were over. Now *he* was the Marquis of Woodbury and he had to behave, and marry, accordingly.

"I do hope there is nothing amiss with you." Charlotte's smooth voice jerked him from his musings. "When you asked to meet with me you seemed quite urgent. Is everything well with your family?"

"Yes." With a nod, he took the tea she offered him. "My family is quite well, thank you for asking. Audrey and her husband are here in London for the summer. My mother is still adjusting to life alone, but she has her charitable work in Woodbury. And Ginny and her husband are on their estate in Northern York."

Charlotte smiled at the quick recounting of Noah's ever changing family, though it seemed to him that her expression was a little less than interested.

"I'm pleased to hear they are all so well. But I still wonder about your need to meet with me today." She folded her hands in her lap.

"I wanted to inform you that I shall be leaving London for a short time. I have business to attend to in my shire."

She tilted her head but he couldn't read her expression.

"How long will you be gone, my lord?"

"Not very long. Perhaps a month." He leaned forward to stare into her eyes and hoped, not for the first time, that he would see something within their depths that captured him.

Nothing.

He leaned back with a small sigh. "When I return, I will be making an appointment with your father. Then I'd like to speak to you about a matter of great importance."

A blush tinged her pale cheeks pink. It was clear they both knew the subject of which he spoke.

"I look forward to that discussion then, my lord."

"As do I." He hoped he sounded sincere. This assignment would mark the end of his previous life. When he'd done his duty for Lord Golding he would settle into his life as Marquis. One that included a new wife.

He smiled and was surprised when she didn't return it, but instead seemed distant. "Is there something troubling you about my news?"

She snapped her gaze back to his immediately. "I have no right to question your decisions."

He arched an eyebrow. "But I value your opinion. Over the past few months I've come to rely on your counsel. Tell me what it is that worries you."

She stood and wrung her hands. "My lord, for the past few months you have courted me in every way that is proper and decent. And I have looked forward to your presence in the ballroom and in this drawing room. But…"

He frowned at her hesitation. Here Charlotte was about to say the only thing that had ever interested him and she paused. "But?"

"You do have a reputation, my lord, that is hard to ignore," she finished, almost apologetically. "And I wouldn't like to look the fool in front of my friends or Society."

His frown deepened. Of course Charlotte knew of his reputation, who didn't? He'd never made it any secret that he enjoyed the entertainments of London, from horses to drink to beautiful women. Enjoyments made more accessible by his life as a secret agent.

"I would never make you look a fool," he said. "Have I behaved in some way that has done so?"

"No, at least not yet. But I wonder if this trip to your shire is really a way to… to finish off your days as a rake and a bachelor."

He leaned back in surprise. He hadn't thought Charlotte would even have such observant thoughts in her pretty head, let alone dare to voice them.

"My dear Lady Charlotte…" Standing, he dared to lean over and touch her hand. "You believe I'm off to carouse in the country as a last-ditch celebration of my bachelorhood?"

She delicately pulled her hand away. "Perhaps. My lord, I am not as naïve as I may appear. I realize after you marry… whomever you marry… you will have your dalliances. But they will be private, not something that would shame your wife. But a public display when it is well-known you seek my attentions could lead to great embarrassment. And I do fear *that* is what you seek while you travel."

He smiled his reassurance. "I am going to Woodbury to take care of some business for a friend, a man who has helped me in more ways than I can ever repay. I assure you my visit is not to sow any wild oats."

At least not the kind she meant. Instead, he was sowing the wild oats of adventure. He could only hope one last turn as an unofficial spy would help him shake the desire for excitement from his blood so he could be a good Lord and Master to his estate and family.

"And what if I hear otherwise, my lord?" Her voice was suddenly very soft.

"You won't," he guaranteed. "My days as a rake are over, and my days as a respectable Marquis have begun."

She nodded slowly. "I hope that is so, my lord."

Then her directness faltered and she dipped her head to return to the subservient miss who he had courted over the past few months. "And now our allotted visit has passed. I wish you good fortune on your trip to Woodbury and a swift return to London."

"Charlotte, if you wish I could stay and we could talk more about this." Somehow he hoped she would say yes and perhaps hold his interest.

Instead, she crinkled her eyes as if confused by such a request. "And why would I wish such an improper thing?"

It was clear she truly didn't want him to remain. With a sigh, he bowed deeply and wished her a good day.

The moment he was back in his carriage and speeding toward his London estate, he dismissed Charlotte from his thoughts. Already his mind spun on the mission ahead of him. A simple one really.

One of his tenants had been married to a much younger woman who was the only daughter of an associate of the head of the War Department. The woman had died under strange circumstances, and her father wished to know if she'd been murdered. Though it wasn't a matter of national security, Lord Golding had taken an interest in helping his friend and called upon Noah. He was the natural choice of investigator. He could return to Woodbury and ask questions without raising suspicions.

As Noah swung down from the carriage and strode into his house to make the final preparations for his departure, the final wisps of concern over Charlotte Ives and the prison of marriage faded from his mind.

For now he was totally focused on solving a murder.

Marion Hawthorne shoved at the creaking carriage window with all her might.

"Open," she ordered with a groan as she cast a sidelong glance toward her father. He was buried in his paperwork and didn't seem to notice her struggle, let alone offer to help with the uncooperative window. Typical.

Finally it opened a crack and a thin stream of cool air blew into the stuffy vehicle. Marion swiped at her brow as she drew in long gulps. How she hated travel.

Why had her father dragged her along on his business to Woodbury? Usually he couldn't have cared less how she passed her time. She had given up being hurt by that fact a long time ago, and taken advantage of the freedom his lack of interest afforded her.

"There it is, my girl," he said across from her, as he set his papers to the side. He wiped some of the dust from the interior window with his shirtsleeve. "*There* is Josiah Lucas's home, Toppleton Square. Isn't it a beauty?"

Marion looked outside with a shrug. It didn't seem to be anything special to her, only a big house on a modest plot of land. Just like a hundred others they had passed in their recent travels. "It appears fine enough. Though I doubt if anyone cares what my opinion of his estate is."

Her father looked at her hard. "You should be more concerned with your betters and your equals, Marion." He turned his fat face away. "You never know where fate will lead you."

"Fate," she muttered under her breath. She was confident her father couldn't hear her. Not with his bad ear turned her way. "I'll make my own fate, thank you very much."

"What was that?"

"Nothing." She gave him a sweet and utterly false smile. "I was just saying how right you were."

He arched a disbelieving eyebrow. "You mind that willful tongue, my girl. Josiah Lucas is an important man, and I don't want you offending him."

"Then why did you bring me?" she asked, again just under her breath.

With a sigh, she turned to look out the window again. The house now loomed up before them. Her father's eyes lit up with anticipation… and what she was sure was a touch of fear. But the fear couldn't have been real. She had never known her father to be afraid of anyone before.

When the carriage stopped, he hardly waited for the footman to open the door. He didn't turn to aid his daughter, so she took the hand a servant offered and stepped down with a sigh of relief. She did hate a carriage.

As her father shifted his considerable weight from foot to foot in anticipation, the massive mahogany front door swung open. A man appeared in its shadow. Marion squinted in the afternoon sun to see him better, curious about this man who could agitate her father so.

When he stepped onto the wide, covered terrace, she was disappointed to see he was just an ordinary man. An older man, at that. At least her father's age, but probably a handful of years older. His dark eyes were hard to read from so far away, but they were most definitely focused on her rather than his business associate. It gave Marion a strange shiver and she adjusted her lacy shawl to better cover her arms.

"Mr. Hawthorne," Lucas said with a thin smile that didn't reach his eyes. "You have arrived at last. And I see you've brought the item we discussed."

"Yes." Her father's voice suddenly grew cold. "I brought it."

"Well, come inside out of the heat and we'll make a proper greeting." Lucas motioned them through the door.

To her surprise, Marion's father offered her his elbow. It had been years since he'd shown her anything that resembled civility. After a wary pause, she took his arm and they followed their host inside.

Mr. Lucas led them to a sitting room where tea was already laid out for them. The small party sat and a maid poured the fragrant brew.

"Now that we are comfortable, Mr. Hawthorne, do introduce me to your charming companion," Lucas said.

Marion shivered under the other man's scrutiny. At

closer proximity she could see his eyes were steely gray and at the moment very focused on her. His hard gaze made her uncomfortable, and she turned to look at a large painting above the mantelpiece. It was of a girl about her age. Marion wondered if this was their host's daughter and if the young lady still remained at home. Any company would be better than that she currently shared.

"This is my daughter, Marion Hawthorne," her father said. "Marion, this is Josiah Lucas, a… business associate of mine."

"I'm very pleased to meet you." Marion gave him the expected smile, then took another sip of her tea.

"As I am to meet you. I must say, Walter, if you had told me just how lovely your daughter was, I would have sent for you earlier." Lucas nodded in her direction as if she were to take the comment as a compliment. When she didn't smile at his pretty words, his nostrils flared a bit.

Her father's ruddy face darkened an even brighter red, but he said, "Thank you. She gets her looks from her mother."

Marion winced at the bitter way he said the word *mother*. Fourteen years after Ingrid Hawthorne's death, Marion's father continued to despise her, though he'd never given Marion a reason why.

"Well…" Her father seemed anxious to change the subject. "How are things in Woodbury, Josiah? I hear your new Marquis has not yet paid a visit to the shire."

Lucas's face fell. "No. The old Marquis has been dead and in the ground for six months now and yet the young man hasn't come to Woodbury to inspect the property nor visit the tenants or the villagers. Still, we may be happy for Noah Jordan's absence."

"Why is that?" Marion asked.

It wasn't that she was particularly interested, but she'd heard a malice in her host's voice that surprised her. Her natural curiosity made her wonder what would cause such strong emotions.

Mr. Lucas gave her another of those leering smiles. They practically dripped with lurid interest.

"Well, my dear, if you must know, our new Marquis has something of a reputation both in London and abroad. Seems he is good with racing and women of a certain type. Those men are seldom as talented with the running of an estate. We'll find out soon enough. He has sent word he will be arriving any day now."

"Perhaps we shall have the pleasure of meeting him," Marion's father chimed in. His face lit up at the thought of rubbing elbows with an important person in the *ton*.

"Perhaps." Lucas's face transformed to one of conceit. "After all, he is interested in touring the shire and making the acquaintance of the important people who reside here. What am I, if not a vital part of Woodbury's future? He's already sent a letter wishing to meet with me."

Marion stifled a yawn. Here she'd thought she was going to hear something interesting about the Marquis, something to pass her time thinking about while she spent a few dreary weeks in Woodbury. Instead all she'd learned was that the new Marquis was nothing more than a washed up rake that could most likely barely stay on a horse in his inebriated state.

How dull.

CHAPTER TWO

With the slight shift of his body, Noah urged his stallion faster. Phantom bounded over a hill and the rush of wind left Noah exhilarated and breathless. By the way the horse tossed his head, it seemed the animal felt the same. The old boy loved to run as much as his master.

"Adventure, Phantom," he murmured. "A last taste of it before we both settle down to stud."

The horse whinnied in disapproval, but continued on. Noah turned him sharply toward another hill where Phantom could leap to his heart's content. After they jumped a few more times over low hillocks and fences, a little lake appeared in the distance.

"I think you've earned a drink," Noah said as he slowed the animal and patted his neck. "So have I, but mine will be much stronger."

The horse trotted to the edge of the water and Noah swung off with a sigh. All adventure had to come to an end, he supposed.

He was almost to the lake's edge with the horse when he noticed the stump of a long-ago fallen tree a few feet away. On its flat surface a few items had been placed. He dropped Phantom's lead and stepped to the stump. Charcoal pencils and a sketch book. He picked up the book and turned it over. On the first page was a lovely sketch of the very lake where he stood. He turned the next and found another of a place he didn't recognize, with bluffs and the ocean rushing up wild on the rocks.

He was about to turn the next page when a woman's voice pierced through the quiet of the afternoon.

"You there, put that down this instant!"

Noah lowered the sketchbook and watched as a young woman came racing from the other side of the lake. She had the hem of a very pretty blue gown caught up in her hand and as she sprinted toward him, he caught a tantalizing glimpse of shapely ankle and a flash of stocking-clad calf.

She had almost reached him when she stumbled and tilted forward onto her knees on the ground. Noah moved to assist her, but she was on her feet again immediately, apparently unaware of her flushed face, locks of chestnut hair toppling around her shoulders and now-dirty skirt that flapped about her feet.

"Are you quite all right?" Noah called out, still too stunned to truly comprehend what was going on.

"Put that down this instant!" she repeated as she stormed up to him, past him and approached his horse.

Phantom was a big animal. Black as night and intimidating as hell. The girl did not seem impressed as she slapped him gently across the nose.

"Give it back!"

Noah rushed over to her and stared. "What in the world are you doing, young lady?"

She glared at him. "Are you daft as well as blind? Your horse is *eating* my pencils!"

Noah blinked as he turned toward Phantom. Indeed, the last remnants of a charcoal pencil clung to his fat lower lip. And there were no signs of the other three that had once sat on the tree trunk.

"Good Lord," he said as he caught the rein and backed the horse away from his chosen snack. Not that it would do any good now. The damage was most certainly done.

"And while we're at it," the young woman said and she reached out and snatched the sketch book from his arms. She clutched it against her chest. "I hope you didn't intend for this to be his second course."

Noah couldn't help it. He laughed. And to his surprise, the young woman's face relaxed a fraction.

"I do apologize Miss…?"

"Marion Hawthorne." She wiped a grass stain from her hand onto her dirty skirt and held it out to him. From the angle it was obvious she expected him to shake it.

Confused, Noah did so.

"Miss Hawthorne," he repeated. "I wasn't paying attention to my horse. Even if I had, I've never known him to snack on pencils, so I will be more careful in the future. My only excuse is that Phantom and I rarely get to run freely and perhaps we were both taken in by the rare experience. I shall certainly make amends for the loss of your pencils if you tell me where you live. I'm afraid I haven't visited this place for many a year now and don't know all the folk who reside here."

Miss Hawthorne's face became solemn as the outrage faded from her eyes. "I accept your apology since I know what it's like to be kept under tight rein. But I don't live here. My father and I are staying with Mr. Lucas at Toppleton Square a few miles away."

"With Mr. *Josiah* Lucas?" he asked in what he hoped was a nonchalant tone. Suddenly this chance meeting had turned into something much more.

Miss Hawthorne blinked once with what could only be described as a condescending smile. "Is there another Mr. Lucas and another Toppleton Square in Woodbury?"

Noah arched an eyebrow. Touché.

It had been a long time since he'd met someone who could match his wit, and a woman especially. The lass was a spitfire. Now that he'd had a good look at her, an extremely beautiful spitfire. Her skin was a warm peach color, her cheeks darkened by just a hint of pink from the exertion of her run.

The sun glistened off her chestnut hair, casting flashes of gold in the tangled locks when she turned her head at certain angles.

As if she sensed his appraising glance, she raised one slender hand to vainly push her locks to the right place. Immediately they fell back into disarray.

"Is there?" she repeated.

Noah shook his head, brought back to the present with her laughter-filled question. "Is there…?"

"Another Josiah Lucas in Woodbury?"

A half-smile tilted Noah's lips. "No, I believe there is only one. And if you'll allow me, Phantom and I will escort you back to Toppleton Square with our apologies yet again for the horse's bad behavior."

She eyed him with mistrust. "The horse I have no quarrel with."

She walked to Phantom's side. Immediately the old boy lifted his head from where he grazed and nuzzled her neck. She rubbed her hand along the entire length of the animal's nose and whispered, "Apology accepted, my fine boy."

With a nicker, Phantom edged a little closer. Not that Noah blamed him. If she touched *him* like that he might just fall under her spell, as well. Her delicate hands looked like they could hold a man captive for hours, playing along his skin as easily as they played a pianoforte.

Noah started. Was it not only a week before when he'd stood in Charlotte Ives' sitting room and told her he wouldn't play the rake during his time in Woodbury? And now he stood a few feet from a young woman he'd just met and already he was concocting ways to have a tumble with her.

Suddenly she turned away from the horse. "Yes, the animal I trust. But you, sir, have no name as of yet, and I have been told never to take walks with strangers."

He bowed low. "My apologies, Miss Hawthorne, I've forgotten my manners. I was surprised to find you here since this lake is little known in the shire. And I was also taken aback by the skill in your drawings."

She blinked. "You liked my work?"

He nodded. "Immensely. You are very good." She flushed and he shifted with a sudden discomfort. She was really very pretty. "Er, at any rate, my name is Noah Jordan, Earl of…" He shut his eyes with a quiet curse at his slip of the tongue. "My apologies, the Marquis of Woodbury."

Miss Hawthorne's eyes went wide and her mouth dropped open. "*You* are the Marquis?"

He couldn't help a grin at her utter shock. "You sound as though you've heard of me."

"Who hasn't?" she said with a laugh. "Even a visitor such as myself has heard about the escapades of the rakish Lord Woodbury."

His smile fell as did his spirits. In the end, it always came down to this. "Ah, my reputation."

For a moment, she only stared at him with her head cocked and little curls tumbling down one shoulder in a most tantalizing fashion. But even still, there was something serious about her expression. Like she was sizing him up and he was desperate to know what conclusion she had reached.

"Well…" She placed a fingertip on her chin as if in deep thought. "Do you promise not to molest me while you walk me home, my lord?"

He choked on his surprised laughter, but her question forced sudden, heated images to his mind that he had been fighting with desperation. Obviously this was a losing battle. He was destined to picture the lovely Marion Hawthorne in various states of undress and pleasure.

He swallowed. "I think I'll be able to manage in the two miles we'll walk together, yes."

"Then I suppose I'll allow you to escort me," she said with a playful curtsey. "As long as it's on your way."

"It is." He caught Phantom's reins in one hand and offered her his opposite arm. "In fact, I was off to visit your host when I came upon you."

"Hmm, that is one way to put it," she muttered, almost

as if she believed he couldn't hear her when she was standing less than a stone's throw from her side.

"What was that?" He tilted his head a fraction.

Her face darkened with embarrassed color. "Nothing."

Noah smiled. No, this young woman was not the usual country miss or city chit. She was entirely original. Unfortunately, that kind of sparkle had always drawn him like a moth to a flame, and usually to the very wrong kind of women. Now he felt that draw to play the rake. Perhaps Charlotte was right, perhaps he would never be able to settle down.

But then again, perhaps his attraction to the young woman had nothing to do with his ability to be faithful. After all, in just a few short weeks he could be tied to one woman forever. That idea would panic the best of men!

"You certainly don't fill the air with chatter, that's one thing I can say about you," Marion said. "In fact, you seem to have forgotten about me entirely."

"I doubt anyone could forget they were walking beside you." Noah cast her a sly smile. He'd never promised Charlotte he wouldn't flirt a little. What harm could there be in that?

To his surprise, she let out a soft burst of friendly laughter. "I suppose this is where I'm to break into titters of girlish glee? Normally, I would my lord, but if you'll forgive me I've had a rather trying morning."

A strange sting whooshed through him that his most dashing manners had no affect on the young woman at his side. In fact, she seemed to find them amusing! He couldn't remember a time when he hadn't been able to charm a lady.

Troubled, he decided to refocus on his case. Somehow in the rush of this encounter, he had all but forgotten that she was staying with a potential murderer.

"Your family must be old friends with Mr. Lucas." He tossed a sidelong glance in her direction.

She met his gaze. "And why would you assume that?"

"You are staying with him, so I thought..."

She smiled and her face glowed. The warmth in her expression made Noah want to smile in return.

"Mr. Lucas and my father have some kind of business together," she said. "But up until a week ago I'd never even heard the man's name. Why Papa insisted on my accompanying him to Woodbury is beyond my comprehension."

Noah frowned again as his intuition pricked. "You don't normally come with your father on business?"

She laughed but the sound was surprisingly bitter.

"No, Papa generally doesn't care what I do…" she trailed off with a frown. "That was an idiotic thing to say, Marion."

"Not idiotic, just honest," Noah said as they entered the last leg of their short walk.

"Honesty is not often valued in a young lady." Marion shrugged one slender shoulder. "And I shouldn't speak so freely in front of a person who I've just met."

Noah found himself wishing he *did* know her a bit better, that she trusted him to tell him more about her father or the reason behind the flash of sadness in her eyes. But there was no sense in desiring a closer relationship with the young lady… except to garner information for his investigation.

"Here we are." She nodded to the large house looming in the distance. "Toppleton Square."

Noah nodded as he looked around the estate. He vaguely remembered the place from his childhood. His father had attempted to teach him about his surroundings, but at the time those details had seemed boring and inconsequential. Any knowledge about the house certainly would have helped him now.

He shook off his regrets before they led to more thoughts of his late father.

"What kind of business is your father in?" he asked.

She kept her eyes focused on the house as she answered, "My father is invested in textiles in Northumberland.

In a little hamlet called Holyworth."

Noah wrinkled his brow. Josiah Lucas was heavily invested in coal. It made no sense why the two men would be in business together. Especially the kind of affiliation that would lead Hawthorne to drag his daughter to Woodbury. Their association must involve something outside of their normal trades. Now the trick was to find out how the two were linked and if it had anything to do with Georgina Ross's death.

They finally reached the road and passed through Josiah Lucas's gate just as the afternoon sun was covered by a cloud. Marion looked up at the sky with an accusatory scowl. "Looks like it will rain."

"It is England," Noah said. He'd been to places in the world where rain rarely fell, so when it did, he rather enjoyed it.

"I shall be trapped in the house all day," he heard Marion mutter under her breath before she approached the house. Before he could ask her about her statement, the front door flew open.

"Marion Hawthorne, where have you been?" the man at the top of the stair bellowed, his red face darkening even further. "Running off like that without a word for anyone. Could you be any more disgraceful to me or to your host?"

Marion stiffened at Noah's side, then she pulled away from his arm and took a step toward the man. Noah was hit by strange urge to pull her back to his side to protect her.

"Oh, Papa, I only went for a walk. I lost track of the time, but I cannot believe it warrants such…"

"You shut your mouth!" the man barked. "I will decide what warrants…"

"It's my fault, Mr. Hawthorne," Noah interjected, unwilling to let the irrational, cruel tirade continue. He stepped forward. "I met Miss Marion at the lake and my horse was not very well behaved. I'm afraid I forced her to keep me company on the walk back to Toppleton Square."

Hawthorne, who had been focused entirely on his

daughter, now looked at Noah with a glare. "And just who might *you* be, sir?"

Noah drew himself to his full height, taller than the other man by more than a head. "I am Noah Jordan, the Marquis of Woodbury."

The man's mouth fell open as if on a hinge and he stared at Noah with wide, unblinking eyes. Noah could have sworn Marion stifled a smile in her palm and a rush of giddy triumph filled him. He'd made her laugh, even after she had been publicly berated.

"My lord," the man finally stammered as he came down to the lowest step with a bow. "My apologies. I had no idea…"

Noah waved off the rest of the man's explanations. "I'm here to meet Mr. Lucas. Why don't we enter and I'll leave a card to ascertain if he'll receive me."

Marion's father nodded.

They entered the house and a harried butler approached. "Mr. Hawthorne, Miss Marion and…" he trailed off with a nod for Noah.

"The Marquis of Woodbury," Noah said with a bored smile as he held out his card, amused when the butler nearly tripped at the sound of his name. "To see Mr. Lucas."

The man bowed to Noah. "Yes, my lord. I shall see if my master is in at once."

"Do that."

"Marion," Hawthorne growled. She jumped just the tiniest bit at his sharp tone. "Go upstairs and make yourself respectable. You look like a ragamuffin!"

"Yes, Papa," she replied with a dutiful smile, though Noah saw that the expression covered embarrassment. She turned to him and her eyes softened. "It was a pleasure making your acquaintance, my lord."

Noah nodded, but found he wasn't overly anxious to see her go. "The pleasure was entirely mine."

"Good day." With that, she turned and hurried up the stairs with her father glowering at her the entire time.

Marion ran the brush through her hair one last time before she gathered her locks into a neat twist. Her father could have no quarrel with her looks now. She'd taken a bit of extra time cleaning herself up. Even a rake like the Marquis would have to appreciate her efforts.

"Now why would you think a thing like that?" she asked with a frown for her reflection.

But thoughts of Noah Jordan had been in the front of her mind since she'd left his side. With his stunning good looks and ability to make her laugh, the man was hard not to consider. Even her humiliation during her father's tirade had been eased when the Marquis set her father down just as handily. She grinned as she remembered Walter Hawthorne gaping like a fish when he realized Marion's savior had been the very handsome Marquis he so wished to impress.

A soft knock at her door interrupted her musings. Sally, the maid who had been helping her since her arrival, entered with a quick curtsey.

"Miss Marion, your presence is requested downstairs in the Blue Room."

"My presence? My father is asking for me?" It was hard to believe that. As always, he seemed anxious to be rid of her.

"No, miss. The Marquis himself is asking that you join them for tea."

Marion's heart leapt. *He* had asked for her! "I'll be right down, thank you."

Once the girl left, Marion took another long look at herself in the mirror. Ridiculous as it seemed, she wanted to make a good impression. But why? Since when did she care what some ill-reputed man so high above her rank thought of her?

Shaking her head because she had no answer to the question, Marion hurried from the room and down the stairs. At the door to the Blue Room she heard masculine voices talking from within. When Noah Jordan spoke, there was a flutter in her stomach.

Chiding herself for being silly, Marion pushed the door open and stepped inside. A man like Noah Jordan would never be someone she could care for. The idea was entirely impossible.

CHAPTER THREE

Noah anticipated Marion's appearance long before she slipped into the drawing room. And the smile she gave him when she finally did left an odd sensation in his chest. She was fresh, like a spring breeze. One that hadn't blown through his life in quite some time. If ever.

Noah noticed that Josiah Lucas followed his line of vision to the door. There was possessiveness on his face as he rose to his feet.

"Ah, Miss Marion," Josiah said. "How lovely you look, and how nice it is for you to join us in our tea. A lady's presence has been sorely missed in these halls since my wife passed."

Apprehension flickered across Marion's face. "I'm sorry, Mr. Lucas, I hadn't realized your wife had died. Your daughter must give you all the more comfort then."

Noah leaned forward, interested by the discussion. Whether Marion knew it or not, she was giving him details for his case.

Lucas's eyes narrowed. "My wife could not give me heirs, Miss Marion. I have no children."

"I beg your pardon." Marion's cheeks darkened with embarrassed heat. "I thought the portrait in your sitting room..."

"*That* was my wife." Lucas's voice was cold as he

motioned for her to sit down on the settee beside her father. As she did so, Noah noticed the two men exchanged a long look before they glanced at her in unison.

To his horror, Noah realized in a heartbeat what the truth behind their "business" was. Hawthorne was making a marriage arrangement between Josiah Lucas and his daughter. A shot of anger pulsed through Noah at the vile thought.

"Lord Woodbury?" Marion's voice forced him to look at her. He found it hard to meet her eyes now that he was aware of the deception she was being drawn into. "Your Phantom is a fine animal. Where did you acquire him?"

Noah told her the story of winning Phantom in a card game, but his heart wasn't in the tale. Instead he watched her every reaction, from her broad smile to her chuckles of pleasure when the horse was finally his. He was sickened that Lucas watched her, too.

Noah turned away. Marion's safety wasn't his concern or his reason to be here. Later he would try to warn her of her father's plot, but for now he had to focus on his assignment. On Lucas's late wife, not on who the man was picking to be the next Mrs. Lucas.

Their host stirred his tea slowly. "Lord Woodbury, I've heard you are about to make an offer of marriage to a young lady in London."

Noah snapped his gaze to Lucas. The older man held his gaze with a clear message. That Marion was his. Noah held back a curse. He was being careless. Instead of encouraging trust and comfort in the man he was hunting, his bold observance of Marion was putting Lucas on the attack. The comment about his pursuit of Charlotte was meant to put him in his place, as well as let Marion know that he was already spoken for.

It worked. Marion drew in a short breath and her gaze dropped away from his.

"I *have* been courting a young lady, yes." He tried to maintain a smile, but it was difficult when he thought of being tied for the rest of his life to a woman he didn't love.

Lucas smiled, but it was a clear challenge more than a friendly gesture. "More than just courting. My sources tell me she will soon be Lady Woodbury."

Noah shifted uncomfortably in his seat as color flooded Marion's cheeks. "That remains to be seen." He rose. "And now I fear I have stayed far longer than I intended. I must be returning to the Green."

He was surprised when Marion spoke next.

"The Green?" she asked as brown eyes came up slowly. But unlike before, they weren't open and inviting. Now that she knew he had found a potential bride, she had shut off a small part of herself.

"My estate, Linton Green. I would actually like to extend an invitation to all of you to visit me there. Perhaps we could have tea tomorrow afternoon since the weather looks to be turning foul." He stared at Marion evenly. "I wouldn't want any of you to be trapped in the house all day."

As he had hoped, her eyes went wide and her face filled with color and a smile. For some reason, Marion Hawthorne muttered to herself and now she knew he had not only heard the words she'd said on the stairway, but *listened* to them.

"A good plan," Josiah said with a nod.

"Splendid, I shall see you all tomorrow afternoon," Noah said as he moved for the door. Before he could bring himself to leave, he looked over his shoulder and allowed himself one last glance at Marion.

At temptation.

Marion attempted to appear interested in the conversation between her father and Lucas, but her mind kept turning on Noah Jordan. He had left a full half hour before, but still his image leapt to the forefront of her mind.

It was the epitome of foolishness. Now she knew Noah Jordan belonged to someone else. Some woman in London. No, a *lady* in London. Probably with breeding and style and grace. Not some merchant's unwanted daughter who spoke too often and laughed too freely.

Marion frowned. There was no reason for her to feel disappointment. The Marquis was a rake, so of course he had flirted with her, but any connection she had sensed between them wasn't real. By now he had probably forgotten all about her.

And so she had to try to forget about him.

"Marion!"

She jumped at her father's harsh bark, then shook away her thoughts and focused on the two men before her. "Yes, Papa. I'm sorry, I was woolgathering."

"Quite all right, my dear." It was Josiah Lucas who answered. His gray eyes slid over her and he inched closer. Even though he was sitting in a chair and she was perched on the edge of the settee, she struggled to keep herself from sliding away. "Perhaps you will share your thoughts with us."

She pursed her lips. Oh, yes. That would be wonderful. She could simply confess to her father and this stranger that she had been contemplating the deliciously handsome Marquis and how utterly out of her realm he was.

Instead she managed a smile and a more proper topic. "I was just thinking about how lovely your lands here are, Mr. Lucas. And how much I'm looking forward to exploring Toppleton Square and Woodbury during my stay."

That elicited a smile from both men and the beginnings of yet another mind-numbing discussion of rivers and hills and valleys. Marion stared into her tea cup as she blocked out her father and Lucas.

Yes, a man like Noah Jordan was not meant for her. But she intended to enjoy his company when she found herself in it. And if she allowed herself a little daydream about him from time to time, it could bring no harm to anyone.

Noah strummed his fingers along the desktop. Though it was only just teatime and his guests could hardly be called late, a restlessness he hadn't felt for years persisted. He welcomed it. It meant his head was in his case, not bored to tears by Society or expectations he wished he wasn't forced to make.

Sliding his hand across the desk, he placed it over the small box of charcoal pencils perched there. He had picked them up in the village to give to Marion as a replacement for the ones Phantom had destroyed. It was the perfect excuse to be alone with her for a moment. And to warn her about his fears for her safety and future.

He liked Marion's humor and couldn't deny a strong attraction to her. Hell, he felt more for her ten minutes after meeting her than he had in all the months he'd courted Charlotte.

The warmth inside him faded. That was unfair. He had made a vow to the woman he intended to marry, and he would keep it. There would be no dalliances during his time at Woodbury. No matter how appealing the prospect.

"My lord?" Basil York, the butler at Linton Green for as long as Noah could remember, stood in the hallway awaiting his master's orders.

"Yes, Basil?"

"Your guests have arrived. I put them in the West Salon as you asked and they await your appearance," he said with a proper bow.

"Thank you. I'm sure Mrs. York has prepared something sumptuous to go with tea." Noah watched with a grin as the old man's eyes lit up at the mention of his wife of thirty years.

"I'm sure she has, my lord," he answered with as close to a smile as the butler would allow himself before his master.

Noah had heard the man laugh many a time below stairs, but above he was the picture of calm and composure.

"Thank you, Basil."

With a pat on the other man's shoulder, Noah strode down the hallway. As he paused for a moment at the West Salon door, his heart pounded with excitement at this continuation of the chase. The chase of Lucas, of course. Marion had nothing to do with it.

With a deep breath, he pushed the door open and gave the guests within a welcoming smile. "Good afternoon, my friends. Thank you for braving this weather to join me here at Linton Green."

He wasn't surprised that Lucas answered him first. The man obviously saw himself as an important fellow. Overly important.

"Good afternoon, my lord. What an honor it is to be invited to your home. Will your mother be joining us for tea this afternoon?"

Noah stiffened as his thoughts turned to Tabitha. His mother was still deep in mourning for his late father, weighed down by days when she could do naught but cry. She claimed to feel better since his arrival, but he had seen no change in her melancholy to support that statement.

"My mother is still grieving," he explained with a sigh. "I have extended the invitation to her, of course, but receiving guests is still too much for her at this time."

He looked over to find Marion's eyes on him. "I'm so sorry for her loss, Lord Woodbury," she said softly.

"Thank you." He was struck by her sincerity. Though her words were the same as a dozen other well-wishers had used, none of them had ever seemed to feel the sentiment behind them so fully. "Perhaps you will meet her before you depart. I'm sure she would appreciate your sympathy, as well."

And he realized he meant the offer. Not only did he feel his mother would take comfort in Marion's genuine sympathy, somehow he wanted Tabitha to approve of her.

Folly. It was absolute folly. And if he wanted to solve his case, he would put it aside forever.

The tea was perfect. But how could it not be? *Everything* at Linton Green was perfect from the food to the efficient servants to their host. Noah's house felt like a home, despite its elegant exterior. It was a place where she could imagine a family laughing or children running through the hallways with wild abandon. Children with bright blue eyes.

"Miss Marion?"

She jumped at Noah's voice, embarrassed he'd interrupted her little fantasy.

"Marion!" her father spit out with venom. "Answer the Marquis! Don't just sit there as if you're daft, girl!"

Marion flinched. "Yes, my lord?"

"Yesterday your pencils were, er, *eaten*. Today I'd like to remedy that destruction. Would you accompany me to the library for a moment?" Noah turned to her father with a decidedly aristocratic glare. "If you have no objection, Mr. Hawthorne."

For a moment, Marion's father looked at Noah without answering, then glanced from at Josiah Lucas. Strange, it seemed to Marion he was trying to determine which of the men was a greater threat. She could have told him it was Noah he should try to please.

Finally, her father answered, "I don't see the harm. Though Marion wastes too much time on her silly sketches. If her pencils got ruined, I say all the better."

With effort, Marion held her tongue. Her father had never encouraged her to educate herself, and that only made her crave art and learning all the more.

"Hmm…" Noah pursed his lips with displeasure. "We shall only be a moment."

Marion rose, wondering why her hands shook just the slightest bit when she took the arm Noah offered her. As they left the room, she threw a glance over her shoulder and saw the anger in Josiah Lucas's eyes.

Refusing to allow the two men ruin this moment, she said, "You really do have a lovely home."

"Thank you. It was my father's pride and joy. I grew up here." Noah paused and his face turned solemn, just as it had earlier in the parlor. "And he died here."

Marion slowed her pace. "Yes, I can see you're still pained by that loss. I'm sorry to see that."

Noah looked at her sharply. "I beg your pardon?"

It was the first time he had taken that arrogant tone with her. The one that said he was a peer of the realm and not to forget it. She stopped walking, forcing him up short at her side.

"I'm only trying to tell you I understand. I lost my mother at a very young age. The loss of a parent is something you cannot help but carry with you. I'm sure you must still feel that heartbreak, just as your mother does. Only you can't show it because you're a man with responsibilities."

His face softened as he reached out to her, but his large hand stopped just short of touching her cheek. Her heart skipped to a faster beat as she felt the warmth radiating from his skin. Suddenly he drew back as if burned.

"You are a fascinating woman, Marion Hawthorne." He hardened his face as he took her arm again. "And here is the library."

She stepped away from him to look up at the tall bookshelves, brimming with books of all kinds and years. She spun in a small circle, craning her neck to see higher and higher up the endless shelves.

"Oh my," she breathed.

He didn't answer for a moment and she tore her gaze away to find him staring at her with a strange expression. One that made a thread of heat curl low in her belly.

Finally, he cleared his throat. "I see you approve."

She shoved away her body's strange reactions and nodded vigorously. "Approve? I'm envious to my very core! It's magnificent. I could lose myself here with no trouble."

Suddenly she had a very clear image of herself curled up in the window seat with a book, very much at home here because it was her home. The image was troubling and completely inappropriate.

He laughed and the sound warmed her. "I often think that, but I always find my way out."

He crossed to a small table and picked up a small box of pencils. "And *these* belong to you." He held it out to her. "With my most sincere apologies. And Phantom's."

Her eyes grew wide at his offering. The weren't the inexpensive ones she'd lost. They were of the highest quality. "Oh no, these are too much. I couldn't take them."

"I insist."

She looked with greedy eyes at the pencils. Things like books and supplies were a luxury she had to fight to afford and keep in her father's strict home. These were a treasure, and not just for their finery. What she drew with them would forever be linked to Noah and the stolen moments she had found here in his home.

"I thank you," she said as she took the box with trembling hands.

"You are very welcome." His smile fell and his voice grew more serious. "Now there was something else I wished to speak to you about and our time grows short."

Marion wrinkled her brow. He seemed so grave. "And what is that?"

He shifted as though he were uncomfortable. "It's about your father."

She thought of her father's embarrassing scene in the salon a few moments before. How she hated it when he berated her in public, and in front of Noah especially. "What about him?"

"Has he ever encouraged you to marry?"

She drew back at his unexpected question. "No. In fact, he's kept me from the marriage market. I am two and twenty and I've never been allowed to have beaux."

"Why?"

She pursed her lips, unsure of what had spawned Noah's sudden interest, yet she found herself too tired to come up with her usual excuses for her father's behavior. "The shortest answer I can give is that he's punishing me for something my mother did. He seems to hate me for being a part of her."

Noah's face gentled. "I-I'm so sorry, Marion."

She started. He'd called her by her name, her given name without prefacing it with "Miss". He was the first man outside of her family who had ever done so.

"I've grown accustomed to it," she whispered. "But I'd rather not discuss it. It's a painful subject."

He leaned closer, but this time he didn't hesitate to touch her hand. His skin was warm and his fingers easily engulfed her own. "Of course. I only ask because I wonder if perhaps he's brought you here for a marriage arrangement."

Marion leaned away in surprise, but couldn't bear to draw her hand away from his. "I don't understand what you mean. With whom would my father make an arrangement? He could have easily done that in our own shire if that was his intent, rather than dragging me across the country to Woodbury."

He took a deep breath as if he wanted to ease her into a bit of unpleasantness. "What about Josiah Lucas? Surely you've noticed the way he looks at you."

That comment drew her up short. She'd be a fool not to mark Lucas's revolting interest. "Mr. Lucas lost his wife very recently. Perhaps he's just coming out of mourning."

Or so she hoped.

Noah snorted. "Somehow I doubt Mr. Lucas mourned his wife excessively."

She frowned. How and why had he come to that

conclusion? "Perhaps, but your hypothesis about me makes no sense. My father and I may not get along, but he wouldn't make a sudden arrangement without consulting me."

Noah looked down his nose at her. "Are you certain?"

No, she wasn't certain. But she couldn't accept that Noah was right. Her own father wouldn't wed her off without speaking to her first. Not to a man like Josiah Lucas. Why his very presence made her skin crawl.

"I won't force you to answer," Noah said when the silence had hung between them for a long moment. "Please know I mention this to you only as a warning so you may be prepared for what is about to come."

Marion nodded wordlessly. Of course, what good was a warning when she had no way of escape? She thought of her aunts. Her mother's sisters had kept up a secret correspondence with her for years, but could she reach them? And would her father follow her if she ran?

"Come." Noah's face was as anxious as her own as he took her arm. "We've have been alone too long."

Mechanically she slipped her hand into his elbow. For the first time she was too distracted to feel the spark that seemed to crackle between them whenever they touched. All she could think about was her father and what plans he might or might not have for her future. And as they walked down the hall, she also wondered how in the world she would get out of them if Noah were right.

She could only pray he was wrong.

CHAPTER FOUR

Marion hadn't believed... or *wanted* to believe when Noah told her that her father might be selling her into marriage. But since he'd said that shocking thing, she had begun to see more evidence that the Marquis was correct.

Meaningful glances between the men, cut off conversations and Josiah Lucas's constant attempts to seek her out for conversation all made her skin crawl.

Her stomach turned at the thought. And with the knowledge that there was nothing she could do to protect herself. Perhaps Noah might have some idea, but in the three days since the Marquis had brought her worst nightmares to reality, she hadn't seen him to ask him his opinion about the matter.

Tonight he was to join them at Toppleton Square for supper, but she feared it might be too late. That afternoon her father had sent her up to her room so he and Lucas could talk. About what, he refused to say, but she was afraid she already knew.

She let out a quiet curse to release her frustration. There were no choices left. She wouldn't do her father's bidding and simply wait while he sold her off to a man who made the tiny hairs on her neck raise with anxiety.

She pushed to her feet and left her chamber. Her hands shook as she slipped down the stairs toward Josiah Lucas's study where the two men were having sherry and talking before supper. Lamplight flowed under the door and through the slight crack where it hadn't been closed completely.

Marion contemplated her options. Eavesdropping on her father and his friend wasn't ladylike. In fact, she was sure her late mother wouldn't have approved in the least. Of course, Marion assumed her mother wouldn't have approved of this marriage arrangement either. Throwing her doubts to the wind, she leaned against the wall next to the door to listen.

"Mr. Lucas I've done all I can to repay my debts to you," her father said in a wavering, almost whining voice. "I've even given you a share in my holdings. What more do you want from me?"

Through the sliver of space in the doorway, she watched Josiah turn from the fire. "You know what I want. You knew before you even came here. After all, you brought your daughter to my estate, didn't you?"

Marion clenched her fists at her sides. If there had been any doubt before this moment, it was gone.

Her father blustered for a moment. "I brought Marion as you asked, but I thought we could negotiate like reasonable men!"

Lucas laughed. "I believe I'm being more than reasonable, Mr. Hawthorne. You give me your daughter's hand in marriage, and I think that will be more than enough to correct the majority of the debt you owe me."

There was a long pause that filled the Marion with ominous premonition. Yet she couldn't turn away. She had to stay and hear her father hear the words.

"You would erase all the debt?" Walter Hawthorne's voice was less certain.

Marion's curled her hand until her fingernails bit into the wooden doorframe. "Please, Papa don't sell me like this," she begged under her breath.

"The *majority*," Lucas corrected. "And I would be very generous in the terms of the remainder's repayment. But…"

33

"But?"

"I'll need proof Marion can provide me with heirs to my fortune, my land and my business. I'm not getting any younger."

Her father gasped. "Marion is a healthy, young woman. I'm sure…"

Lucas rose with an angry grunt. "My late wife, Georgina was also healthy and young. Younger, even, than Marion when we married. And she did nothing but complain about her lot in life and avoid my touch whenever possible. Her womb was barren. Youth and health aren't always indicators of a woman's cold soul. This time I'll need evidence."

Marion eyes stole to the picture of the pretty girl above Josiah's head. She must have gone through so much, only to die so young. And now Marion seemed to be steered to a similar fate.

Her father's shaky reply returned her attention to the men. "And how would I provide you proof of my daughter's fertility?"

Lucas let out a low, sinister laugh and Marion's heart sank. "I must be allowed my husbandly rights before our marriage. If she becomes with child within three months, I'll wed her."

Even Walter Hawthorne balked at this. "You would have her before you have taken vows with her?" She heard him swallow hard. "No."

A surge of unfamiliar gratitude toward her father flowed through her. Noah was wrong, even Walter didn't have the greed to barter her in such a callous way.

Her father continued, "If she doesn't bear you a child, then she will be a worthless commodity to me. She'll be ruined and I'll have no chance to make a valuable match with her in the future."

Marion's gratitude faded.

Lucas's voice was smug. "Of course I realize that, Walter. And I would be fair. I'd still reduce your debt by half as my appreciation for her... services. And my repayment plan will be generous. You have nothing to lose and everything to gain by my plan."

Sickened, Marion's hands began to shake. She prayed her father would turn the offer down. That he would forget whatever animosity he had toward her mother and remember she was his child.

"Yes," his replied quietly.

She lurched back as her heart broke. Once again he'd let her down. And all for money.

"Good." Through the crack in the door, she saw Lucas poor her father a drink. "After Lord Woodbury departs tonight, you will bring Marion to my quarters and our bargain will begin."

"No," her father said hastily. For a brief moment, Marion hoped he'd changed his mind. "My daughter is willful and will fight like a cat if you spring this 'courtship' on her so suddenly. Give me a few months and I can convince her..."

"If your daughter is willful, perhaps she needs a firmer, less loving hand than the one you've bestowed."

Hawthorne snorted. "Trust I've been the best disciplinarian I could be. But I still think she'll be more willing in a few months."

Lucas hesitated, as if pondering the wisdom of waiting to bed her. "I can see how a few weeks of coaxing might make the conquest all the easier. I will give you *one* month to convince her, but no more. If she still doesn't come willingly, I'll take her to my bed by whatever means necessary."

"One month," her father repeated under his breath. "I'll do my best."

"Very good. Lord Woodbury should be arriving at any moment. I'll ring for a maid to fetch Marion. I'd like to see your convincing begin as soon as possible."

Marion turned to run up the stairs, but with every step, tears blurred her vision and her heart ached with disappointment. Now what in the world was she to do?

When Marion entered the dining room with her brown eyes cast to the floor and her skin a sickly pale, Noah knew something had happened. But there was no way to ask what had transpired without drawing unwanted attention to their tenuous friendship.

"Good evening," he said.

She met his eyes with a weak smile. "My lord." Turning to the other men, her smile fell and her voice became more brittle. "Father, Mr. Lucas."

"Are you well, my dear?" Lucas stepped forward to hold out a hand. She sidestepped his touch and took a seat without his aid. "You seem weary."

Her eyes went very cold. "It's been a long few weeks, Mr. Lucas, between the travel and being in a strange bed."

Noah frowned. "I'm sorry to hear that. I hope being able to sketch has helped."

Her smile finally seemed genuine. "Very much so, and I thank you again for your kindness."

How he wanted to take her aside and ask what had happened. If he could, he would have, but Josiah Lucas watched the two of them with just the slightest hint of jealousy. Alienating the man who was his target didn't seem wise. Not if he intended to complete the mission he'd been sent here to do. Which wasn't to save Marion.

However, when the starched butler came in to announce supper, Noah didn't hesitate to take Marion's arm. Her father and Lucas went ahead and he quickly whispered, "What happened?"

She gave him a fleeting glance. "Not now, it's too complicated. Meet me later."

"Where?" he whispered, but she left his side and took the seat the footman offered her before she could answer. By her exasperated expression, she, too, was frustrated by their inability to communicate further.

When the food arrived, Marion forced herself to eat, though everything tasted like sawdust. All she could think of was her father's promise to Josiah Lucas. In just four short weeks she would be made to share a bed with Lucas, and probably a life if that joining produced a child. The thought was repulsive.

Her gaze stole to Noah. He was talking to her father about some member of Parliament's latest financial scandal. Noah Jordan was a rake, a man who had made the pursuit of women a life's mission. Surely *he* could help her think of some way out of the situation she currently found herself in.

A plan began to form in her mind as she looked even closer. Yes, he was exactly the kind of man who would take pleasure in the challenge of a virtuous woman like herself. The kind of man who expected to flirt and woo a woman, then discard her. Ruin her.

Noah glanced down the table and was surprised that Marion's expression had lightened considerably. In fact, she looked positively pleased with herself as she stared at him. His stomach lurched that she would look at him like that. As if she believed he held the key to her welfare.

What could be further from the truth. As much as he wanted to help her, he had to concentrate on Josiah Lucas. Already, Marion was proving to be too much of a distraction to him. Even now he had to force himself to turn away and listen to Lucas.

"Well, it was a wonderful meal," Walter Hawthorne said as he set his napkin to the side of his plate with a satisfied sigh. "We're lucky to be able to partake in such a sumptuous feast, aren't we, Marion?"

She stiffened at the comment, her brown eyes narrowing slightly. Noah could see contempt in every inch of her.

"Thank you, Mr. Lucas, for your hospitality. Unfortunately, my head troubles me a bit tonight. I hope you gentlemen will excuse me if I go up to my room and rest my eyes," she said in a voice devoid of the emotions so clear in her eyes.

Lucas took in a short breath through his teeth, an almost imperceptible noise, but Noah heard it.

"Of course, Miss Marion," their host said with a tight smile. "Go with my hope that you'll feel better in the morning."

Marion bobbed out a quick curtsey to the group and a hard look at Noah before she slipped from the room. It left him wondering even more what had happened in the span of a few short days that she would so desperately want his help... seemingly *need* his help. And why being needed by Marion Hawthorne was such a pleasant prospect.

"Psst!"

Noah turned on his heel to look around the dark hallway.

"Lord Woodbury!"

Marion peeked her head around the corner of the doorway a bit further. He nodded when their eyes met and she skittered away from the door so she wouldn't be seen. The room was dark except for the one candle she'd dared to light. Sheets covered the furniture and the fireplace was long cold and unused. Though the servants didn't seem to pay much attention to the neglected sitting room, she couldn't take any chances.

"I'm glad I found you." Noah's voice was low as he shut the door noiselessly behind him. "I've been looking for quite some time."

She nodded. "I'm sorry about that. I tried to hide in a place where I'd see you leaving the library after you shared port with my father and Mr. Lucas, but where I wouldn't be caught. This room was the only option."

Noah looked around them. "How long have you been here?"

"For over an hour," she confessed, stretching her neck and massaging the tight muscles behind it.

Standing with her head cocked around the doorway was most uncomfortable. To her surprise, Noah mumbled something that sounded like "drive a man mad", then turned away to walk to the fireplace. The candle that flickered restlessly on the small escritoire by the window barely illuminated his face.

"My apologies, Marion," he said. "I tried to break away sooner, but Lucas and your father seem to enjoy the sounds of their own voices immensely. Then I had to sneak back inside after I *finally* managed to say my farewells."

Despite her worries, Marion giggled at the observation. Noah was very much right. Her father had never known the virtue of a quiet moment, and since she'd arrived at Toppleton Square she had been haunted by the grating tones of Josiah Lucas's voice.

Noah turned from the window to look at her with a cocked eyebrow. "But I'm sure you didn't ask me to find you to discuss your father's talkative ways, did you?"

Her mouth suddenly dry, Marion reached behind her to grip the covered back of a high chair. "No."

He stepped a bit closer with a curious tilt of his head. "Then why did you ask me to meet you in private?"

Her thoughts raced. What right did she have to drag this man... this near-stranger, into her humiliating problems? Then again, he was her only hope. Part of her desperately wanted to trust Noah Jordan, to believe he could help her out of the situation her father had cast her into.

She glanced down at the carpet with unseeing eyes. "It's a bit awkward."

"We've become friends, haven't we, Marion?" Noah asked, his voice husky in the darkness.

"As much as two people could be in such a short time." She didn't dare to look into his blue eyes for fear he'd see her tremble. "I consider you a friend."

He cleared his throat as if uncomfortable, then continued, "Then tell me what's happened as you might tell any friend."

She finally dared to look up and found him staring at her. He seemed to be closer, though she hadn't heard him move. His bright eyes shown in the dim candlelight. They held her captive as if he'd woven a spell around her.

Taking a deep breath, she blurted out. "I want you to ruin me."

CHAPTER FIVE

Noah nearly choked at her blunt request. He staggered back. "What?"

Marion's face flamed red as her hand came up to cover her mouth. The very same mouth he'd been contemplating kissing just a few moments before. God's teeth, now she was offering him the chance to do that and much, much more. His treacherous body grew heavy with just the thought.

"I'm sorry." With a little sob, she turned away from him. "I didn't mean to blurt it out like that. I should explain."

She took several long breaths before peeking over her shoulder at him. The distress on her face softened his heart.

"Go ahead," he encouraged her gently.

"Not ruin me exactly," she said. "I only want my father and Josiah Lucas to *believe* you've taken my virtue."

Noah didn't like where this discussion was going at all. "Why?"

She hesitated and her gaze fluttered downward.

"You know why."

He let out a low growl. So, his accusation had been correct. Somehow he'd hoped he was wrong about Walter Hawthorne, that the man wouldn't go through with such a distasteful arrangement without his daughter's consent. But Noah's instincts were almost always correct, they had been honed by years of spying.

Damn her father. What kind of man would submit his own child to the lecherous attentions of an old man?

"Marion."

She shook her head, though she didn't move away from him as he reached for her. Though it was entirely inappropriate, he wanted to comfort her, to feel her warm skin against his own and her pulse beat through her veins.

"You were right about my father." Her voice barely squeaked past her throat. "He's arranging for a marriage between Josiah Lucas and me."

As she lifted her stinging eyes to Noah's kind face, Marion briefly considered telling him the whole truth. Including the part about Josiah wanting to 'taste' her before they were wed. She took a breath to do so when Noah touched her hand. Electricity seemed to crackle between them.

No, she couldn't confess the most humiliating part of her father's scheme. She couldn't look into Noah's beautiful eyes and tell him she was to be Josiah Lucas's whore before she was his wife. If she did, he'd never again look at her as he was at that moment.

"I can't marry him, Noah… Lord Woodbury."

He caught her upper arm with a gentle grip. "I want you to call me Noah."

With a shiver, Marion looked up at him, her brown eyes soft with unshed tears. He couldn't tell her how much he longed to hear her say his name again. How he wanted to throw propriety to the wind and have her call it out as he kissed her, touched her… ruined her in reality the way she asked him to ruin her for show.

"Why don't you want to marry Josiah Lucas?"

"How can you ask me that?" she gasped, her voice filled with indignation.

He smiled at her strong response. "Because I need to know you've thought this through, Miriam. Once you've been ruined, pretended or not, that act cannot be undone."

She nodded. "I could never marry him. The thought

makes me… sick. He's too old for me. And even if he weren't, I don't *like* him."

"But he has money."

"That's unimportant to me," she said, her tone just a touch haughty. He'd obviously hit upon a tender subject for her.

"People always say that, Marion, until they have none," he pointed out gently.

He wagered she'd never done without. Her fashionable wardrobe spoke volumes about that subject.

Her eyes narrowed. "So you won't help me?"

"I never said that." He stepped a bit closer. "It's a significant decision for us both."

She clenched one hand into a fist at her side. "I'm not a ninny, Noah! I know what I'm asking."

"Then tell me," he said. "Where will you go if I help you? Once you're ruined and you'll never be able to make a match, where will you run? Or do you think your father will happily allow you to live with him indefinitely?"

She opened and shut her mouth and her pale face answered his question. Noah shook his head.

"I won't leave you to a life on the street. I've seen too many good women whose lives and dreams were destroyed by men who took what you're offering me."

"I didn't think…" She took a step toward him. Now they were only a few feet apart. He could smell the soft peachy scent of her skin even from a distance. "I never thought you would care what happened to me… *after*."

That comment stung him more than he wanted to admit. "What kind of man do you think I am?"

"A rake," she whispered.

Noah winced. She had him there. He was a rake. He'd taken immense pleasure in many women without giving much thought to their future. But he had never, not in England nor on the continent, taken a woman's innocence. He'd never condemned a woman to a life on the streets or in shame.

"Perhaps I am," he said with a sigh of regret. "But I'm not a monster. I've seen what kind of consequences your request can bring. So I need to know that you'll be taken care of if I do as you ask."

She swallowed hard. "What I'm about to tell you, you must never tell my father."

He let out a harsh laugh. "As if I'd run to your father with anything that transpires between us!"

"Of course you wouldn't," Marion said, more to herself than to him. "I don't know why I worried."

He smiled and motioned to one of the dusty chairs. She nodded as he lifted the drop cloth away, sitting down as if she were weary.

"My father and mother didn't suit." She stared at her hands. "He is… well, you've met him, you know what he's like. Brash, loud, uncouth and often unkind. My mother, on the other hand…"

She paused with a soft smile that made Noah's chest clench. He wished he could keep that smile on her face always. He hated seeing her filled with fear. "Your mother?"

"Ingrid was her name," Marion sighed. "I know that and little else. She died when I was only eight years old. But what I remember of her was gentle, very kind. She feared my father, and he loathed her for all her best qualities. When she died, he didn't mourn for her."

"But you did," Noah said. "And still do."

Marion allowed herself a look at him. She hadn't spoken much about her mother to anyone, the subject was simply too painful. Yet Noah seemed to understand her heart.

"Very much." She nodded. "For a long while I was cut off completely from the life she'd lead, from the *person* she'd been. My father forbade her name to be spoken in his house, so I couldn't even garner any information from the servants. I had all but given up when I found a packet of letters in my father's office."

Noah smiled at the thought of Marion, the little girl spy,

searching her father's desk. "Quite the little snoop, were we?"

She laughed despite the pain in her eyes. "Yes. Finding information about her was my obsession and I'd stop at nothing to find out the truth. The letters were a boon to me, the first information I'd found about her in years."

"How long had you been looking?"

"A few years," she sighed. "I was fourteen when I found the correspondence. The letters were from my mother's sisters. They were addressed to me mostly, though a few begged my father to allow me contact with them. I stole them from their hiding place and devoured them all in a two-day period, then put them back so he wouldn't miss them."

Noah looked at her again. He was just beginning to understand what a lonely existence this lovely young woman had experienced. All the love in her life had faded with her mother's death, leaving behind an uncertain future guaranteed by the ugly man who she called father.

"What are their names?" he asked, hoping to keep her in whatever state of happiness the subject brought her.

She smiled. "Lavinia and Hester. Hester is the one who tells me the most about my Mama. Lavinia writes far less, but she's always very kind to me. They're unmarried and live in a little cottage by the sea that was provided for them in my Grandfather's will. He'd made his fortune in shipping, so they seem to live comfortably."

Noah barely resisted the urge to touch her cheek. "And why didn't your father allow you contact with these women?"

Again Marion's face grew sad. "He doesn't want me to have anything to do with my mother. He doesn't even know I correspond with my aunts. I enlisted our cook's help in getting the letters in and out. I'm fortunate to be able to communicate with them at all."

"But how will this provide for your future if I..." he paused as a quick picture of Marion across his bed flashed into his head. "If I do as you ask?"

"My aunts have told me many times that if I could

escape my father they would provide for me, but I've never been able to do so." She took a sidelong glance at Noah. "But if I were ruined he would have nothing to gain by keeping me with him. I could escape to my aunts and be free of his schemes."

"Are you sure he'd release you?" From the sound of her description, Marion's father might keep her just out of spite.

"He would be so angry if I was ruined." Her voice grew soft and her eyes lit up with just a twinge of fear. "I would ruin all his plans, but I think he'd be more than pleased to send me away. The idea of me rotting away on the streets would probably appeal to him."

Noah gritted his teeth. He was going to have to work very hard at making Walter Hawthorne's life hell after Marion was safely away from him.

"Why hasn't he tried to make a match for you earlier?" he asked. "After all, you're very beautiful. I'm sure other men have been interested in your hand."

Marion blushed. This man who had probably been with a hundred far more lovely women called *her* beautiful. Suddenly she wished he would touch her hand again, or that she was brave enough to take his.

She gave a shake of her head to clear her foggy mind. "I'm not certain why he hasn't made a match with me before. He's never encouraged me to court. In fact, he's always discouraged it. I believe he liked having a free servant and hostess. But I know why he's selling me now."

"Why?" Noah leaned forward as if this piece of information was very important to him.

"When I overheard him making his… *arrangement* with Mr. Lucas, they said it would settle a debt."

Noah nodded. "I thought as much. Cads."

He said the damnation with such heat that Marion jumped. The man with the flashing blue eyes and dangerous look wasn't the same one who'd teased her as they walked through the rolling hills of Woodbury. He seemed much darker now.

"Will you help me?" she asked.

He shook his head as if he'd forgotten her existence for a brief moment. "I'm not certain." He looked her up and down as if sizing her up. "What would *I* gain from this arrangement?"

Noah could name several benefits from pretending to ruin Marion. At least he'd get a few kisses from the deal, and that should have been enough. But there was something more. The chance to free her was just as powerful a draw as any physical one.

She blinked at him, stunned. "I don't understand."

"I mean, if I'm to help you, I would expect repayment in some way." He smiled. "You said it yourself, I'm a rake. I'm not a respectable man."

Her surprise turned to humor as she realized he was teasing her. "Isn't helping a lady enough repayment?"

Noah paused. Looking at Marion with her dark eyes focused on him, her slender hands resting so close to his own and smelling her intoxicating fragrance, he could almost believe helping a lady would be more than enough. But his promise to Lord Golding gave him pause. If he thwarted Josiah Lucas's plans, Noah would certainly lose any chance he had of proving whether or not Georgina Ross had been murdered.

Then he thought of the vow he'd made to Charlotte Ives, and his pause became greater. He'd sworn he wouldn't behave in a way that would embarrass her once she was his Marchioness. And publicly ruining an innocent... a very beautiful innocent... even if it weren't real, would certainly embarrass Charlotte. He was torn.

But perhaps there was a way.

"I'll have to consider it," he said.

Her face fell. "But I thought..."

"I just don't know, Marion. You don't know what you're asking of me." With a frown, he rose to his feet. "Give me a day or two to think it over and I'll return to you with my answer." He couldn't bear to look at her disappointed face. "Goodnight."

"Ye-Yes. Goodnight, my lord."

Marion watched him go, trying to hold back tears of disappointment until he was gone. She'd been so certain Noah would be her salvation, but he'd suddenly turned much colder, as if she'd asked him to do something that tried on his soul.

But Noah was a rogue, well known for his behavior with women. How could pretending to ruin her harm him in any way? Unless…

Her mind flitted back to Lucas's mention of Noah's fiancée in London. Noah seemed loath to talk about the young woman. Perhaps *she* was the reason he couldn't pretend to ruin her. Perhaps his days as a rake were over now that he'd found love.

Choking back a sob, Marion hurried back to her room. She could only hope the friendship she'd forged with Noah over the short time she'd known him would be enough for him to help her. If not, she was on her own and her chances for escape were very small indeed.

CHAPTER SIX

Noah paced his office like a tiger in a cage. The ice in the tumbler in his hand tinkled against the crystal as he spun on his heel. Since the previous night when Marion asked for his help, he'd been unable to think of anything but her. Yet he couldn't do as she asked, or at least, not without a great deal of consideration.

Consideration he'd been unable to achieve while she stood only a few feet away. Her presence made rational thought completely impossible. He needed time alone to reflect on what she'd asked.

But a night of brooding left him with no new solutions. He had no idea how to assist her, yet still stay true to his case and keep his vow to his future bride.

Well, he had *one* idea, but it was dangerous.

While Marion had told her story about finding her aunt's letters, a vision of her as a little girl spy had made him smile. Now it made him think. She was quick-witted and graceful, two qualities essential to a good spy. His own sister had demonstrated both, and Audrey had been a successful agent for the crown. Could Marion do the same?

If so, she might help him find the evidence he needed to prove Lucas was a killer. Instead of ruining her, Noah could free her from her father's debts by arresting the man who held them. And even if it turned out Lucas was innocent of murder,

Noah could easily buy Marion's freedom. He was sure Walter Hawthorne could be persuaded to let his daughter go. For the right price.

Neither option would require Noah to 'spoil' her publicly, He wouldn't have to kiss her or touch her to make their deception look real. Because if he started down that path with Marion, he wouldn't want to go back.

Working alongside her would be difficult enough. They would have to meet in secret to exchange information and were bound to get into confined situations. But being pressed up against Marion Hawthorne in order to solve a murder wasn't the same as humiliating Charlotte with some country tart.

Was it?

"Noah, there you are."

He turned to find his mother at his door. Normally Tabitha Jordan kept to herself during the day, tending to her gardens or her charitable works. She didn't often seek out Noah's company, or anyone else's for that matter. Since his father's death, she'd been reclusive, though Noah told himself it was natural for her to mourn. He could do nothing to ease her pain while his own was still so great.

"Good afternoon, Mother," he said. "I didn't expect to see you until tea time."

She arched one dark eyebrow with a smile. "But my dear, it *is* tea time."

Noah flipped his pocket watch from his waistcoat. He hadn't realized the hour had grown so late. "By God, Mother, you're right. I'm sorry you were forced to seek me out."

He offered her his arm and led her to that salon where their tea would be served. It was the same room where he'd shared tea with Marion, her father and Lucas a few days before. Marion had sat across from him, her eyes sparkling with mirth when he said something amusing…

"You seem distracted, Noah," his mother said as she smoothed her skirts and motioned for the maid to pour their tea. "Is anything wrong?"

He forced his focus back to his mother. "No, I'm sorry. I was just thinking about my tea with Mr. Lucas a few days ago."

Her cheeks darkened with distress. "Yes, I'm so sorry I couldn't make it down. The idea of facing a group of strangers was a bit overwhelming that afternoon."

With a sad smile, Noah touched her hand. "I realize this is still difficult for you, Mama."

She nodded. "I don't know why. I did plenty of things without your father's presence while he was alive. I hosted teas and ran charity guilds. But now that he's gone, doing anything without him seems…"

"Wrong?" Noah finished for her.

She nodded as their eyes met in sad understanding. "Wrong."

"I'm sorry you feel that way. I know he'd want you to continue with the things that give you pleasure," he said, thinking about what his father would want for *him*. To fill his shoes, and Noah was doing his damndest to try. Whether or not he was a success was another issue.

"Perhaps in time that will get easier," his mother said with a sigh. Then she seemed to push aside her sadness. "It wasn't only Mr. Lucas who had tea here, was it?"

"No, a Mr. Walter Hawthorne and his daughter, Miss Marion, also attended. They aren't from Woodbury, but are visiting Mr. Lucas." He paused to appear indifferent. "Lucas has lived in the shire for over ten years hasn't he?"

His mother nodded as she sipped her tea. "Yes, since he took over Toppleton Square from Squire Green. The poor man lost everything in some kind of gambling problem. Why do you ask?"

"What kind of man do you take him to be?"

His mother knew most of the people who lived in his father's shire… *his* shire. He doubted she had any useful information, but something was better than nothing.

"I haven't had many occasions to talk with him

personally." His mother's voice grew cold. "But he's always been pleasant enough when I have."

Noah cocked an eyebrow at her tone. "Mother?"

"I don't like the man," she admitted. "He married that poor young woman, Georgina I believe her name was. The girl seemed miserable. She died not long ago."

Noah nodded. "So you don't think their marriage was a happy one?"

"No." Tabitha's answer was quick and firm. "Her parents made the match without any thought for her happiness. He was far too old for her."

He shivered. Marion would face a similar fate if he couldn't find a way to help her.

"Noah?"

He glanced up. "Hmm?"

His mother set her teacup down and leaned over to look at him. "Why are you *really* here in Woodbury?"

With a start, Noah stood. He hadn't realized his mother found his visit odd, though perhaps he should have. He hadn't come to Woodbury since his father's death. He'd certainly never asked in-depth questions about the inhabitants of the shire. It seemed sacrilegious, like he was dancing on his father's grave.

"I'm... I'm only here to take up the duties I've neglected for so long," he said. "It's time for me to behave responsibly, to take the mantle of the Marquis of Woodbury and put it around my neck." He had a sudden vision of a noose slowly strangling him and amended his statement. "Er, around my shoulders."

Tabitha folded her arms with an incredulous smirk. "Somehow I doubt that. Tell me, are you on a case?"

Noah coughed. "What are you talking about?"

Though he assumed his parents might have guessed about his duties in the War Department over the years, neither one had ever confronted him about the life he lead. It was a subject they all avoided, for both their sakes.

She folded her arms. "Don't pretend as if I don't know what you and Audrey were up to all those years. If you're here to catch some spy, at least I have a right-"

"No spies, Mother. I promise you that," he interrupted as he took her hands. "I'm here because I've neglected Woodbury too long. And you." He saw the lingering doubt in her eyes.

She pursed her lips. "If you're truly here to take up your duties, I'd be happy to arrange for a party in your honor. You'd have the opportunity to meet the country folk and local gentry, as well as do whatever *other* activities you're trying to keep from me."

Noah laughed at her saucy expression, but was touched by her offer. She loathed a crowd now, it troubled her to be surrounded by people without his father beside her. In life she hadn't depended on the man for support, but in death she longed for what she'd taken for granted. So did Noah.

"We could even invite the Ives family," his mother continued with a sidelong glance at him. "It's been some time since I saw Lady Charlotte."

The thought of Charlotte coming into his case and his home left him uneasy. The last person he wanted to see was the woman he planned to marry when Marion filled his every thought.

"No, no parties right now." He waved off her suggestion. "If you'd like to host a small event, perhaps we could have a picnic with a few selected families from the shire. There will be plenty of time for parties and balls later."

"Later when you make your offer for Charlotte?"

Noah stiffened at this second mention of his future bride. How he'd tried to keep her from his mind, her and his blasted promise. It was impossible.

"When I return to London at the end of the month I intend to speak with her father," he admitted.

Tabitha sighed. "Well, I'm pleased with your choice, of course. There's nothing unpleasant about the young woman.

But as I look into your eyes, I wonder if this is the right decision for you?"

"Why would you say that?" Noah's tone was sharper than he'd intended it to be. His mother's concerns were valid. Plus, there was that twinge of guilt he felt. He'd been trying his best to forget the other woman existed, let alone that he planned to marry her.

"Although I encouraged her to match for other reasons, Audrey found love. And she's never been so happy or content," his mother said. Her eyes grew sad when she continued, "But Ginny did as she was told and matched with a man who could bring her the security I thought was so important. She's miserable and blames us… *me* for her lot in life. I don't want another one of my children to make that same mistake."

Noah thought briefly of his youngest sister, Ginny. Before his father's death, his mother had been much more driven to marry her children to mates who would move them forward in Society. Ginny had obeyed, and now was truly miserable with a man who didn't love her.

"I'm certainly not Ginny. And I'm sure I'll grow to love Marion." He stopped in horror as he realized he'd said another name instead of his intended's.

"I mean, Charlotte," he corrected, but his mother's gaze was already honed in on him and there was a startled look on her face.

"Noah…"

"I'm sorry." He set his cup down. "I would love to continue this discussion, but I have something I must do before supper."

With that, he walked out on his mother. He heard her call his name one more time as he hurried down the hallway, but strode on. Once he'd reached the front door, he whistled for Phantom to be brought to him. As he rode off, he shook his head. He'd never left his mother like that before. It was wrong. But she said things that hit too close to the mark. Things about marriage. Love.

Love was something he didn't want to consider. It didn't fit into his carefully laid plans.

Marion tossed the book in her hand aside, letting out a soft curse as it hit the floor and skidded under a chair across the room. As interesting as the matchmaking attempts of *Emma* were, Marion could no more concentrate on them than she could a boring treatise on commerce in modern England. All she could manage to think about was Noah Jordan.

"Ridiculous girl," she chided herself softly. "As if a man like him would ever think twice about a no one like you."

"Beg your pardon, miss?"

Marion turned with a blush at being caught muttering to herself. "Nothing, Sally," she said to the girl at the door. "Was there something you needed?"

"There's a message for you, miss." Sally held out a silver tray with a note.

Marion barely resisted the urge to grab it greedily. "Thank you."

When the other woman was gone, she turned the letter over to look at it carefully. Her name was written in a bold hand across the face of the envelope and her heart began to beat faster. Noah, only Noah would send her a message.

She nearly tore the note in half as she opened it and threw herself into the nearest settee. As her eyes scanned the paper, she noted the strength that even his handwriting exuded.

Meet me in the rose garden, N.

She read it over once more. Her father and Lucas had gone out for a few hours, so she had time for a secret meeting. She thrilled at the adventure of that thought as she stuffed the note into the pocket of her pelisse. As she hurried into the foyer, Sally looked up.

"Is everything all right, miss?"

Marion turned back. She had to calm down or the whole house would suspect her! The smile on her face seemed false and stiff, but she said, "Oh yes, just going for a stroll in the garden."

"Very good, Miss Marion," the girl said with a tiny curtsey. "You just seem a bit flushed."

"It must be this humid heat." She waved her hand around in the air. "Perhaps I'll find some relief in the shade."

Sally nodded as she returned to her duties. "I hope so, miss. Have a nice walk."

Marion nodded, then turned and strolled casually to the door. Seemed she had much to learn about sneaking around. She didn't want the household to become suspicious of her activities and report them to Josiah Lucas or her father.

Once she was outside, Marion gave two quick glances around, then took off at a brisk walk toward the rose garden. Noah had chosen a spot that was close enough to the house that it seemed casual, yet private enough where they could talk.

When she finally reached the small area where tended roses bloomed in their last gasp of summer, Marion didn't see Noah. With a frown, she took a few more hurried steps through the bushes.

"You look as though you're trying to escape a fire, not meet a friend."

Marion spun around to find Noah sitting on one of the low benches in the middle of the garden. He was sprawled out with one foot pulled up on the bench. He held a red rose in his hand. As she took a step closer, he held it out to her.

"We'll have to work on the expression of panic on your face, as well," he teased as she took the flower with a blush.

"I'm sorry." Marion sat down on the bench, but left a respectable amount of distance between them. "I was just so happy to get your message. After you left yesterday, I wasn't certain you'd come back, at all."

A guilty look crossed his face. "I'm sorry to have worried you, Marion. You must understand your proposition surprised me. I needed some time to consider your request."

"And have you had enough time now?"

He nodded slowly. "I believe so."

She waited for him to continue, but he was silent. In frustration she asked, "Well, what was your decision? I don't think I can bear the tension any longer."

He let out his breath slowly and nodded. "You were very honest with me yesterday, Marion. You shared an embarrassing secret about your father and Mr. Lucas, and then a pleasant one about your aunts. I assume that means you have some level of trust in me."

Marion bit her lower lip as she thought of some of the details she'd left out when she'd told Noah about the marriage arrangement she so wanted to avoid. But that wasn't a matter of trust, that was a matter of avoiding complete humiliation.

"Do I take your silence to mean that you don't trust me?"

Marion shook her thoughts away. "Oh no, I *do*. I wouldn't have asked for your help if I didn't."

"Good." Relief swept over his face. "Then I feel I can trust you, as well. What I'm about to tell you is something very few people know. I need it to stay that way."

Marion's eyes widened. "I won't breathe a word."

"I'm afraid I've been misleading you." Noah held her gaze. "I'm not here in Woodbury for the reasons you believe me to be."

She was drawn in by the serious seductiveness of his tone and the gleam in his eyes. "Then why are you here?"

"Marion, I'm a spy for His Majesty's War Department. I'm here on a case."

CHAPTER SEVEN

Noah had been forced to tell people about his role in the government before. Most took the news with the seriousness afforded it. Marion tilted her head back with a peal of laughter.

"Marion."

He glanced around to make sure her outburst hadn't drawn unwanted attention to them. Had she become hysterical after the stress of the past few days?

"You know." With a sigh, she wiped away her tears of mirth. "If you don't want to help me, you only have to say no. You don't have to concoct some kind of silly story meant to impress and mislead me."

Noah opened and shut his mouth. Women cooed over him, they fawned over him… they did *not* laugh at him.

He stood up. "I-I'm not concocting a story. I've served the government for ten years."

She giggled.

"On dangerous missions," he insisted.

She nodded as she tried in vain to control her laughter. "I'm sure you have."

"I kept the Prince Regent from being assassinated not one year ago!" His voice went up two levels as his frustration grew. With a grimace, he checked the immediate area for listeners.

Marion looked at him with pinched lips and eyes full of

wonder, but didn't say anything for a moment.

"Well?" he snapped.

"I'm trying to decide if you're being serious or if you're simply daft." She folded her hands on her lap. "I no longer think you're lying, though."

"Well, thank God for that." With a grunt, he threw himself back into the seat. "I so enjoy being called crazy rather than a liar."

"I'm sorry, Noah," she said with a small smile for his sarcasm. "You must admit it's difficult to believe."

He frowned. It had never been difficult for the women he'd told before to believe. In fact, they'd been so impressed with the fact that many had fallen into his bed because of his status in the Department alone. But Marion wasn't like those women. Marion wasn't like anyone he'd ever known.

"I can see why it might be difficult for you to believe," he said through clenched teeth. "But I promise you, it's true. I can provide references if you wish."

When she looked closely at him, something in her face changed. "No. I believe you. I'd forgotten yesterday…"

"What about yesterday?"

"Yesterday there was a moment where you looked so dangerous." She shivered. "I can believe you're a spy when I think of how you appeared in that instant."

Noah's blood moved quicker through his veins at her words. There was something very sensual about her finding him dangerous. Something that made him want to prove just how dangerous he could be.

He cleared his throat. "A-at any rate, the reason I'm telling you this is because I need your help."

"*My* help?" Marion eyes widened. She'd been so focused on him telling her about his secrets that she'd almost forgotten how they related to her.

"Yes." Noah smiled as if he could read her thoughts. "I'm here in Woodbury not only to begin my duties as Marquis, but because I'm hunting a dangerous man, a man who may have committed a murder."

Now she again wondered if he was teasing her. "Are you trying to impress me by being vague?"

Noah opened and shut his mouth again, just as he had when she'd doubted the truth of his story a moment before. Really, it was almost too easy to make him speechless.

"No. I'm investigating Josiah Lucas."

The color drained from Marion's face and all the humor she'd felt faded with it. Noah thought Josiah Lucas was a killer and yet she was forced to share a home with the man. And perhaps a bed if she couldn't escape his advances soon.

"Whom do you believe he killed?" She fought to remain calm.

Noah's voice grew quiet. "His wife."

She closed her eyes to absorb the shock she felt hearing all this information. Shaking her head to clear her thoughts, she asked, "Aside from terrifying me, how does this relate to my quandary?"

"You must be frightened if you don't see the answer to that question," Noah said with a humorless laugh. "If Lucas goes to prison, the debts he holds over your father will be gone as if they never existed."

She nodded slowly. "I suppose that's true. But you said Lucas was only a possible suspect in Georgina's death. What if he's innocent? I would still be forced to marry him."

Noah sighed as if he were uncomfortable with what he was about to say. "If we cannot prove Lucas is a killer, then I'll do what you ask of me. I'll make it appear you've been ruined."

Marion covered her mouth with a little yelp of joy. "You'll help me?"

His eyes narrowed at her emotional outburst. "Yes. Don't worry, Marion. I'd never let you come to any harm."

She lowered her hand slowly and looked him up and down. "Yes, I know that. Somehow I know it."

His face darkened, and for a moment she thought she

saw a flicker of desire in his gaze. With a quick movement, he got up from the bench and turned away. His action broke the spell he'd held her in, and Marion remembered that by the end of the month Lucas would claim her body whether they were married or not.

"How long do you think this will take?" she asked.

He didn't look back at her. "Probably no more than a few weeks, why?"

She paused, weighing the benefits of telling Noah the whole truth about her father's agreement. But then, it seemed like the whole situation would be taken care of before she was forced to do anything unsavory. Why tell him if Lucas's bargain would never come to be? It was so humiliating.

"Father is planning on beginning our – *engagement* - at the end of the month, so my time is limited," she said.

"I see." Noah rubbed his chin. "If you're helping me, we should catch him before you're forced into something so vile."

Marion stood up and rung her hands in front of her. "I'm not sure I'll be very good at this. Perhaps I'll hinder you."

He shook his head. "I've had women as partners before, I'm sure you'll do wonderfully."

A pang of jealousy shot through her. Noah's former partners had probably been gorgeous, sophisticated women. After a long night of spying he probably returned to his rooms with them, repaying their efforts with kisses and…

She shook her head. The thoughts were making her angry.

"My sister Audrey and I solved many a crime in France," he continued with a reminiscent smile.

"Your sister?" Marion gasped. Powerful relief poured through her.

"Yes."

"But-but isn't she married? Isn't she respectable?"

Noah laughed. "She is both. She married Viscount Berenger last year and is one of the most respected ladies in all of London." His smile broadened. "She was also one of the best spies the Crown ever had the privilege to employ."

Marion shook her head in mute shock. What was there to say?

He sat back down next to her and touched the top of her hand. All her fears fled instantly at the gentle gesture, replaced by a strange warmth that curled in her belly.

"Marion, I'll help you. You won't be in danger." He brushed a few loose curls away from her face with the back of his hand. "Will you be my partner in exchange for your freedom?"

She shut her eyes and hoped that by breaking visual contact with him, she could form words. His touch certainly wasn't helping. Finally, after a few short breaths she managed, "Yes. What will I need to do?"

Noah stared at her before answering. It had been a long time since he'd wanted a woman so much. He couldn't help but remember what his mother had said about the lack of passion in convenient matches. He had no doubt a joining with Marion would be passionate.

"Noah?"

She opened her eyes and stared at him. He pulled his hand away to rake it through his hair. He had to focus, focus on the plan. Not on the way her stare heated him. Not on the way the tip of her tongue darted out to wet her lips.

"Uh," he stammered, hoping the proof of his desire wasn't as evident to her as it was to him. "You would obtain information about Georgina."

She nodded. "Yes."

"You'd keep your eyes open for anything you see or hear that could be incriminating," he continued. "And you'd become friendly with the servants to ascertain if they have any information involving Georgina's life here at Toppleton Square and her death. And you can help me get access into the house."

She frowned. "Is that all?"

He nodded. She didn't seem to be concerned by what

he was asking for, even though any one of those requests could put her in danger. If Josiah Lucas really had killed his wife, he wouldn't want his houseguest asking too many questions.

"I don't know if you fully comprehend what I'm asking you to do."

She shrugged. "But I do. And all those things should be fairly simple."

He arched a brow. "Are they?"

She nodded. "There are reminders of Georgina in all corners of the estate, from all those massive portraits Lucas has hung up everywhere, to the lady's sitting room we were in last night. I believe it may have been hers. If I asked about those things it wouldn't seem out of the ordinary, especially since my father is so desperately trying to get me to show an interest in Lucas. They hope I won't fight them when they announce their plans to me."

Her face twisted in disgust and horror at the thought of her upcoming nuptials to the older man. Noah again felt the urge to comfort her, but he used every ounce of strength in him to keep from doing so.

"What about the other tasks?" he asked. "They might be more difficult for you."

She glared at him with a snort of derision. "Very unlikely. I've always got my eyes open, Noah, so I'm sure to notice what you call 'incriminating items'. I'm already friendly with the young lady who tidies my quarters. And as for helping you obtain access to the house." She smiled. "You don't seem to have any trouble with that, but I'll leave my chamber window open if it would be of assistance."

She was teasing him, but the thought of climbing into her bedroom window gave Noah another jolt of awareness. The last thing he needed was a constant reminder that he had access to her bedchamber night and day.

"Yes, it might help." He edged closer to her. "But there may be one part to your plans you haven't truly prepared for."

Her eyes widened. "What's that?"

"If we're ultimately forced to pretend I've ruined you, will you be ready for that?" He raised his hand to wrap one loose strand of chestnut hair around his finger in slow, steady circles.

"I believe so," she said, but her voice was suddenly hoarse.

"Hmmm?" With his opposite hand, he gently cupped her chin. "Because even a false seduction must appear real."

"I think I'll be able to handle it," she whispered as she swallowed hard.

"Are you certain?"

With aching slowness he lowered his mouth toward hers. She lifted her face immediately and he brushed his lips against her mouth. At first he meant only to kiss her lightly then release her, but when she sighed and her hands came up to grip his elbows, he couldn't seem to control his reaction.

"Marion," he whispered against her lips, pulling her up flush to his chest. Her body molded naturally with his own.

She hesitated for just a moment. With timidity, she brought parted her lips a fraction. He flicked his tongue between them, testing the sweet softness of her lips before delving into the cavern of her mouth. She tasted like peaches as much as she smelled like them. It was a heady flavor and made him yearn to taste her skin, to explore her body until her scent filled him.

"Noah." Slowly, she wrapped her arms around his neck. He could feel her pulse pounding wildly through her veins.

What was left of his rational mind screamed at him to stop, to think of his promise to Charlotte or his duty to his country. But when Marion relaxed in his arms and began to return his kiss with as much fervor as he gave, those thoughts were dashed.

He ran his hands up her sides and gripped the nape of her neck. She stiffened at the boldness of his touch, but let out a gasp of pleasure when he deepened the kiss. How he wished he could press his skin against hers, but he certainly couldn't do that here in the garden where anyone could see.

Anyone could see.

Startled, Noah pulled back as his sensible side finally won the battle with his hungry body. He jumped off the bench as if on fire and took a few long steps away from Marion. She looked up at him with dazed, hurt eyes.

"I'm sorry. I shouldn't have done that."

Marion reached up to brush her lips with her fingertips, as if reliving their kiss. Noah's muscles tensed, but he didn't return to her side as he would have liked. At the moment, he couldn't trust himself to be so close to her.

"Wh-why?" She dropped her eyes to the grassy ground.

Noah groaned. How could explain all the reasons why he couldn't continue his seduction?

"Because if I'm not forced to ruin you, I won't."

"Oh."

Marion sat gathering her tangled thoughts for a moment. What a wanton she must be, for all she desired was for Noah to sit back down beside her and take her in his arms again. She stole a quick glance at him. If his scowl was any indication, that was the last thing he wanted.

Pinching her lips together into a determined line, she stood up. She wouldn't show him how embarrassed she was or how much she wanted his touch. Marion Hawthorne had some pride.

She straightened her hair and adjusted her dress as if what had occurred between them was an everyday event. "Where do we start with your plan?"

He looked out over the garden silently. She took the opportunity for a greedy glance at his broad shoulders and big hands. Hands that had just done things to her she'd only dared to dream about. Her father's refusal to let her out into the marriage market had convinced her she would never experience either love or a physical union. But then, that was before she met Noah.

"We should start by my leaving Toppleton Square right

now." He turned back to her. His eyes were dark as they moved over her body. At his quick perusal, blood rushed hot to Marion's face.

"Why?" she asked, suddenly desperate to have him stay.

He smoothed his crisp linen shirt with an uncomfortable shuffle of his feet. Marion realized she was throwing herself at him. Her actions obviously made the Marquis uncomfortable.

"I don't want Lucas to find me here and become suspicious. Feeding his jealousy too early might only result in him demanding to marry you sooner."

The blood drained from her face as she rose to her feet. "Do you think he would do that?"

Her mind spun horrible images of Josiah Lucas holding her the way Noah just had, touching her. It was all she could do not to let out a cry of dismay at the thought.

"Marion." Noah closed the gap he'd made between them earlier. He took her hand and raised her cold fingers to his heart. "I would never let anything happen to you. If I got even a hint you were in danger, I'd come for you."

She nodded slowly as she extracted her fingers from his hand before she couldn't help but throw herself into his arms.

"I believe you," she said as she turned away from him. She heard his quiet sigh behind her.

"Very well. I'll contact you in a few days with more information. Until then, be careful."

She nodded. "I'll try."

Standing silently for a moment, she contemplated if she should say something more. Perhaps she *should* tell him the whole truth about Lucas's plans for her, especially if he was promising to protect her.

"Noah…"

She turned, but to her surprise he was gone. He had slipped away in total silence, leaving her alone in the garden with only her thoughts and memories.

CHAPTER EIGHT

Marion took a quick glance up and down the hallway, but found it empty. With a grin, she slipped inside Josiah's study and tapped the door shut behind her. The past few days had afforded her little chance to search Toppleton Square for the evidence Noah had asked her to find. Her father and Lucas kept her busy with long card games, boring carriage rides, and unbearable picnics.

The time with the two men was tedious. It took all of her self-control to play the innocent while her father tried to convince her of Lucas's good points.

Their host, himself, was insufferable. He made overtures of friendship toward her even while his beady, gray eyes devoured her body whenever he thought she wasn't looking. She always was.

It motivated her all the more to find some evidence of Lucas's crimes and get out of Toppleton Square. Only Noah hadn't yet met with her to tell her what it was she *should* look for, except for his vague reference to something 'incriminating'.

"Some help he is," she muttered to herself.

Her muscles tensed as the image of him kissing her returned to her mind. She'd relived the moments they shared too many times to count. Each time she felt an equal mix of desire to kiss him again and guilt that she'd let things go so far to begin with. Noah was practically engaged. He wasn't someone she could ever have a future with.

With a shake of her head, Marion looked around the room for anything that might implicate Lucas in the death of his wife. The large portrait on the wall caught her attention as she paused before it.

The picture had obviously cost a good deal of money, for the quality was excellent. But more than that caught Marion's eye. The girl in the picture was so young.

"Just like me," she whispered as she rubbed her arms. The room suddenly felt cold.

But that was ridiculous. She looked nothing like Georgina Lucas. The other young woman was much taller and fuller-figured, with a sadness in her eyes that made Marion want to weep. Perhaps it was a life with Josiah Lucas that made the girl seem so forlorn.

"Miss Marion, what are you doing in my private office?"

Marion jumped straight up in the air with a little scream as she turned to find Josiah Lucas glowering at her from the door. At her outburst he smiled as if amused and came two steps into the room.

"Oh, you gave me a fright, Mr. Lucas. I was so focused on the painting I didn't hear you enter." She covered her heart in the hopes she could slow its wild beating.

"Very amusing," Lucas said. "But it doesn't answer my question. Why are you here? I thought you were reading in your chambers."

Marion gave him the friendliest smile she could muster. "Yes, I *was* reading. I was reading a very sad poem about youth taken too soon. It made me think about your poor late wife and I came downstairs to look at the painting."

Lucas frowned. "How did you know there was a painting of Georgina in this room? I don't think you've ever been here before."

Marion winced. Of course she had been eavesdropping

when she noticed the second portrait. Lucas didn't know she'd seen it. She grasped for a believable explanation.

"The door was open as I passed and I noticed it from the hallway. I was drawn in by how beautiful it was."

"Yes." He looked up at the portrait with distant eyes, as if recalling old memories. "The picture is lovely. But then, as you can see, my wife was a very beautiful woman. It would be difficult not to paint a flattering image of her."

Now that her heart wasn't fluttering with fear, Marion was becoming immersed in the game of cat and mouse. "I hope you don't mind talking about her."

Lucas shrugged one shoulder.

"What was she like?" She sidled a bit closer to her host.

His eyes darted over to her. "Why do you ask?"

"No particular reason." Marion accentuated her remark with a tilt of her head. "Only that she and I were close in age. It makes me wonder if we had anything else in common."

Lucas's eyes narrowed, but with a grunt he nodded. "Yes, I'm sure you did. Georgina was also from a family of wealth but not title. She was a little younger than you are when we married, just twenty."

"Hmm."

Marion wondered how he knew her age, but of course, her father would have told the older man. Just like a piece of stock at auction, she was sure her attributes had been discussed in detail from age to the health of her teeth. It made her so angry she wanted to swear.

Instead, she smiled in encouragement. The best way to keep her father and Lucas from taking what they wanted was to assist Noah.

Josiah stole another look at her from the corner of his eye. "Like you, she had dark hair and brown eyes. I was pleased to discover your coloring was similar to hers."

"Th-thank you, Mr. Lucas." With a demure glance down at her slippered feet, she broke their stare.

Until that moment she hadn't realized what a delicate

game she was playing. In order to help Noah, she had to make Lucas believe she was interested in him. In order to protect herself, she had to make sure he thought she was *disinterested* in him so he wouldn't force her father to give her to him earlier than planned. It was a thin tightrope she walked. One that could spill her over at any time.

"You're welcome, my dear." The older man smiled at her with gleaming eyes. "I must say again your presence here is most welcome. Since her death-" He glanced up at the picture with a forlorn glance Marion assumed was meant to gain her sympathy. "I've been so lonely."

"I can imagine." To put more distance between herself and Lucas, she stepped closer to the picture. "May I ask how your wife died?"

She glanced over her shoulder in enough time to see the small smile that passed over Lucas's face and the glimmer in his eyes at her question.

"It was an accident." His face returned to the mask of sorrow. "Georgina fell down the stone stairs in the foyer."

With a swallow of fear, Marion thought of the staircase. It was very high and the stairs had sharp edges.

"How terrible," she whispered as her hand stole up to her throat.

"Yes," Lucas said with a nod before he lifted his eyes back up to his late wife's painted image. "Terrible."

The flat, emotionless tone of his voice made Marion glance at him again. Was he so troubled by Georgina's passing that he was numb? Or maybe he just didn't care.

A question that plagued her more sent a shiver down her spine. Was the man before her capable of pushing his young wife to her death? Even though she didn't like him or his vile plans, she wasn't sure if he could have committed such an awful crime.

"We've spoken of the sadness of the past for far too long." Lucas's face cleared as if they'd been talking about something commonplace. "I'd much rather consider the future."

Marion blanched as his eyes moved over her. "Yes."

"I've just accepted an invitation from Lord Woodbury and the Dowager Marchioness Lady Woodbury to picnic on their estate tomorrow afternoon if the weather is pleasant."

"Oh, that sounds divine," she burst out as her whole attitude lightened.

Lucas pinched his lips together with displeasure at her immediate response. With a grimace, Marion inwardly cursed her too quick expression of pleasure.

"You know, my dear," Josiah said. "Lord Woodbury is practically engaged to a very respectable young lady who is the daughter of a *titled* gentleman in London."

"Yes." It took effort to keep the jealousy from her voice. "I've discussed Lady Charlotte with Lord Woodbury. It sounds like a good match for him and I wish them much happiness together."

Her mouth filled with the bitterness of her lie. She *did* want happiness for Noah, and if this Lady Charlotte brought it to him, she wished them joy. Still, the thought of Noah kissing the other woman set Marion's teeth on edge.

Lucas offered his arm. With hesitation she took it and allowed him to lead her to the hallway. He glanced at her.

"It does sound as though they make a perfect match. You never know when you'll find a perfect match, Miss Marion. You shouldn't limit your choices."

She took one last glance at the picture behind her as they left the room. The artist had painted the portrait so Georgina's eyes seemed to follow a person wherever they went. Now she wondered if the dead woman's eyes were pleading for her help.

"I expect you are right, Mr. Lucas," she said as she turned away from Georgina's painted gaze with a shudder. "You never know what the future will bring in life or in matters of the heart."

Noah nodded to one of his guests before he stepped away to lean over the terrace railing. Down below he saw the gilded gate of his estate open and Josiah Lucas's carriage roll inside. His heart pounded a bit faster at the sight of it. No matter how many times Noah tried to convince himself his excitement had to do with his duty alone, he acknowledged Marion had some part in it. He'd spent the past few days running over their encounter again and again in his mind. When had he last lost control like that with a woman?

Or had he ever?

"You seem distracted, Noah," his mother said as she came to stand beside him and lay a hand on his arm.

"No, Mother." He smiled down at her. "Only watching our last guests arrive."

Tabitha leaned over the rail with interest as the carriage door opened. Lucas and Hawthorne stepped out, then Lucas turned back to offer Marion assistance. Noah's pulse jumped as she appeared from the vehicle dressed in a pink gown with little sprigs of green throughout it. The color accentuated the peachy warmth of her skin and reminded him of her taste.

"Oh my, is that the famous Miss Marion?" his mother asked.

Noah winced. It was a reminder of his slip of the tongue before. "Yes, though I wouldn't call her famous. We've spoken of her twice, haven't we?"

He said a silent prayer that he appeared bored.

"Well, she's breathtaking." Tabitha patted his arm before she turned back to the small crowd behind them. He could see the trepidation in her eyes as she took in the group.

He put an arm around her small shoulders. "Does it trouble you to have so many visitors?"

She shook her head. "No. I'm sure I'll remember my talent as hostess. I'm only a bit rusty now."

The sadness in her voice cut Noah like a knife. He'd tried to convince her that she didn't have to trouble herself with the picnic, but she insisted that she play hostess at his side.

He would have said something more, but the veranda doors opened and Basil stepped into the doorway with a stiff bow. "Lords and Ladies, Mr. Josiah Lucas, Mr. Walter Hawthorne, Miss Marion Hawthorne."

"Well, introduce me then." His mother took his arm and led him over to the three latecomers.

"Ah, Lord Woodbury," Lucas said with a bow as they neared the small group. "And Lady Woodbury, how nice to see you about. We're so sorry we're a bit late."

Walter Hawthorne cast a greedy glance around him. "You know how a young gel can be. My Marion takes hours getting ready and slowed us considerably."

Marion's face darkened a shade as she muttered, "Wasn't me who took hours to get into his corsets."

Tabitha coughed at his side, though Noah couldn't be sure if his mother was covering a laugh. For his part, Noah concealed his smile with a bow for his guests.

"We're glad you're here. Now the festivities can truly begin. Let me present my mother to our new friends, as she's not yet acquainted with the Hawthornes.

"Mother, this is Mr. Walter Hawthorne, a business associate of Mr. Lucas's. And this is his daughter, Miss Marion." He motioned to his guests.

"Mr. Hawthorne," his mother said, disregarding Hawthorne with a sharp nod of her head. She stared at Marion for a short moment. "And Miss Marion, how nice it is to meet you. I've heard so much about you."

Marion blushed as she curtsied. "I thank you, Lady Woodbury. I've heard much about you as well, and I'm so happy to finally make your acquaintance."

Noah smiled as his mother's face opened up. She liked Marion, not that he would have expected less. His mother was an excellent judge of character. But somehow he felt relief the young woman had lived up to her scrutiny. He wanted Tabitha to like the lady he'd agreed to protect.

"Miss Marion, perhaps you'll take a turn around the terrace with me before we go down to the lawn for our picnic?" Tabitha tilted her head with a smile. "I'd be happy to introduce you to some of our other guests."

Marion nodded though she stole a quick glance toward Noah. She wanted to be alone with him and tell him everything she'd learned in her discussion with Lucas. But there was no way to refuse Lady Woodbury's kind offer. Especially when the woman in question seemed to *need* to introduce her. She'd caught a glimmer of fear in the older lady's eye and sympathized. For a woman like the Dowager Marchioness, life without her husband had to be an adjustment on many levels.

"Of course, my lady," she said. "I'd be pleased to meet your guests."

Noah smiled as Marion took his mother's arm and the two strolled away. The look she tossed him over her shoulder told him she'd rather be with him, but his mother would never guess that. And perhaps having a stranger to dote on would relieve Tabitha's own worries. Already she seemed more at ease, smoothly introducing Marion to a boring Earl and his ugly Countess.

"Lord Woodbury," Lucas said beside him, his tone as soft as a snake's.

Noah immediately turned his attention back to the men beside him with a smile. It was time to turn on the spy in him. "My apologies, gentlemen, for not being more attentive."

Lucas returned his smile, but the expression was thin and tight. "I'm sure you must be worried about your mother. After all, people have begun to talk since she's not been out in Society much in the months since your father's death."

The blood drained from Noah's face as he clenched his fists. How he hated the idea that his mother was the topic of any kind of gossip. Her mourning had been deep, but her love for his father was great. She only needed more time before she'd be back to her old self. No one, especially not a blackguard like Josiah Lucas, had the right to question her actions.

"If people talk then they obviously lack the intelligence to find a more interesting topic," Noah hissed, barely reining in his anger. The last thing he needed was to destroy his own investigation and perhaps put Marion's life in danger by losing control.

"Of course, *I* don't believe the rumors." Lucas placed a hand on his breast as he took a drink from one of the servers. "But it's difficult not to hear the whispers."

Walter Hawthorne looked from one man to the other nervously. If Noah hadn't been so angry, he would have found Hawthorne's predicament amusing. After all, he was indebted to Lucas, but obviously strove to impress Noah. Now that the two men were at odds, Hawthorne couldn't decide where his allegiance should lie.

Noah refused to stoop to Lucas's level by asking him what the rumors about Tabitha were. He already knew. Friends had told him some of the crueler members of the *ton* said his mother had lost her mind.

The echo of Tabitha's laughter floated over the crowd and he spun around to face her. He hadn't heard that sound for months, yet there she stood, laughing as Marion grinned and nodded her head. A surge of pleasure shot through him at the sight. Marion's presence was a good influence on his lonely mother.

"Lords and Ladies, you may proceed to the South lawn for sustenance when it pleases you," Basil said from the terrace as he motioned to the stairway with a short nod.

One by one, the guests trailed past Noah and meandered their way toward the South lawn for their picnic luncheon. Finally Marion and Tabitha reached the men.

"Mama." Noah took her hands and kissed both her cheeks. "Seeing you laugh is a gift."

Tabitha smiled. "Marion was telling me the most

amusing story of how her pencils were eaten by the horse of a perfectly *dreadful* man."

Noah glanced at Marion. Her brown eyes danced as their gazes met and she winked at him brazenly. The tiny gesture sent heat rushing to his loins and he shifted uncomfortably to cover the reaction.

Tabitha turned to Lucas and Hawthorne with a wide smile. "Will you gentlemen be so kind as to escort me?"

Lucas opened his mouth as if to protest as he shot a look toward Marion, but Tabitha had already taken his arm and was leading the two men down the stairway before his complaint was out of his mouth. For a brief moment Noah and Marion were alone.

"Your mother is an angel," Marion said as she watched the little group disappear around the terrace stair. "She adores you and your sisters."

Noah smiled as he offered her his arm. "Yes, sometimes to excess."

She laughed as they began to descend the staircase. "How is that possible?"

"She and my sister Audrey didn't always get along," Noah explained. "And my sister Ginny made a very bad match at my mother's urging. Mama blames herself for it."

Marion dipped her head. "I suppose I'd never considered there might be disadvantages to a mother who was so involved in a person's life."

Noah let out a curse under his breath. Here he was acting as if his mother's intrusions were inconvenient when Marion had never had the benefit. He'd been insensitive to her feelings about her mother's untimely death.

Marion blinked back unbidden tears. Why did spending time with Noah's mother make her think of her own so much? She should have become accustomed to the sting she felt, not allow it to wipe away any control she had over her emotions.

With a tiny shake of her head, she forced a smile to her lips. "I wonder if we might have a moment alone together later to talk about that matter we discussed?"

With a tilt of her head, she indicated Josiah Lucas and her father.

"Yes." He nodded. "That was already in my plans."

She smiled broadly. Wouldn't he be surprised when she told him she already had information from Lucas's own mouth?

"When?"

Noah smiled. "In half an hour the rest of the guests will be so involved in eating and gossiping they'll hardly notice if you slip away. I'll meet you in the library where I gave you the pencils. Do you remember where that is?"

Marion held back a laugh. She'd memorized all the rooms and passageways of Linton Green, at least all the ones she'd been in. The library had been particularly interesting to her. She closed her eyes and pictured it perfectly. Into the foyer, down the short hall to the left of the stairs, turn right…

"Marion?"

Her eyes flew open to find Noah staring at her with an amused smile on his face. His blue eyes sparkled.

With a blush she said, "I remember. And you'll meet me there?"

"That's my intention," he said as he released her arm to motion to the chair the footman held out.

As she sat, she looked around her in relief. The rest of the guests had already been served their first course and were eating and chatting around her. Marion was pleased her father and Lucas had been seated two chairs away from her, while Noah was directly across from her and his mother to her right.

Now that she knew he would meet her, Marion gave a happy sigh and quickly fell into conversation with Tabitha Jordan. Later she could surprise Noah with all she knew, later she could have a moment alone with him. Perhaps a moment when he would look at her in that way that made her knees go weak.

No one could begrudge her just that bit of stolen time.

CHAPTER NINE

Marion ran her finger across the spines of a line of books, inhaling the scent of their aged pages and devouring the beauty of their lettering. There was nothing she loved more than a library. After her mother died, her father had destroyed or given away all the books she owned. He'd turned her mother's library into a stuffy parlor where no one even bothered to have tea anymore. It had been a first of many crushing blows to Marion, losing the things her mother had loved.

She shook her head. Now wasn't the time for melancholy remembrances of the past, but preparations for the future. If only she could do what Noah asked of her she would be free of her father forever, free to travel to her aunts and live a life too wonderful to even fathom.

"Why does that feel so empty?" she whispered as she pressed her forehead against the books.

She should have felt joyful at the thought of escaping to the life she'd planned for so long. Instead, the idea of going to her aunts wasn't as thrilling as helping Noah or being near him.

The sound of a man clearing his throat jerked her from her scandalous thoughts. Marion spun around and found Noah leaning against the doorjamb, a crooked grin on his handsome face and his bright eyes sparkling.

"I knew you were enamored with my library before, but

I never thought I'd find you embracing my books." He entered the room with wink. "I may be a touch jealous."

Marion blushed as she backed away from the bookshelf. "My apologies, I was lost in thought."

"Apparently." Noah shut the door behind him and motioned to two chairs beside the fireplace. "Would you care to share with me what took you so far away from Linton Green?"

Marion shook her head. What was she to say, that she was dreaming of Noah's touch? She highly doubted the Marquis would appreciate that.

"A secretive lady is always so interesting," he said as she sat down. "But I won't intrude on your thoughts right now. We have very little time to talk and need to discuss our plans for Josiah Lucas."

Marion nodded with enthusiasm. "Yes, I have so much to tell you!"

He wrinkled his brow. "*You* have so much to tell *me*? I haven't even talked to you about the specifics of what to do yet."

"I know that, but I was getting so frustrated waiting the last few days. I want to find out whatever Lucas did to Georgina and move on with my life."

Noah leaned forward, his eyes flashing and his tone sharp with disapproval. "What did you do, Marion?"

She jumped. He seemed angry, not pleased that she'd begun prying into Lucas's life.

"I went into his study to look around for incriminating items," she began. Her excitement returned with the memory. "By the way, you should try to be more specific with a beginner. 'Incriminating items' is about as vague as you can get. At any rate, Lucas came in-"

Noah sprang to his feet. "What?"

He'd never been so furious in his life, not even with Audrey who loved to put herself in dangerous positions.

Marion looked up at him with bright, brown eyes. "I

said Lucas came in while I was looking around."

"He found you in his private quarters?" Noah snapped, trying to rein in his anger and worry.

She nodded as if the fact that she'd foolishly put her life in danger rather than wait for his instructions and protection was normal.

"I thought that was what you wanted." She stood up and her head barely reached his chin. "You told me to look for incriminating items, so I did."

"I didn't mean for you to burst into Josiah Lucas's office and put yourself in danger!" He ran a hand through his hair. "My God, Marion what were you thinking?"

He stared at her a moment, wondering if he was wise to allow her to participate in his investigation. The last thing he wanted was to put her in further danger. But it was too late. She already knew about his case and had waded knee-deep into it.

"What did he say? What did you say?"

She shrugged. "I told him I was reading a poem about-"

He threw his hands up in the air. "You talked to him about *poetry*?"

She pursed her lips as irritation lit up in her eyes. "If you'll allow me to finish, I'll explain exactly what I did. Then you can scream and bellow like a barbarian." With a frown, she crossed her arms and continued, "I simply told him I was reading a work about life taken too soon and it reminded me of his late wife. I explained that as I walked downstairs, I caught a glimpse of her portrait in the office and came in to look."

Noah stepped back. For a novice, Marion had come up with a fairly reasonable explanation. If he hadn't been so furious with her impulsive nature, he would have been impressed by her ingenuity. "And he accepted that?"

She shrugged. "He seemed to. He even talked to me about Georgina." Marion paused. "Why are you so angry? I thought you *wanted* my assistance in this matter. That was our bargain, was it not?"

"It was." With a sigh, he turned toward the picture window that looked down on the party below. "But I never wanted you to put yourself in danger."

She gave a humorless laugh. "Every moment I'm in that house I'm in danger." He turned in time to see a shiver wrack her body. "The only way I can protect myself is by helping you."

Noah frowned at the fear in her eyes. A forced marriage was certainly distasteful, but it was no reason for her to be so frightened, or worry she wouldn't be protected. Hadn't he already promised her that?

"In the future-" In one step, he closed a little of the gap between them. Her scent wafted over toward him and dulled his anger. "You'll depend on me for protection *and* instruction before you go running off and doing something so foolish like invading Lucas's office."

Her eyes narrowed as she brought her hands up to cover her hips. He followed their movement, wishing he could mimic their action with his own.

"Now wait just a moment, Noah Jordan," she said, completely oblivious to the lust she inspired in him. "You aren't talking to a child! I'm a grown person and if you trust me to be your partner, even for a short time, you must trust me to make my own decisions. Right now you're being as narrow-minded as my father."

Noah moved even closer. Now they almost touched. "See here, I'm *nothing* like a man who would sell you for his own foolish debts."

"No? He doesn't feel I'm capable of making my own decisions either," she retorted.

He pursed his lips. "You're not experienced enough in this field to do anything without some guidance."

"That is so pompous," she said with a sigh. "To think that because I don't have training, I somehow don't have instincts."

She began to turn away from him but he caught her arm

in one smooth motion and spun her back around to face him. "I know you have instincts, but I can't see you hurt. Do you understand?"

Marion gazed up into intense blue eyes that refused to set her free from their imprisoning gaze. Noah's warm, sensual scent enveloped her, and his hands felt like fire burning through the thin silk of her gown. She flashed back once more to his mouth on hers and instinctively wet her lips at the thought.

Noah let out a low groan and without warning, brought his mouth down to hers. Marion's surprise lasted only for a moment as the heat from his mouth washed away any other senses, any other thoughts, anything in her mind but him. For that moment, he was everything. And she gave in willingly, bringing her arms around his neck with a soft sigh.

This time Marion wasn't surprised when Noah's tongue caressed her lips. In fact, she opened hungrily to him, clutching at him harder when he delved inside her mouth to taste every hollow. Meanwhile, his hands crept to her waist and he tilted her against him until their bodies touched in the most scandalizing way.

Through the haze of desire, she noted Noah was guiding her backward across the room. He stopped when her back flattened against one of the high bookshelves. Now she felt the full length of him as he pressed against him. His broad, muscular chest touched hers, his hard stomach and hips molded to her quivering body and his muscular thighs, so well defined in his tight breeches, pressed against her most intimate place. Never had her body felt more alive, tingling at every nerve ending.

He moved his mouth to kiss the corner of her lips, then her cheek before moving down to skim along the curve of her throat. She tilted her head back with a soft sigh. Her hips lifted with the motion and she felt the hard thrust of Noah's erection against her thigh.

Her eyes flew open at the contact and she looked at

Noah's face through heavy lids. "I..."

He shook his head, though he continued to keep her wedged between his body and the bookshelf. "I'm sorry."

"Don't," she pleaded as she buried her face against his shoulder to place a light kiss just above his cravat. "Please don't say you're sorry."

With a grunt, Noah tilted her face back toward his and kissed her again. He simply couldn't control himself around this woman. He needed her. Despite the promises he'd made to Charlotte and the fact Marion was an innocent who he could plan no future with, he wanted to hold her in his arms and fill his senses with her scent and taste.

There was a bustle in the hallway and a burst of laughter through the door. Immediately he pulled away to leave Marion staring stunned at him.

"Servants," he explained when no one intruded on the awkward scene.

She dipped her head with a slow nod. "Yes."

"I'm sorry, Marion, I don't know why I got carried away."

Already, he longed to touch her cheek and brush away the stray curl that twisted against the satin of her lip. Of course he knew why he'd gotten carried away. Marion Hawthorne was beautiful, honest, light and he wanted her more than he'd wanted any other woman in he couldn't remember how long.

She sucked in her breath through her teeth. "I told you," she said, accentuating each word. "Don't apologize."

She pushed past him to halt before the fireplace. Staring at the flames, she didn't say anything for a long moment, then finally she whispered, "Do you want to know what he told me?"

"Who?" Noah answered. She had to know any thread of conversation they'd had previously was hopelessly lost in a haze of passion.

"Josiah Lucas."

With a shiver, she glanced over her shoulder. Quickly

she recounted their conversation. Noah answered her with nods and few non-committal grunts. Nothing she said was news to him, but the idea that Lucas had compared Marion to his dead wife was deeply troubling. If he saw her as some kind of replacement for Georgina that could mean he would repeat whatever patterns he'd played in his first marriage. Including murder.

"Is that all?"

"Yes." She kept her eyes down.

He winced, hating that he'd embarrassed her. This was exactly why he was so reticent about ruining her, even in name only. If a stolen kiss in private left Marion shaken, how would she survive a blight on her name that would follow her forever?

Of course, a false ruination wouldn't make him as hot as their stolen kiss had. And she'd responded, too. There was no doubt in Noah's mind Marion desired him and, gauging from her reaction, it terrified her.

He cleared his throat and snapped, "In the future I again ask you not to do any investigation without my instruction."

Her shoulders stiffened and her eyes came up with slow, angry purpose. "And what am I allowed to do then, my lord?"

He stifled a smile at the return of her spirit. "Why don't you start by asking a few discreet questions of the servants and see where that leads?"

She nodded. "And I can continue to probe Lucas when I have the chance."

Noah's heart leapt at the thought. "No, no, no. Didn't you hear what I just told you? Don't talk to Lucas about anything unless I'm in the room. Don't confront him at all. And above all else, don't go sneaking about his private rooms anymore. Do I make myself clear?"

She stared at him for a long moment. Her eyes flashed with emotion as she struggled to rein in control. Finally she ground out, "Perfectly. Now I'm going back to the party."

Marion turned and stalked toward the door. How she

would like to prove to Noah Jordan that she was more than some pawn in the game he played. She was intelligent and could be of better use than simply questioning the servants. Why just a few moments of conversation had opened Josiah Lucas to her. She could only imagine what more time and questions would reveal.

"Good, I'll be behind you in a moment," Noah said. "If we return together it will only spark questions."

"Fine." She pulled the door open. Muttering under her breath, she added, "I don't want to walk back with you anyway you overbearing lout."

"Marion!" Noah said, his voice heavy with surprise and laughter.

She turned back with a sweet smile on her face. "Yes, my lord?"

"I am standing right here! I can hear what you said perfectly well."

Marion stiffened. She straightened her back in defiance and nodded her head at Noah.

"Good," she said. "I wouldn't want you to think I was talking behind your back." With that she closed the door and strode down the hall, her ears tickled by the sound of Noah's belly laugh from behind her.

***

Marion slipped into her seat with a quick smile for Lady Woodbury. As she straightened her napkin on her lap, she noticed the other woman continued to look at her.

"Marion." Tabitha tilted her head as she glanced at her son's empty seat then back. "Is anything amiss?"

"Why?" Marion's heart beat faster. She'd been very careful to return with as little fuss as possible.

"You're a bit flushed."

Marion looked away. Oh dear, she was a bit too

obvious it seemed. The last thing she desired was for Lady Woodbury to know what a wanton she'd made of herself in the library. She enjoyed Noah's caresses. No, she craved them. When he pushed her aside, it had left her feeling bereft and aching for his kiss.

"I'm sure it's just the afternoon sun." With a false smile, she smoothed her pelisse and began a covert search for Noah.

Tabitha's well-defined eyebrow arched up. "I'm sure."

Marion shifted in her chair, refocusing her attention on the plate a footman set before her. Lady Woodbury's dark eyes continued to watch her as if she understood far more than Marion wanted her to. Finally she returned her attention to her other guests.

Marion let out a small sigh of relief as she began to pick at her dessert. Lying to her father and Josiah Lucas was one thing. The two men were conspiring against her, so turnabout was fair play. But lying to Tabitha Jordan was quite another. For some inexplicable reason she wanted Noah's mother to like her.

She glanced up with a smile as Noah returned to the table. He shot a quick wink at her before turning to the man to his side and beginning a political conversation. With a shiver, Marion realized the reason she wanted Tabitha to like her was sitting across the table from her, his blue eyes sparkling and the little dimple between his cheek and chin making him even more charming. The reason was Noah Jordan.

The man she was falling in love with.

CHAPTER TEN

Marion sat in the window seat in her chamber and stared out at the overcast day. Though she should have been doing many other things, she was lost in thought as she watched the gardeners trim the rose bushes in the distance.

"Where Noah first kissed me," she murmured, before growling at herself with displeasure. Surely she'd been mooning over the man long enough. It was time to forget the girlish crush.

Except it was more than a girlish crush. Two days before she'd dared to think that she was falling in love with the handsome Marquis. Since then that notion had grown until it filled her mind and shadowed her every thought, word and action.

"Stupid, stupid girl," she chided herself before resting her forehead on the cool glass. Over the years her father had kept her from being courted. Of course her natural reaction to the first man she met was to believe he was the man of her dreams. And the fact that he looked like a Roman god and made her blood run hot only served to further bolster that silly idea.

But nothing could ever come of it. Even if Noah weren't practically engaged to another woman, he certainly wanted to marry someone of aristocratic blood and gentle breeding. Men of his ilk didn't fall in love at all, much less with the daughters of indebted merchants who would sell their only child.

She almost burst into tears right then and there, but the somber moment was interrupted by a light knock on the door behind her. Wiping her eyes, she called out, "Come in."

The door opened and Sally stuck her kerchiefed head into the bedroom.

"I'm sorry, miss. I'll come back to change the bed linens later."

Marion scrambled to her feet with a shake of her head. "No, no. Please come in now. I'll stay out of your way."

This was just the distraction she needed, the opportunity to chat with the maid. Noah had said the servants might hold the key to finding out what had really happened to Georgina Ross. The key to Marion's salvation.

"If you're certain, miss." Sally came into the room with a pile of folded linens in her arms.

"Of course. It certainly isn't your fault that I'm hiding up here in my room," Marion said with what she hoped was a light laugh. "I wouldn't want to keep you from your work."

"Thank you, miss."

Sally gave her a brilliant smile before she stripped the bed with an efficiency born from many years of practice. Marion moved over to her dressing table and sat down in order to watch Sally in the mirror as she hurried about her duties.

"How long have you been with the household?" She pretended to fiddle and rearrange the items on her table.

"Going on three years, miss," Sally said. "Since I was fifteen."

"A long while then," Marion said with a smile. Perfect.

"A while." The girl nodded and her brown eyes flashed up before she went back to her work.

"Then you knew the last Mrs. Lucas?" In the mirror she saw Sally's back stiffen and her hand clenched into a fist to smash the corner of the blanket she held.

"Aye," she whispered. "Mrs. Lucas had just married

Mr. Lucas when I came to Toppleton Square."

"It's sad that she died so young."

Sally returned to her work, though Marion couldn't help but notice how much slower she moved, as if unpleasant thoughts waylaid her. The maid glanced over to meet Marion's eyes in the reflection.

"Very sad."

"What was she like?" She turned in her chair to look Sally in the face. Now that the mirror didn't distance them, the maid dropped her eyes to the floor.

"Like?"

Marion stood up and came a few steps closer. She didn't want to frighten the girl or push her too far so early in their acquaintance, but she felt the young woman had something to reveal. Something important.

"Yes. She and I were nearly the same age," she explained. "I wonder if we had anything else in common."

Sally bit her lip as she turned to look Marion up and down. "Well, you look a bit like her, I suppose. In the hair and eyes, but you aren't as curvy as Mrs. Lucas was. Begging your pardon, Miss Marion, but why do you want to know?"

Marion backed away and gave a careless shrug. "Bored, I suppose. My father and Mr. Lucas aren't exactly stimulating companions. Poor Georgina's portraits have drawn me to her. I wonder what a woman her age must have done here to relieve her own ennui. Or perhaps she was too much in love with Mr. Lucas to suffer boredom?"

Sally laughed but it was a brittle sound that came from the back of her throat. "No, I wouldn't say that. Madam was certainly not enamored with Mr. Lucas."

Immediately Sally gasped and stared at Marion while she covered her mouth with one hand. "Oh, pardon me! I shouldn't have spoken so freely."

"No." Marion stepped forward to touch the girl's arm. She was surprised that it trembled. "You may trust me. I'd never repeat anything you said to me in confidence."

Except to Noah, she added in her head, feeling just a little guilty that she was forced to lie to the girl. But she assured herself that her actions were honorable. How could they not be when Lucas was the prime suspect in a murder?

Sally lowered her hand and looked at Marion through wide eyes. Finally she nodded. "I suppose you *should* know, considering..."

"Considering?"

"Mr. Lucas was obsessed with his wife, Miss Marion," the girl burst out. "He followed her everywhere, and had a man on her when he couldn't go with her. He was afraid she was off cuckolding him with some young man. Any young man who looked in her direction was suspect."

"That poor girl," Marion whispered. "Had she given him cause to be so suspicious?"

"None except to be young and beautiful." Sally set her jaw defiantly. "And honest, perhaps too much so. She didn't want to be with Mr. Lucas and never pretended otherwise."

Marion's eyes grew wide. "If that is the case, she must have been very unhappy."

The maid nodded sadly. "She was. Her father and mother had given her to Mr. Lucas against her will, though I heard they came to regret their actions far too late."

Marion thought of what Noah had told her. Georgina's father had asked that the case be investigated, probably out of guilt. She had to wonder if her own father would even care enough to do the same if his arrangement with Josiah Lucas led to her death. Sadness filled her at the answer. Probably not.

Sally sighed. "Madam was a fighter and she fought him every chance she got. Oh, the screams from that bedroom..." The girl tilted her head down and wiped her eyes with the corner of Marion's blanket. "I shall never forget them."

Marion shivered as she realized what Sally was describing. Lucas had forced himself on his young wife. Just as he promised to force himself on her if she ultimately refused his advances.

"Poor Georgina," she whispered hoarsely.

"Over the two years they were married, she grew more and more unhappy. She cried nearly every night, though she never spoke to any of the servants about her troubles. She was too proud for that. But then she had her accident." Sally's eyes narrowed and hatred filled them. "Or what was called an accident."

Marion's heart leapt to her throat and kept her from speaking for a moment. "Y-you mean you don't believe it *was* an accident?"

She held her breath as Sally stared at her. Her cheeks were flushed and her eyes uncertain and guilty. Marion couldn't blame her. As a servant, Sally could lose her position... even her life, if she spoke too freely. But still, Sally seemed to *want* to confess whatever she had kept inside for so long. Finally, the maid set down the blanket and took two hesitant steps toward Marion.

"Oh please, Miss," she whispered, looking around her even though the door was securely shut. "You mustn't tell anyone. You must swear to me."

Marion nodded. She took both Sally's hands to reassure the young woman that her vow was one she meant to keep. "I would never endanger you, Sally."

The maid swallowed hard. "I don't think Mrs. Lucas fell."

"Why?" Marion was surprised to realize just how tightly she gripped the other woman's hands. Releasing them, she repeated her question, this time with gentleness. "Why do you believe that?"

The young woman lifted her face. Her brown eyes were brimmed with unshed tears and she looked as miserable as any person Marion had ever seen. "Mrs. Lucas was the most graceful woman I ever knew. She held herself like a lady. She *never* would have tripped and fallen like they said she did. She didn't have that kind of clumsiness in her."

For a moment, the young woman cried, then she

straightened and wiped her face. Her eyes locked with Marion's as she said, "I swore I'd never say those words, but you're so much like her, Miss Marion. And you've been kind to me when I've received no kindness in this house for a year. I see the way *he* looks at you, Miss. The same way he looked at her."

Marion's spine stiffened. Suddenly their conversation had turned to the uncomfortable subject of her own personal safety. That was a topic she didn't much like to think about, let alone chat about with the servants.

"The way he looks at me?"

Sally nodded adamantly. "Mr. Lucas wants you, just the way he wanted her. And not to offend you, Miss Marion, but your father don't seem like the kind who would go out of his way to protect you, especially if money was on the line."

"Why do you suspect money is involved?" Marion forced past dry lips.

Sally shook her head. "With Mr. Lucas, money is *always* involved.

"I see."

"If you can get away from here I'd go before you're forced into the same trouble as the last Mrs. Lucas."

Bile crept up Marion's throat to taint her mouth. She wasn't willing to confess that the same life had already been planned for her. Not when she couldn't even bring herself to reveal it to Noah.

"You think those are his plans for me?" she asked.

"If I didn't I'd keep my thoughts to myself," Sally said. "I hope I'm wrong, Miss Marion. But if I'm not I'd advise you to keep your bedroom door locked and leave this place as soon as you can."

Marion nodded slowly. "I appreciate your concern, Sally. I assure you, I'm doing my best to do just as you say, but I'm afraid it might take some time."

The bravado and candor left Sally's eyes. "Excuse me for speaking out of turn then, Miss Marion. I didn't mean to frighten you or say too much. I hope you won't go back on your promise and tell Mr. Lucas or your father about what I said."

Marion smiled to reassure the girl. "I made a vow that I wouldn't tell Mr. Lucas, and I intend to keep it. If you want honesty, I despise the man, too."

The fear eased from Sally's gaze. "Then perhaps we can help each other."

"How?"

"We could look out for each other. If that isn't too forward a suggestion."

Marion's smile broadened to a grin. "On the contrary, I think it's a very good idea. From now on I'll watch out for you and you'll do the same for me."

She held out her hand to the girl who stared at it for a long moment. Finally she took it and they shook. "Thank you, Miss Marion."

As Sally blushed and returned to her bed making, Marion hugged herself. Once again, Noah had been right. The servants were a fount of information and she had just befriended one who not only had intimate knowledge of Georgina Ross's life and death, but was willing to share it. Noah would certainly be impressed by that when she got the chance to tell him.

Noah glanced over the latest message from London with a frown. Lord Golding had given him more information about the case, but none of it made Noah feel any better about leaving Marion in Josiah Lucas's house to garner evidence. The more he found out about Lucas and his dangerous obsession with his late wife, the more uncomfortable he felt.

He ripped the missive in half and tossed it into the glowing flames in the fireplace, watching as the sparks ate away the words on the page.

What choice did he have about leaving Marion where she was for the time being? His first allegiance was to Golding and the case he'd taken on. If he removed Marion, his intervention would completely cut off any ability he had to investigate Lucas. A man like Lucas would be less than understanding that Noah had stolen the woman he intended to marry.

He strode to the door and yanked it open. "Rothschild!"

The hulk of a footman appeared from out of nowhere and scurried to his side with a short bow. "Yes, my lord?"

"Have you been keeping abreast of the actions of Mr. Lucas and his houseguests?"

He smiled at the eager look on the boy's face. After a few years of service, he trusted the young man. And his huge size and intimidating strength made him an asset.

"Yes sir, just as I said I would," the boy replied with a wide smile.

"And what have you discovered?" Noah motioned for the young man to come inside the study for his report.

"Yesterday Mr. Lucas and Mr. Hawthorne went into the village for a game of cards. I believe Mr. Hawthorne lost a small sum of money."

Noah shook his head. "The man never learns," he muttered.

He'd never been one for games of chance. He preferred to play where he knew he could win. Where depending on his wits and his intelligence would lead him to victory, not the lucky throw of the dice or the turn of a card.

"Beg your pardon?" the boy asked with a tilt of his head.

"Nothing, continue."

"Yes, my lord. Miss Marion stayed in her chamber most of the day reading. She did come down for supper, but she barely ate."

Noah frowned. He hated to think of her upset with no

one to talk to about her feelings. But he wasn't sure if he was the best confidante for her, even if they could be alone. It seemed whenever he had a few moments with her, all he could do was accost her, and that probably wouldn't help... although the image was a pleasing one to him. He could still feel the soft curves of her body molded to his, her breath coming short as he kissed and touched her.

"My lord?"

Noah jumped as the boy brought him back to reality a second time. "What was that?"

"Nothing sir." He cocked his head as if he were unsure of his master's state of mind. "I just asked if you were pleased with what I found?"

"Yes, of course." Noah waved his hand in dismissal of the question. "But what about today? Do you know of their plans?"

Rothschild nodded. "Yes, my lord. Mr. Lucas asked their cook to prepare a picnic luncheon for three. Apparently he and the Hawthornes are going to be going for a ride across the estate and the shire. They plan to lunch by Perchta Lake."

Noah smiled. "When do they plan to depart?"

"I believe sometime before noon, my lord. Would you like me to find out a more specific time?"

Noah glanced at his pocket watch. It was already nearly eleven. "No, Rothschild, that will be all. Tell the groom to have my horse ready and find my valet. I'll be riding today and won't be home for luncheon."

"Yes, my lord." Rothschild gave a smart bow before he hurried from the room to make the arrangements.

Noah strummed his fingers across the oak desktop with a smile. If Josiah Lucas thought he would get some time alone Marion at the enchanted 'fairy' lake, he was wrong. Noah would make sure of that.

With a laugh, he bolted from the room and climbed the stairs two at a time. He had to change to look his best when he broke up Lucas's party.

CHAPTER ELEVEN

Marion closed her eyes and let the cool afternoon breeze rush across face. She was trying to block out her surroundings, but the attempt was unsuccessful. It wasn't the beautiful sunny day she wished to banish, nor the rolling hills of Woodbury, nor the chirping birds. All those things by themselves would have been enchanting. Unfortunately, they were coupled with the sound and sight of her father and Josiah Lucas, both of whom droned on and on endlessly.

From time to time her father would say or do something designed to make Marion like Josiah Lucas, but those attempts only made her shiver with disgust. Even if she hadn't known Lucas wished to possess her body, she wouldn't have cared one whit about his supposed 'power' in the shire. Or his love of battle paintings. Or his damned riding skills.

"Marion!" Her father cracked his riding crop against his horse's neck to get her attention. She just barely missed being slapped by the leather whip and instantly returned her concentration to the two men.

"Yes, Papa?" she asked, her voice smooth and sweet as honey.

Over the years she had perfected the dutiful daughter exterior, though little good it did her. All that devotion hadn't kept him from using and abusing her. Now her resentment was almost impossible to mask.

"Pay attention! Mr. Lucas was talking to you."

He motioned his head toward Josiah. Marion winced. Their host did seem annoyed.

"I'm so sorry, Mr. Lucas." Slowing her mare's pace, Marion moved closer to her host. "I was enjoying this ride so much I nearly lost myself. What were you saying?"

His lips stretched thin and tight across his teeth in a false smile. "I was asking if you like the mare you're riding?"

She nodded instantly. "Oh, yes. I was disappointed we couldn't bring my own mount with us on this trip, but Satin here more than makes up for her absence. Thank you for allowing me to borrow her for the afternoon."

Lucas and her father exchanged smug smiles which chilled Marion's blood.

"How would you like to have Satin for more than just an afternoon?" Lucas asked as he leaned in closer.

She swallowed hard, clutching at her horse's bridle as she willed herself not to move away from Lucas's hot breath on her cheek.

"What do you mean?"

As subtly as she could, she looked to her father, expecting him to tell Lucas to back away from her. He was being far too forward. But Walter had ridden a few feet ahead of the pair and rode with his eyes straight ahead.

"I would very much like to make Satin a gift to you."

The lurid light in Lucas's cold eyes made her reel back. The man thought he could buy her affection, her body with a *horse*? A truly magnificent horse, yes, but no animal was worth enduring his touch.

"That would be highly inappropriate, Mr. Lucas," she snapped and she didn't have to pretend offense. "I'm surprised you would make such a bold suggestion without consulting my father. I'm sure he would have told you I couldn't accept a gift from a man I barely know, much less the gift of an expensive mount."

She glanced at her father again for confirmation, but he

was pretending as if he couldn't hear the exchange.

Lucas licked his lips with a chuckle. "My dear, I did speak with your father. He approved my present. After all, he and I are closely related business partners, and there may be a time in the future when you see me as more than a man you barely know."

Promise to Noah or no, Marion couldn't just sit by and pretend this man wasn't making a blatant overture to her. "Until that day, I cannot accept your gift."

His gray gaze went from amused to angry in a blink. Suddenly he looked less like a doddering old man and more like a person capable of pushing his wife down a flight of stairs.

"You accepted a gift from Lord Woodbury and you barely know him. And you had no leave from your father to take what he offered."

She drew in a breath of outrage. "Taking a collection of pencils meant to replace those I lost is nothing like taking a horse!"

"No," he agreed as he grabbed her arm in an iron grip and pulled her closer to him. She teetered on Satin's saddle and had to grip harder to keep from falling. "The horse comes with the promise of a future if you take it. Woodbury's pencils come with nothing but the guarantee of seduction and desertion."

The blood drained from Marion's face at his implication. She hadn't realized Lucas had been following her budding relationship with Noah so closely. In his mind, the Marquis couldn't be a threat. Marion already belonged to him, it was just a matter of *when* Lucas made her his, not if.

"Release me." She pulled on her arm as she gripped the ladies saddle horn with her opposite hand.

"Good afternoon, Mr. Lucas, is there a problem?"

Noah drawled the question as if he were asking about the weather, but as Josiah Lucas turned to look at him he knew what the other man saw in his eyes. The rage that Noah was barely keeping in check. When he came around the corner to see Marion being manhandled by the villain while her father rode on without a care in the world, his blood had begun to boil. And seeing her fear had nearly driven him over the edge. Only the need to keep perspective on his case had kept him from pummeling Lucas and taking Marion away with him that very moment.

"No." Lucas released Marion with a glare. "Not a problem. I was just helping Miss Marion, she seemed to have forgotten a number of things about riding."

"Noah."

Her eyes lit up as they met his. The utter trust he saw there made him swell with protectiveness, but it also fed his guilt. Her faith was a gift he shouldn't take.

"*Miss* Marion," he said with a smile, hoping his proper address of her would remind her that they weren't in private and it wasn't prudent for her to say his Christian name.

"What a lovely surprise to run into you today, my lord," she said, smoothly shifting from frightened young woman to cool partner with nary the blink of an eye. "Papa, look who's here. It's Lord Woodbury!"

Up ahead Walter Hawthorne pulled his horse to a short stop and turn to face them. His skin blanched when he caught a glimpse of the threesome behind him. Marion had walked her horse over to stand beside Noah, and Lucas now looked angry enough to spit.

"Er, Lord Woodbury," Hawthorne stammered as he trotted his animal back to the group. "We didn't expect to see you today."

"I was taking a little excursion around the shire." Noah lied. He held Hawthorne's gaze and hoped Marion's father could read this utter disgust. "It's a happy coincidence we were all riding the same way."

"Yes," Lucas hissed as he glared at Noah. "Very happy, my lord."

"And where are you three off to this fine summer afternoon? There won't be many of these warm days left, I wager." Noah motioned in the gentle air around them.

"We're off to Perchta Lake," Lucas said in a flat tone. "To picnic."

"Ahh, the Fairy Lake." Noah nudged Phantom into a walk, which forced the rest of the group to do the same. He'd seamlessly inserted himself into their party and Lucas would be hard pressed to force him out.

"Fairy Lake?" Marion asked and a twinkle in her eye returned that made Noah's heart swell.

"Yes." He urged his horse next to her dark mare to cut her father and Lucas off. Now he and Marion rode together in front, leaving Lucas and Hawthorne to follow them. He hoped they were fuming over their thwarted plans. "Haven't you ever heard of Perchta Lake?"

"No," she admitted. "I'd never even heard of Woodbury until we arrived."

"Tsk, tsk." Noah glanced back over his shoulder at the gape-mouthed Walter Hawthorne. "You shouldn't have neglected her geographical studies, Hawthorne. You never know where a lady may end up in the world once she's of age."

"Uh…" Hawthorne stammered, but Noah turned away.

"Perchta Lake is named after the fairy goddess of sun…" He paused for the greatest effect. "And fertility. Though a man shouldn't talk about such things in front of a lady."

Instead of making Marion giggle as he'd thought his dramatic recitation of the lake's supposedly magical powers would do, she paled. "Is that really what people believe? That the lake makes a person more fertile?"

"Quite," Lucas said from behind them.

When Noah turned he saw that any defeat Lucas had shown when he rode up was gone, replaced with a knowing smugness that made Noah want to resort to physical violence.

Lucas continued, "It's a villagers tale, of course, but even the most pragmatic of men has been known to take his wife… or future bride… to the river to increase her chances of bearing him a son."

Marion shivered though the breeze was warm on Noah's skin. Why she was so troubled by the discussion? Yes, the thought of marrying Lucas was a terrible one, but Noah would never let the man lay a finger on Marion's skin, let alone taste the pleasures of her lips or body. It would *never* go that far.

"Silly tales," he said as he locked eyes with her. His gaze seemed to calm her fears. She rewarded him with a soft smile.

"Yes, very silly. But I do like the idea of a Fairy Lake."

He nodded. "Then you'll like the reality all the more. It's quite beautiful there. I loved to go there with my friends when we were children. There may even be remnants of our tree fort, though it's possible it's rotted away after so many years."

Marion smiled again. This man had the capability of calming her worries with just a word or a smile. She had a feeling his intrusion on her father and Lucas's party was no coincidence as he'd claimed. He had come to protect her.

She shook her head at the silly thought. Protect her? That was secondary to Noah's mission. He'd come to find out more about Josiah Lucas, but then, why was he riding beside her, completely ignoring the older man?

"It's just over this hill." Noah motioned to the low mound before them.

When they crested the hillock, Marion drew in a deep breath and quickly forgot all her own worries and thoughts. Noah was right, the lake was beautiful, exactly the place where it was easy to imagine fairies living. Bright sunlight streamed between the gently sweeping boughs of willow trees, making shadows dance across the water. The lake itself was large, walking around it would take quite a while. Perfect spots of shade and flat areas for a picnic were all around the water's edge.

"My..." Marion slowly slid from Satin's back. She

dropped the mare's reins to allow her to graze and took a few steps toward the water.

"It's exquisite, isn't it?" Lucas asked.

Marion was shaken from her own world by his harsh voice. When she turned to watch him dismount, she saw the jealousy and anger in his even stare.

"Yes," she said, once again dancing the thin line between politeness and interest. "Thank you so much for thinking to bring me here, Mr. Lucas."

The older man's glare became less harsh. "I'm glad you like it. Perhaps later you'll allow me a turn around the water's edge."

Marion nearly gagged at the idea, but quickly smiled to cover her initial reaction. "That would be lovely."

"But first, we'll have our picnic," her father interrupted with an apologetic look at Noah. "I'm afraid we only brought enough food for three, my lord."

Marion grimaced at her father's uncouth ways. Even if he hadn't been trying to get rid of Noah to force her to spend time with Lucas, he would have embarrassed her.

"Oh, father, I'm sure we've brought enough for one more guest."

She smiled at Noah. The last thing she wanted was for him to leave her alone with the other two men.

"No need to worry about sharing your feast." Noah returned her smile and added a sly wink. "My cook, Mrs. York, packed me a luncheon in case I didn't return until the afternoon. The woman spoils me. I probably have enough food for all of us in my saddle pack."

Her father's face fell at Noah's smooth answer. "Well, then I'm sure we'll be able to make room on our blanket for you, Lord Woodbury."

"Very good," Noah said as he offered his arm to Marion. "Perhaps while you and Mr. Lucas find a place for us to lunch, Miss Marion and I can try to find that playhouse we spoke of earlier."

Without waiting for either man to answer, Noah led her away from them and began a slow walk toward a small grove of trees a few hundred yards ahead of them. As soon as they were out of earshot, Marion let out a laugh.

"Did you see my father's face when you came over the hill? He was as white as a ghost when you disturbed his plans for Lucas and me."

Her giggle faltered a little when she remembered the way Lucas had grabbed her. He was getting bolder.

Noah's hold on her elbow tightened, a reassurance to her that he was there and wouldn't let her come to harm. But what about later, when he wouldn't be there?

"Marion, look at me," he whispered. When she did so, he said, "I'm here now."

She nodded. "Yes, a happy accident."

He chuckled. "Well, not a complete accident. I thought you might be tiring of only your father and Lucas's company so I arranged to have a meeting with your little party today."

"So you *did* come for me?" Marion whispered before she realized she'd spoken out loud. Dipping her head, she tried not to look into Noah's eyes. What a cake she was making of herself. "I'm sorry, that was a foolish thing to say."

He glanced over his shoulder toward her father and Lucas. They'd entered a thicker part of the woods and no one could see them. Turning her toward him, he tilted her chin up and made her look into the face that had haunted her dreams for weeks.

"Marion…" His breath came shorter than it had been. "I will always come for you. You need to believe that."

She searched his face for emotion, wondering what he felt when he said that. Did he consider her a source of information that he lusted after? Or was there more to the relationship that was brewing between them? But she could read nothing from his hooded expression.

Finally she sighed, "I do believe that."

"Good." For a moment he only held her gaze then

leaned down and gently brushed his lips against hers.

When he pulled away, Marion blinked a few times to cast away the haze before her eyes. Here she'd just been telling herself how Noah only desired her, and then he kissed her in a tender way that made her heart melt. Before his kisses had swept her away on a wave of heat. This one made her truly confront the fact that she loved him. She loved him. It was as simple and as complicated as that.

"Your-your fort?" she choked out, dropping her gaze from him as the power of her emotions rocked her.

"Yes." His voice shook. "It was through this clearing over here."

Noah cleared his throat as they passed through a cluster of trees and saw the dilapidated shadow of his former playhouse before him. He released Marion's arm and went over to the area, pretending to examine the spot in a fit of nostalgia. In reality, he needed a moment to himself to digest what had just transpired between the two of them. One moment he'd simply been comforting her, the next kissing her. And not a lusty kiss he could dismiss as desire-driven, but the kind of kiss that claimed her in more ways than even a night in his bed would have.

"You must have had a great deal of fun here as a child." Marion climbed up the slight slope to lay a slender hand on what was left of the fort's front wall.

"We did."

Noah suddenly wondered if his own children would play here. He could almost picture his hellions revamping the place. Only instead of having Charlotte's pale looks, his image had Marion's brown eyes and sweet smile.

What the hell was wrong with him? Obviously his mother's lectures about marrying for love, not convenience were beginning to addle his mind. He needed to get back to London where his friends would renew his sanity.

"I did what you asked me to do," Marion said, bringing his attention back to her.

"What was that?"

"I made friends with one of the maids on the staff. Sally."

She ducked under the doorway of the dilapidated fort to get out from under his stare. The roof of the little building was long gone so her head stuck up above the walls.

He blinked. "Really? I'm impressed. That didn't take you long."

"No. I already liked her and I believe I remind her of Georgina, who she apparently cared for a great deal." Her voice grew sad. "Everyone says I remind them of Georgina."

The last comment trailed off with a twinge of fear. Noah touched her arm. "Your end will be a much happier one."

Marion's nostrils flared as she looked down at his hand against her skin. "I hope so," she whispered. "Because Sally doesn't believe Georgina Ross fell down that flight of stairs."

Noah's breath caught in his throat. "She told you that already?"

He wasn't sure why he was surprised. Marion inspired trust in other people. He certainly trusted her even though he'd only known her for a short time. A frightened young maid with a secret she longed to tell might easily see Marion as an outlet for her fears. But could the maid have some ulterior motive to sharing her secrets?

"She told me Georgina was too elegant to trip and fall. She also warned me to get away because of Lucas. Even she can see his plans for me."

Noah winced at the tears that gathered in her brown eyes. Marion had felt very alone in the past few days and he'd done nothing to assure her he was making sure she was safe.

"Did I tell you I have a man watching the house?"

Her eyes lit up with surprise. "You do?"

"Yes. One of my footmen has connections to Lucas's footman. They're... brothers I believe. So I'm always aware of what is happening at Toppleton Square." Her quiet smile relieved him.

Marion nodded. "I'm glad of that. It makes me feel better to know you're tracking what's going on."

"I am, so you needn't be afraid," he said. "This won't go on for much longer."

Her eyes narrowed. "How much longer do you think?"

He shrugged one shoulder, though the catch in her voice caught his attention. Why was she worried? "Perhaps a few weeks."

Marion swallowed hard. Lucas had only given her father until the month's end to convince her to come to his bed willingly. A few more weeks would be far past that deadline. August was fast waning and September would soon be upon them.

"Noah."

She was determined to tell him the whole truth about what Lucas truly planned to buy from her father. Even if Noah was angry she'd kept the truth from him, he would understand why she needed his timetable advanced.

"Yes?"

She ducked back out of the playhouse to take his hand. "Noah, I can't wait for…"

"Marion, Lord Woodbury?"

Marion jumped at her father's voice. She dropped Noah's hand as if it burned her and called out, "We're here."

"Well, come back. We're ready to have our luncheon and Mr. Lucas is tired of waiting for you," he snapped.

Marion rubbed her eyes in frustration. Once again, she couldn't tell Noah about Lucas's planned seduction. At least for the time being. And there was little time left. She had no doubt Lucas was tired of waiting, not just for his lunch, but for her. And whatever it took, she wouldn't allow that.

CHAPTER TWELVE

Noah watched through narrowed eyes as Josiah Lucas strolled around the lake's edge with Marion on his arm. If only he wasn't on a case he would...

Well, there were a good many things he would do. None of which he could even consider since he *was* working for the War Department. His one consolation was that with him sitting just feet away, Lucas wouldn't dare touch Marion again.

But what about when he wasn't around? Marion shared a home with Lucas, even if it was temporary. Noah had thought her father would protect her from the man's advances until she was legally wed. Obviously, he'd underestimated Hawthorne once again. After all, the man hadn't been ten feet away and allowed Lucas manhandle Marion like she was already his.

He shifted his gaze to Walter Hawthorne. The other man was stuffing his great, red mouth with chunks of venison Mrs. York had put in Noah's lunch. He had to wonder how the man didn't choke. But fate was never so kind.

"What kind of business interests do you and Mr. Lucas share, Mr. Hawthorne?" Noah watched the other man's face carefully even as he maintained a bored expression.

Hawthorne coughed and his piggy hazel eyes widened at the question. When the man was quite purple, Noah leaned over and pounded him on the back a few times, sending a chunk of meat flying across the lawn to plop into the water.

"Thank you, Woodbury," Hawthorne wheezed as he took a long draught of ale from the flask by his side. "Now what was that?"

Hawthorne remembered the question perfectly well, but Noah gave him a bemused smile and repeated, "I simply wondered what business interests you share with Lucas. It seems odd to me that a textile man and a coal baron have something in common."

Hawthorne opened his mouth, but Noah continued, "Some kind of business so pressing that it required you to travel all the way from your home with your daughter and stay with Lucas for… how long has it been now? A fortnight, at least."

Walter nodded. "Er, Mr. Lucas and I have… that is we're both invested… that is we have some mutual interests."

"Which are?" Noah picked up a ripe, red apple and tossed it in the air only to catch it just before it hit the dirt. He repeated the action over and over while he waited for the other man's response.

"I say," Hawthorne said after a moment of being mesmerized by Noah's action. "There are some things, even in business, that are too delicate to be discussed in the open."

Noah barely held back a growl. Obviously selling his daughter was one of those subjects too delicate to speak about, but not too delicate to do. It made Noah sick.

"Is that so?" His voice never wavered or betrayed his anger. "Perhaps I might be interested in your investments, as well."

He stopped tossing the apple and met Hawthorne's eyes evenly. The time had come to test this man.

"But you don't know what they are," Hawthorne stammered.

Noah smiled. "I know you have some things I wouldn't mind owning," he said with a glance toward Marion.

She and Lucas were nearly all the way around the lake now, heading back toward them on the opposite side from where they'd started. Hawthorne followed his line of vision and started when he saw Noah look at his daughter. His gaze immediately narrowed in thought. Noah was sickened that Hawthorne was now trying to find a way to use Noah's relationship with Marion to his own advantage.

"I-I might be willing to negotiate with other parties if they made it worth my while," Hawthorne said after a long pause.

Noah swallowed back his rage. "Perhaps. First I'd need to know the amount being asked."

"Understood," Hawthorne said with a grin. "What I'm offering is a rare commodity. I couldn't settle for anything less than its worth. We could talk about specifics later, if you'd like." His eyes shifted to Lucas. "I wouldn't want the other party to catch me bargaining with you."

Noah bit back a retort. "I need time to think about whether the investment was worth the price."

Hawthorne nodded. "But don't wait too long. You never know when what you seek may be lost to you. Especially if other investors make their decision first."

The muscles in Noah's shoulders twitched with the anger that boiled within him. Though he'd learned Hawthorne had a price for Marion's freedom and her body, somehow that didn't make him feel better. The man had no scruples. But why did he have so little feeling for his own flesh and blood?

"I wonder if you might be able to put your other interested parties off for a while." He hoped to buy both Marion and himself some more time. He was sure they could uncover the evidence he was looking for if they just had a few extra days. "Until I make my decision."

Hawthorne shook his head. "Oh no, my lord. Mr. Lucas has made it clear that he wants M-, that is to say, he wants what he's earned by month's end. I was pushing my luck by asking for that long. If you want what I have to offer, you'll have to make your decision quickly."

Noah pursed his lips in displeasure. This was like

talking to a farmer about a cattle auction, not a father about his only child.

"You're a mercenary, sir." He hoped he sounded amused rather than disgusted. "We aren't talking about cotton here, are we?"

Hawthorne didn't even the decency to look ashamed. "A commodity is a commodity."

Before Noah could utter the curse about to escape from his lips, Marion and Lucas reached the picnic blanket. Immediately, she released the older man's arm and edged toward Noah.

"Thank you, Mr. Lucas. I enjoyed our little walk. You know so much about the history of Woodbury."

She met Noah's eyes. He could see by her pained expression that she'd heard an earful of nonsense, but nothing that could help them on their mission. Poor girl, he'd have to school her in the fact that most of the time spy work was frightfully boring.

"What were you two talking about?" She looked from her father to Noah, then back again. "You looked awfully serious as Mr. Lucas and I approached."

Noah frowned. It was bad enough Marion knew her father was willing to sell her to pay his debts. She didn't need to hear he was now auctioning her to the highest bidder.

"Mind your business, girly," her father growled as his eyes shifted to Lucas with an uneasy smile. "What Lord Woodbury and I were discussing is none of your affair."

"Yes." Noah rose to his feet. "It wasn't important, Miss Marion. But the afternoon is growing late and I'm sure we should all be returning to our respective homes. May I escort you all to Linton Green at least?"

Lucas frowned, but propriety gave him no choice but to agree. "Of course, my lord. We welcome your company."

Noah acknowledged the man with a nod, but his attention was still focused on Marion. How the young woman had come through life with her father and still maintained her sanity and sense of humor was more than he could comprehend. But it made him all the more determined to help her in whatever way he could.

Noah strode into the foyer and started down the hall. He needed to write a letter to Lord Golding explaining his situation with Marion and ask for his former superior's advice. Seemed Noah could no longer trust his own judgment.

He grasped his door handle when he heard his mother's voice from the parlor behind him.

"There you are!" He turned to find her in the door with a wide smile on her face. "Come in and tell me about your day."

She was watching him with expectant blue eyes and he knew he couldn't deny her. Golding would have to wait.

"Of course." He placed a kiss on her cheek and motioned her back to the parlor. Sitting down, he smiled at her. "I'm sorry I couldn't share luncheon with you."

She waved his apology away with a smile. "Nonsense. I'm perfectly capable of eating on my own. But I wonder if *you* ate alone?"

He smiled at her arched eyebrow and the knowing twinkle in her eye. "I did not, but I can tell you'd already guessed that. I was lucky enough to bump into Mr. Lucas, Mr. Hawthorne and Miss Marion while I was on my ride. We ended up picnicking together at Lake Perchta."

Tabitha smiled again. "Bumped into them, eh?"

He gave one shoulder a noncommittal shrug. He knew better than to lie to his mother.

"I like Marion," his mother said with a sigh. "She's a lovely girl with a bright and quick wit. She reminds me of Audrey in some ways."

Noah nodded. "I never noticed it before, but you're

right. Audrey would like Marion."

"She would, indeed," she answered. "It's unfortunate they'll never meet."

His smile faded at that thought. "Why wouldn't they?"

"I would assume after her father's business is done, the two of them will return to Northumberland. Unless…" she trailed off with an arched eyebrow.

Noah blinked. "Unless what?"

"Unless you have other plans for her," his mother finished with an even stare. He squirmed under the direct look and question. "Do you?"

What was the correct answer? Especially since he didn't yet know his plans for Marion himself. She wanted him to take her to her aunts, but that thought was no longer as comforting as it had once been. With her so far away, he'd likely never see her again.

"I-"

"And if you *do* have plans for Marion, where does that leave Charlotte?" his mother interrupted. Her tone was very gentle for such direct questions.

Noah shifted in his chair. These were the very questions he'd been asking himself. The thought of losing Marion forever was an unpleasant one, but promises had been made to Charlotte in London. Though they weren't binding, they were honorable.

"You don't fully understand the relationship Marion and I have, Mother."

Hell, he didn't fully understand the relationship he and Marion shared, either.

"I'm well aware of that," she said with a laugh. "I was hoping you might explain it." She folded her arms as if she were ready to wait.

"I can't," he said as he rose to his feet to pace to the fireplace. "But trust I'm not doing anything to jeopardize my plans with Charlotte. Just because I happen to like Marion doesn't mean my intentions have changed."

Tabitha stood up with a shake of her head. "*Like* her? I know I'm speaking out of turn, but it's obvious that it's more than that. For both of you."

"Mother!" he said, eyes widening. He'd never known her to be so frank. "Propriety…"

"Bah!" she scoffed with a shake of her head. "Propriety has its place, but so does love. Look at the life your father and I shared."

"And how unhappy you are now that he's dead. Is that what love brought you?" he snapped before he considered his words.

His mother's face twisted with pain, and Noah immediately wished he could take back his harsh words. Until he'd said them, he hadn't realized how much he equated love with loss.

"Do you think my sorrow now makes me want to change even one day I shared with your father?" A tremor broke her voice.

Noah turned away from her pain with a wordless shrug of one shoulder. She grasped his elbow and forced him to face her again.

"I wouldn't! My grief now is a testament to the love we shared. In time my pain will ease and I'll be left with the very happy memories. I wish you even half the joy we shared."

Noah felt a tightness in his throat and could find nothing to say to his mother. Behind the grief in her eyes, he could see her strength and her love. They were things he hadn't noticed since his father's death, but they'd been there all along.

"Promise me you won't throw away a chance you have for happiness just because you think propriety risks less," she said with a sigh. "There's been enough of that in this family."

"I can only promise you I'll consider what you've said." Noah slipped his arm from her grip. "I know you mean well, but you don't understand the totality of the situation. Now if you'll excuse me, I have a bit of work to do and I'd like to finish it before supper."

His mother opened her mouth to say something, but after a moment, closed it again with a nod.

He looked away and walked out into the hall, knowing her sad eyes followed his every step, willing him to make a choice he couldn't make.

CHAPTER THIRTEEN

Noah scribbled his initials across the bottom of the note he'd just written. He stared at it for a long moment before folding it in quarters and handing it to Rothschild.

"Do you know what to do with it?" Though the correspondence was a routine one, anxiety overwhelmed him.

"Of course," the young man said with a jaunty grin. "I'm to give it to my brother at Lucas's, and I'm to tell him not to give the note to anyone but Sally Howard for Miss Marion."

"Very good. Be careful. The last thing I need is for this message to fall into the wrong hands. It could endanger Miss Marion's life if that happened." He stared at the man with a menacing glare. "Do you understand?"

The cocky sureness in the boy's grin faded. "Absolutely, sir. I'm very clear on how important this is. And I'll tell my brother to keep an even closer eye on Miss Marion to be certain she's not in any danger."

"Very good. Now be off." Noah waved the other man away to deliver his missive, then sank down into his office chair with a groan.

Since his troubling conversation with his mother the day before, all he'd been able to think about was Marion and the feelings she inspired in him. The friendship he could understand. The desire he understood, too. But this new sensation of needing her, he had no idea what to do with. It was completely foreign.

He'd run over and over in his mind what to do about it. His only answer was to solve his case as quickly as possible, buy Marion's freedom and send her to her aunts. There, at least, she would be happy and he wouldn't have to face the way she made him feel. He would return to London and marry Charlotte as he had planned. Eventually he would forget about Marion Hawthorne.

With a shake of his head, he rose to his feet and mixed himself a drink. Tonight he planned to sneak into Toppleton Square through Marion's window and do a thorough search of Lucas's study. Going there was about finding evidence. It had nothing to do with her.

"Damn and blast."

He downed his drink in one fiery swig. When had things become so complicated? He'd come out to the country to have one last taste of adventure. Instead he'd found a woman who captivated him and created more problems than he wanted to fathom. But the idea of being with her was a powerful draw, and in the recesses of his heart, he had to admit it drove him to Toppleton Square more than any case could have.

Marion sat on the narrow window seat looking out across the misty night toward Linton Green. In just a few hours Noah would ride through those trees and climb into her room. She thrilled at just the thought of being alone with him again.

"May I help you get undressed?" Sally asked from behind her.

Marion turned to face the servant with a giddy smile. She'd almost forgotten the young woman was there in her excitement to receive and read Noah's note. She continued to clutch it against her breast, unwilling to let it burn in the fire as she knew she must.

"No, I'll stay as I am for a while." She attempted to regain a firm hand on her composure. "I'll read for a bit. I can undress myself."

The last thing she wanted was for Noah to see her in her boring, high-necked night shift. She wouldn't even be able to look at him after that.

"I don't know, miss," Sally began. Her lower lip twisted in question. "It may not be proper."

Marion wrinkled her brow. "What might not be proper? Undressing myself? I assure you I do it all the time back at home. I don't have a maid of my own there, and-"

"No, miss," Sally interrupted her with a shake of her head. "Not undressing yourself. I meant being alone with a gentleman in your chamber isn't proper."

The blood drained from Marion's face to rush to her heart, where it pounded out a staccato beat against her ribs. She took her time before answering. "What on earth are you talking about?"

Sally gave her a sly smile. "You know as well as I do that Lord Woodbury will be coming through that window in just a few hours."

Marin drew in a sharp breath and reflexively clenched Noah's note in her palm. The paper crushed in her fist and the corner bit into her skin as she frantically decided what to say.

Sally's eyes softened with pity. "Sit down, Miss Marion, you look as though you'll faint away."

Marion drew in a sharp breath. "Why did you open my letter?"

"Everything surrounding its arrival was so mysterious," the girl admitted as she watched Marion sink back onto the window seat with a thump. "I wanted to make certain you weren't doing anything that could get you hurt."

Marion briefly wondered if allowing Noah so far into her heart wasn't the most potentially hurtful action of all, but quickly pushed the thought aside. "Will you tell anyone what you read?"

Sally drew back as if offended. "Of course not, miss! I'm surprised you'd even ask me such a thing after I told you all I know about Mrs. Lucas and my ideas about her death. You've been kind to me." Her eyes narrowed before she continued, "And I hope my own kindnesses won't be forgotten should you get yourself out of Mr. Lucas's control and into a better situation."

Marion bit the inside of her lip until she could taste the faint tang of her own blood. Sally was asking her for her help to get out of Lucas's employ. It was something Marion had never even considered, and she wondered how Noah would react. But perhaps he needed a new maid at one of his estates or knew of someone who would provide her helpful friend with kind employment.

"I'll do my best to help you any way I can."

She wished she could offer Sally a place to go, but she had no money to hire a maid. And she doubted her aunts could offer her a place.

Sally's eyes filled with relief. "Thank you, miss. I'd appreciate any word you could put in with your Lord Woodbury. I'm sure any position in a household you two governed would be-"

Marion's eyes grew wide. "What? No, no, you misunderstand. Lord Woodbury and I have no promises between us, nor plans for a future together. He's promised to help me in return for my cooperation on another matter."

With a tilt of her head, Sally looked her mistress up and down. "Is that so? Hmmm, by the way you two looked at each other, I thought sure…"

Marion swallowed hard at the thought of anything more than a stolen moment with Noah. She'd only allowed for brief dreams of what a happy life that would be haunt her nights, she would never dare voice them to anyone.

"You were mistaken." She turned away with a dark blush. She would have to be more careful in the way she treated Noah in public or Sally's belief might become a common impression. "At any rate, I'll be fine with the Marquis. He's an utter gentleman, and we won't be alone in my chamber for long."

The other woman nodded, though Marion could still see the doubt in her eyes. "Very well. Goodnight."

Marion barely acknowledged the farewell as she turned back to the window to lean against the glass. Noah's note hadn't indicated when he would arrive, but it couldn't be immediately. It was barely midnight and some of the servants buzzed around the house finishing their daily duties.

She turned from the window to go to the fire. As it warmed her skin, she opened the note again and stared at each word. Noah's hand was bold and sure, just as he was. She could imagine him leaning over his desk as he scribbled the words, his bright eyes scanning over the missive before he folded it.

Stealing a quick glance around her, Marion hesitated, then lifted the page to her nose and took a deep breath. She smelled nothing and felt silly for her girlish action. With a growl at herself, she tossed the letter into the fire and watched the flames devour the paper bit by bit until it was gone.

"Stop thinking these overly romantic thoughts."

With a sigh, she crossed over to her bed and threw herself down on the coverlet. She flung her arms over her eyes and tried to think of anything else. Anything but Noah.

It wasn't possible.

Would he kiss her during their visit? He had in the woods and it had nearly melted her. She craved the same caress over and over. She dreamed about him putting his lips to hers. Even at supper while her father and Lucas rambled on and on, she found herself drifting away to a world where only she and Noah existed.

Yanking her hands down, Marion forced herself into a sitting position. The thoughts she'd been having lately were utterly scandalous. Certainly not the kind her mother would have approved of. Only fallen women dreamt of a man's touch, didn't they? Not a properly raised girl. Probably Noah's fiancée, Charlotte Ives, would be scandalized by Marion's forward thoughts.

Now why had she thought of the mysterious Charlotte? The other woman only made her painfully aware both of her position in Society and in Noah's life. He might desire her, as a virile man of his age and disposition would any woman, but in the end he would take Charlotte into his life, his home and his bed… permanently.

She hopped back to the floor with a frown and paced the room, her restless legs carrying her back and forth from the fireplace to the window, then back to the bed again.

"But Charlotte isn't his wife yet," she muttered. "And he's here with me now."

She flushed at the thought, wondering what Noah would think if she were so bold as to kiss *him*, to touch *him* in the same ways that made her flame with desire. He'd probably take her for a wanton, but would he refuse her?

She strummed her fingers across the mantel with a shake of her dark head. These thoughts were ridiculous! She wasn't about to throw herself at a man who was already promised to another. No matter how he made her knees weak and her stomach flutter. She'd help him, he would help her, and then she would move on to her new life with her family. A life where Noah Jordan had no place.

Noah shimmied up the tall oak tree adjacent to Marion's window. After years of practice, not a twig cracked beneath his foot nor a leaf fell beneath his weight. When he reached the end of the sturdy limb before him, he reached out and tapped her window. He grinned when it opened easily. She had followed his instructions and left her window cracked.

With a little hop, he stood on the ledge and jumped inside the warm room. He pulled the window shut with a tiny click, then turned to look around Marion's chamber.

"Marion," he hissed into the dark as his eyes adjusted to the dwindling firelight. "Marion?"

Finally he saw her and his breath hitched in his throat. She lay on the bed, her dark hair tumbling out of her bun onto the pillows. She was still dressed, a fact Noah didn't know whether to be grateful for or disappointed by.

The firelight danced across her face, making her look softer in her relaxed state, more fragile than when she stood toe to toe with him in a game of playful verbal sparring.

He crept closer to the bed. If she woke up when he came back into the room, she might cry out. Worse yet, she could close her door after he'd gone and end up locking him in the house.

"Marion?"

He sat down on the edge of the bed. Being so close to her, especially in a place where he could easily have her, easily show her how much he wanted her, was proving more difficult than he'd imagined.

"Marion, wake up sweetheart."

As he repeated her name, he reached his hand out to touch her face. God, her skin was soft. With a sigh, she turned into his palm and rubbed her cheek against his fingers. Hot blood rushed through his body, and he immediately grew hard at her innocent response.

He wanted this woman more than he'd ever wanted any woman in all his thirty-two years. He wanted to pull her up into his arms and rain kisses down on her until she begged him for more. He wanted to peel off her clothes and touch her entire body until she shivered in release. The intensity of his feelings was overpowering.

Instead, he simply stared at her, memorizing every curve of her face and body. Soon enough she would be gone. He wondered if he would suffer the way he'd seen opium addicts suffer. Marion was certainly like a drug pumping through his system.

He shook his head as he forced himself to withdraw his hand from her cheek. "Marion!"

He was pleased when her eyelids began to flutter. He leaned forward, preparing to cover her mouth if she screamed in fright at finding him in her room. Instead, she opened her eyes with a small stretch and a smile.

"Noah," she sighed with a yawn. "I knew you'd come for me."

Now it wasn't just desire that he felt clenching at his body, but that strange emotion he still had no name for. Her blind belief that he'd somehow save her was something he'd never expected to find at Woodbury, but it wasn't entirely unpleasant. In his line of work he'd always played the rogue, not the hero. He was finding the hero a pleasant fit.

"I'm here, my sleepy lady," he whispered. "And now I'll go downstairs and tend to my business. Leave your door open a crack so I may return when I'm through. I should be no more than half an hour."

Marion's eyes flew open.

"Noah!" she cried out, sitting bolt upright. "You aren't leaving me here, I'm coming with you."

He winced as he lifted one finger to her soft lips to hush her. "No, you'll stay here."

She lowered her voice. "If someone hears you moving around downstairs and I'm with you, I can more easily explain my presence while you slip away," she reasoned but her voice faltered.

Marion suddenly realized Noah was leaning on the edge of her bed. It was an intensely intimate position, something more fitting to a lover than a partner or friend.

His face twisted at her reasoning and he seemed to be considering her plan, but then he shook his head. "You've never worked with me. No one will hear me."

She drew in a breath at his utter confidence. Over-confidence, she would say.

"I'm coming. There's no time to argue."

Noah's mouth thinned into a hard line she'd never seen, and a fire came into his eyes that she was sure had frightened hardened criminals before. It did nothing for her except cause a little ache in the very pit of her stomach.

"Fine, Miss Marion." With a low growl he rose from the bed and offered her a hand. "But don't hinder me."

She stifled her grin at his serious face. If she was going to have to live in Josiah Lucas's house and endure his leering looks, the least Noah could do was allow her to help him apprehend the man. And convincing him was less difficult than she'd imagined.

"Are you coming, then?" He turned at the door with a raised eyebrow.

"Yes." She scrambled to her feet and hurried after him.

He lifted his finger to his lips again and whispered, "Stay behind me and don't make a sound."

Marion huddled closer to his back as she tried to ignore the heat coming from him. She watched as he cracked the door, pressing his ear to the space he'd made and straining to hear even the faintest sound. When he seemed satisfied, he peered out, looking left and right several times. Then, with a nod in her direction, he grasped her hand and began to lead her down the hall.

Every nerve ending in Marion's fingers came to life at his warm touch. Though the gesture was innocent enough, it sent heat flashing through her like lightning, touching every tender part of her until she was filled with it. She barely breathed as he led her silently through the hallway and down the stairs toward Lucas's office.

They entered the dark room together. Noah sighed as he shut the door behind them. Moonlight was the only illumination in the room for the moment, and in it she saw his face clearly outlined. He turned and it was as if he suddenly remembered she was there.

"Well, that's part of the job done," he whispered, still clinging to her hand.

"Yes."

She glanced down at their intertwined fingers with a smile. Somehow their hands fit, despite how much bigger his were than hers. He followed her gaze, then let go of her to light a candle and bring a soft glow to the room.

"We'll have to work quickly." Marion could hear the slight choke to his voice. "Getting caught at this juncture could be devastating."

She nodded. "What are we looking for?"

"*You...*" he said with emphasis, "Aren't looking for anything. Hold the candle for me so I can see." He handed her the smoldering tallow stick.

She followed him to the desk where he began sorting through papers one by one. She was amazed by how quickly he could glance over a sheet and decide if it was worthwhile or not. In no time he'd cleared everything on the desk top, returned the papers to their original position and shifted his attention to the desk drawers.

"I was glad to know my message got to you." He looked up at her briefly with a small smile. "I worried it might put you in danger."

She started at his words. By the way he seemed singularly dedicated to his search, she'd thought he'd all but forgotten her presence.

"No. It reached me fine. Sally seems to be a reliable friend." She paused, thinking about the fact that the maid knew of their tryst. "Er..."

"Yes?" he asked as he opened another drawer with an almost imperceptible squeak. He grimaced, muttering, "Out of practice."

She smiled at his perfectionism. "About Sally, she knows you were coming here tonight."

Noah's search came to a complete halt as his blue eyes rushed to her face. "How?"

"She read your note. Apparently she's worried for my safety. I'm sure she only did it out of protectiveness." With a grimace, she explored Noah's angry face, worried about the expression in his eyes.

"Damn." His voice went up a level in the quiet room. "If she breathes a word about this to Lucas or to anyone else…"

Marion shook her head. After the bargain she and Sally had struck, she couldn't believe the young woman wouldn't keep her word. "She won't."

For a long moment he said nothing else and she could tell he was mulling over what she'd said. Finally, he looked at her again.

"Perhaps we can use her to our advantage," he said, rubbing his brow. "After all, she's aided you in doing something wrong."

Marion's mouth fall open in surprise. "No! I won't *use* her. She gave me her word she won't tell, and that's enough for me."

His frown lengthened. "It shouldn't be. You don't know that this woman isn't a spy for Lucas sent to find out all your moves and report back to him."

She laughed. "That's ridiculous, Noah. Where do you come up with these ideas?"

He glared at her. "From years of experience you do not have the benefit of. Sometimes using people is a necessary evil."

Marion felt as if she'd been slapped. Was this the same man who'd kissed her, awakened her heart? And if he explained away using her maid, did he also explain away using Marion for his own gain. Suddenly things seemed much clearer to her.

"You have no problem using people?" She lowered the candle back to the table.

He frowned. "When it's necessary."

"Like you are now using me?" she asked.

Noah's face darkened and his eyes flashed blue fire. "I'm not using you, Marion," he said, his voice dangerously soft. "In fact, I would say you're using me. You came to me, remember? You asked me for *my* help."

She turned away. "And you only agreed to help me if I would assist you with your case. But I wonder, when will you do as you agreed and make me appear ruined in front of my father? My time is running out."

She shivered as she ticked off the days in her mind. In only a short week, Lucas would come and try to make his claim on her body.

She spun to face Noah with tears pricking her eyes. "You know I'm weak to you. What if you're only using that weakness to get what you want?"

"I told you I'd protect you and I shall."

The anger in Noah's eyes faded slowly. With a few steps he was just in front of her. He reached out his fingers to brush them along the curve of her jaw, sending a quick, intense thrill through her entire body.

"And as for your weakness... it's one we share."

With a quiet groan he brought his mouth down on hers. Without hesitation, she gripped her fists around the lapels of his jacket and returned the kiss with as much passion as he gave. Their mouths merged, tongues parrying until both were breathless. Finally, Noah pushed her back gently. He looked at her with eyes glazed by desire.

"You see?" His voice was rough as he took two steps away.

For a moment, silence hung between them as Marion tried to regain her composure and find her voice. Before she could do either, the clock in the hallway began to gong, ringing off the time. At three strikes, it stopped.

"And now I've stayed too long and found nothing. At least nothing of great use." He held out his hand to her. Marion thought it trembled, but when she looked again it was firm. "Come, I'll exit through your window."

She blew out the candle before putting her fingers in his. Again, a feeling of safety filled her as he began to lead her back up the staircase toward her room. A foreign feeling, a feeling of coming home. It was so strong it nearly knocked her from her feet. She was happy when they reached her chamber and he released her.

"I'm sorry you didn't find anything." She closed the door behind her and leaned back against the wood.

"It's not your fault," he said with a sigh as he returned to her window to open it.

She almost pointed out that she'd been a distraction, but didn't. It was painfully obvious he already knew what a diversion she'd been and still was.

"Well, goodnight."

"Wait!" In a few light steps, she hurried to the window. Noah already had one muscular leg out on the ledge, but turned back to her with questioning eyes.

"Yes?"

Marion looked at him, so handsome, so much everything she'd ever wanted, and would ever want. She ached for the fact that she could never have him. With that regret in her heart, she leaned forward, cupped his strong jaw in both her hands, and kissed him.

This time it was Noah's turn to be surprised, and hers to be in control. She enjoyed the juxtaposition of their usual roles. Pulling him closer, she deepened the kiss, darting the tip of her tongue between his lips as he had done to her. To her surprise, Noah uttered a deep, guttural moan and clutched her closer to him. His arms came around her waist like a vice to crush her against his chest. For a moment she lost all sense of time and place. The only thing that existed or mattered was the two of them and the small world they created in each other's arms.

But the moment passed. Noah was in danger if he stayed in her room, so against her own desires, she pushed back away from his chest and the heavenly prison of his arms. He blinked a few times to clear his eyes as he stared into her face, searching for… something. She didn't know what.

"I know you aren't using me." With trembling hands, she reached out to run her fingers along the harsh curve of his jaw. "Go safely."

Noah wrinkled his brow and opened his mouth as if he wanted to say something. Then he hesitated with a shake of his dark head.

"Goodnight."

Turning away from her, he took a short jump to the nearest tree limb and disappeared from sight. She took a few steps to close the window and saw that he had already made it down the tall tree and was hurrying to a circle of trees where Phantom awaited his return. At the edge of the circle, Noah turned back. When he saw her waving from her window, he flashed her a grin, then disappeared.

She dipped her head with a sigh. The situation was only spiraling out of control with each passing day. With each moment she spent with Noah, she wanted him even more. And she couldn't have him.

She was surprised that fact hurt more than any betrayal from her father ever had.

CHAPTER FOURTEEN

Marion swore as she made another crooked stitch on a piece of cloth that already looked like she'd run it through a wash ringer. Though she didn't enjoy it as much as sketching, normally she had no problems making a pattern work, but today she was completely incompetent. She'd tried to convince herself it was only because of lack of sleep the past few nights. In her heart she knew it was so much more.

Too many thoughts tangled together in her head. She had three more days before Lucas would claim her, whether she fought him or not. Already the man watched her with predatory eyes, desire-filled eyes. Her stomach turned with the thought.

And she'd no chance to remind Noah of her ticking clock because he hadn't made contact with her since the night he snuck into her bedroom. She was beginning to wonder if he meant to help her at all, or if, his help would come too late. After all, he had no knowledge of the real nature of her predicament. He only thought she was walking into an arranged marriage, not that Lucas would take her virtue within days if she didn't escape his house. The idea of the old man laying a finger on her was enough to make her drop her needlepoint with a shiver of disgust.

"You seem distracted, my dear."

Marion paused midway from reaching her discarded

handiwork. Over the weeks, she'd come to know Josiah Lucas's voice as well as she knew her own. The coldness of it haunted her.

Steeling herself to another boring and disturbing conversation, she rose to her feet and turned to the door with a half smile.

"Mr. Lucas. I didn't hear you come in."

He smiled that thin, skeletal smile of his. "No, I expect not. Most young ladies do a better job of hiding their thoughts when they're around other people. You're most unique, Miss Marion."

The lump in her throat made her swallow hard before she could speak again. "Are my thoughts so very clear to you, Mr. Lucas?"

He entered the room and tapped the door shut discreetly with his heel. She eyed the miniscule crack in the door with an arched eyebrow. This wasn't good.

"Often they are very clear." He moved steadily toward her. Marion fought the urge to back away just as quickly. "But that's part of your charm."

He halted directly in front of her, mere inches from her body. She could smell a strong odor of some kind of cologne. It hung heavily on the old man's skin and hair. It was entirely unpleasant, especially when he was so close that Marion had to breathe his air.

Just as she was about to point out the impropriety of his proximity, he bent down and picked up her long forgotten needlepoint. When he straightened up, he took a long time looking at her curves, from her feet to the top of her head.

She took her work with a forced smile. "Thank you, Mr. Lucas."

He clucked his tongue as he motioned for her to return to her seat. She did so warily, feeling his gray eyes on her every step of the way.

"Now, now Marion. You've lived in my house for nearly a month. Don't you think we've grown close enough that you could call me Josiah?" He took a place on the settee beside her as he spoke, ignoring the two other empty chairs further from her.

Marion edged away. "Oh no, Mr. Lucas, I don't think that would be appropriate at all. My father and mother were very clear to me that I should always address my *elders*," she paused with special emphasis on the word. "With respect."

Lucas's smile fell and a flicker of rage lit up in his eyes. Marion's heart skipped at the sight. Was that what Georgina had seen as she drew her last breath?

"And what of your suitors? Would you not offer them such an allowance if they were serious about you?" His voice was more a hiss than a normal speaking voice.

Marion balked. She rose to her feet and backed away. She was flailing wildly and yet she couldn't seem to be able to control her arms. She raised them as a guard to his words and his intentions.

"You are not my suitor."

His grin returned at her statement. "Surely you haven't been blind to my desire to know you better these last few weeks. You may be..." He swallowed hard and his eyes moved over her body again. "You may be an innocent, but you're still a woman. A woman is always aware of the power she wields over a man."

Marion found she'd backed herself into the mantel and had nowhere else to go. Taking a few long breaths, she tried to calm herself. She had to return to the position she had taken before she cowered. Lucas stood and moved toward her with terrifying slowness. Like he was stalking her. Showing him fear was like running from a rabid dog. It would only encourage him.

"I'm sure I hold no power over you. And I always felt that your interest in me was an indication of your friendship with and your respect for my father. I'm pleased to be your friend." She cursed her shaking voice. It revealed too much about her frightened state of mind.

"Yet you've expressed an interest in my late wife," Lucas said. His smile widened as he came closer step by small step. "Don't you think that could send a message to a man that you had some interest in him?"

She froze. Damn, this was exactly the situation she'd been trying to avoid.

"I-I told you," Marion stammered. "Your wife was close to my age. I was only interested in her as my peer."

"You're very much like her." Finally, he reached Marion though he kept a respectable distance. "You look a little like her, though there's more fire in your eyes than there was in hers. I trained her fire out of her."

She cringed at the smile that accompanied his words. Her thoughts trailed to what Sally had told her about poor Georgina's screams in their bedroom. Of her fighting against the very man who had now neatly boxed Marion in with no hope of escape.

"I'm certain that's none of my business," she stammered. She needed an escape route but there was none.

"Don't you want to know about my wife?" He placed one large hand on the wall beside her head. "You wanted to know before."

"Th-They were impertinent questions." A sob caught in her throat before she could swallow it back. "I shouldn't have asked them."

"Having a young wife has advantages," he continued, almost as if she hadn't spoken at all. His finger strayed toward her cheek and he traced over the curve there. She turned her head away, but his hand followed. "And disadvantages. Other men notice her. Other men covet her and the things she hides under pretty dresses and demure smiles."

A wave of nausea hit Marion and a cold sweat broke over her brow, but she fought to remain calm, measuring her breathing as she tried to think of way out of the situation. "I'm certain Mrs. Lucas was admired for her charms by both men and women."

He laughed, though the sound was far from pleasant. "Men like your Noah Jordan wanted her. Men who were young and virile and willing to make her empty promises. But I made sure she could have nothing."

His eyes narrowed as he put his face directly in front of hers. Even as he spoke, his fingers trailed down the neckline of her gown. Then lower until the tips brushed the curve of her breast. Marion bucked at the touch, but Lucas leaned forward to keep her from escaping.

"Stop," she whispered, too afraid to say it louder. She felt like she was underwater and couldn't get enough air to fight or speak.

He ignored her plea. "You must understand, I won't allow what is mine be taken. *Ever.*"

Marion couldn't control the shaking of her entire body now. Even her toes trembled as Lucas slowly removed his hand and backed away. He smiled as if he were satisfied his message had been received and understood.

"I'll let you return to your needlepoint, Marion." He motioned toward the settee with relish. "And I look forward to the next few days when I'm sure we'll come to understand each other all the better. Good day."

With that, he left the room. Marion sank to her knees as soon as he was out of sight. Silent tears streamed down her cheeks as the full gravity of her situation became clear to her. Lucas wasn't the kind of man who would hold to the promise he'd made to her father. Any night he could have burst into her room and taken her, and any night he still could.

Yet she'd told Noah nothing of the full horror of his plans for her. The one person who could save her didn't know the hideous truth. And for what? Because of a girlish crush that could lead to nothing?

But even if she told him the truth, would he save her? Especially if it endangered his case? After all, her father lied on a regular basis, Lucas lied. Perhaps Noah lied, too. It had been his suggestion to use the only other friend she had, Sally.

The situation was untenable.

Sally bustled through the door with concern clear on her face. When she saw Marion huddled by the fire, she rushed to her side.

"Oh, miss. What did he do to you? When I saw him come out of the room looking like a cat in the cream, I just knew something terrible had happened." The maid lifted her hand to feel Marion's brow. "He didn't... he didn't touch you, did he?"

Marion shook her head as the other girl helped her to her shaky feet. "No. Not yet."

Sally's eyes widened a fraction. "Do you think he means to?"

Marion nodded in response as she worked her way back to the settee. She gripped the back of every chair and edge of every table along the way. She didn't trust her legs would hold her.

"I *know* he means to." She swallowed past the bile in her throat. "I must find my own way out of this mess, I can't trust anyone else will come through for me."

"What do you mean to do, Miss Marion?"

The young woman's voice was thick with concern. When Marion turned to look at her, she could see Sally was trembling. She couldn't help but think of what Noah had said: that the maid could easily be her enemy not her friend. And that she should use the young woman before her.

"I'll need your help." She eyed Sally closely for her reaction and was relieved when the girl nodded immediately.

"Of course, what can I do?"

"I must send a message to Noah Jordan, but I don't know which member of Lucas's household is under the Marquis' employ. If I write a note to the gentleman, could you give it to the correct person and ask that it be delivered immediately?"

"I... suppose... so." The girl cocked her head. "But are you sure you want to bring Lord Woodbury into this? He doesn't have the best reputation and you already told me there are no promises between you."

Marion nodded, though a sharp shot of regret moved through her at Sally's blunt appraisal. "I'm positive. Noah is the only person who can help me, whether he wants to or not. Now, go fetch me some ink and a few pieces of paper."

After Sally had scurried from the drawing room to find the items she'd ordered, Marion rose to her feet and crossed to the window to stare in the direction of Linton Green. She planned to tell Noah the whole truth when he came to her, but this time she wouldn't give him the chance to refuse her plea for assistance. No, Marion knew what she had to do, and though Noah might be furious at her for it later, she had no choice but to protect herself.

"When did it arrive?" Noah read Marion's note a second time.

"Just a short time ago." Rothschild stood at attention in front of his master's desk while he awaited orders. "I tried to find you, my lord, but all I knew was that you'd gone riding."

Noah shook his head in reassurance. "Don't trouble yourself any longer, Rothschild. No damage was done. I'll ring for you to deliver my response, so be ready."

"Yes, sir." The young man gave a quick bow and scurried from the room.

"What are you doing, Marion?" Noah muttered.

Her note was brief, telling him she had new information to share, but he had to come to her room that night. He had the strangest premonition that Marion's missive was a trap, but Rothschild and his brother had made it clear Marion remained unharmed. She certainly wasn't being influenced by Lucas or her father. And there was no doubt the note was written by her. The handwriting was smooth and rounded, flowing over the page in delicate spirals and curls. Exactly as he would have expected her hand to be.

With a frown, he crumpled the message into his pocket and sat down at his desk to write his reply. Seeing Marion was the only way he'd find out the truth. Even if she hadn't written him asking for his presence, he had planned on coming to her that night or the next. Her time was ticking away and she'd soon be forced into an engagement with Lucas. He wanted to spare her that.

It wasn't as if his investigation was going anywhere. Though the servants had whispered Georgina hadn't fallen, there was no evidence she had been murdered. The death had been so long ago, Noah worried it was a dead-end case. Not the way he wanted to end his career in the War Department, but it couldn't be helped.

He scribbled a quick reply to Marion's message. He should have contacted her earlier, but had been reticent to see her. When she'd kissed him at her window a few days earlier, it had shocked his entire system and he'd spent hours since contemplating what to do about her. He hated the idea of her rotting away in the country with her aunts, with no prospect of a better life. But the idea of launching her into Society and watching her marry one of his own acquaintances or, God forbid, *friends* was little better.

He was so desperate he would have gone to his mother, but Tabitha had departed to visit friends a few days before and wouldn't be back until the following afternoon. Her wise council couldn't be depended upon.

With a frustrated growl, Noah rang the bell at his door with relish. He would know what to do when he saw Marion. Somehow he would just *know* what decision was the right one for her future… and for his.

CHAPTER FIFTEEN

Marion's dressing gown twisted around her calves each time she pivoted across her room. Wasn't it one yet? Noah had said he'd come to her at one. Everything else was in place. Sally knew her role in Marion's plan and was ready to do her part. Though she was wracked with nervousness and doubt, Marion was resigned to her decision. All that was missing was Noah.

With a groan, she flopped onto the soft chair by the window. He had promised he would come. She would just have to trust he was telling the truth. Not that trust was a commodity she easily came by. It was why she was forced to play out their agreement the way she planned.

A movement in the bushes below caught her eye in the faint moonlight. At first she believed she'd imagined the motion, but when it came again and a man stepped from the shadows to creep over to the tall oak beside her window, she breathed a sigh of relief. Noah was there and she could relax.

At least until he reached the top of the oak tree and entered her room. Then her plan would be set in motion and she would be anything but relaxed.

He looked up as he hooked one booted foot into a notch in the tree. Their gazes met and Marion was drawn in by the pleasure on his face. He grinned, then began the task of climbing the tree to reach her window. She admired how his muscular body moved effortlessly up the tree trunk. He had natural balance and athletic grace. Before she had time to breathe, he'd pushed open her window and was standing before her with a grin on his face and not a drop of sweat on his brow.

"Thank you for leaving the window unlocked."

"Y-your note."

She was suddenly very aware she was in her dressing gown. The man always made her conscious of her body and of the way it reacted to him.

"Yes, our little correspondence." His mouth thinned into a frown as he retrieved a wrinkled sheet of paper from his pocket. Holding it out in front of her nose, he shook his head. "*This* was a dangerous thing to do. You should have known I'd come to you soon, you shouldn't have taken the risk to contact me."

Marion drew in a breath as he crossed to the fire and tossed her note in.

"And how was I to know that, Lord Woodbury?" she snapped, her nervousness making her short-tempered. "You haven't spoken to me since you were last in this room. For all I knew you had abandoned me completely."

Noah turned from the fire. "Why is it you assume I won't keep my promise to keep you from harm? Have I done something to prove my deception?"

He watched her face twist at his words and instantly regretted his sharpness. But how was he to react when he came through her window and found her in a thin cotton wrap? It was all he could do to concentrate on why he was there, not wonder what was under that robe. The woman was a test of his self-control and he failed miserably every time he was near her.

"No." She sat down hard on the edge of her dressing table and folded her arms across her chest as a barrier. "But my time is running out. I was afraid of…" she trailed off, leaving Noah to wonder once again why she was so reticent to talk about her father and Lucas's plan for her.

"Afraid of what? Shortly your father will force an

engagement with Lucas, but I promised you I wouldn't let the man marry you." He took a few steps closer. From the miserable expression on her face, he could see that promise wasn't enough.

She stood up. "You said you wouldn't let him become engaged to me. *That* was your promise. You told me you would stop this before it went that far!"

He shrugged one shoulder. "A few days more or less won't really make any difference, will it?"

Marion made a little gasp in the back of her throat as the color drained from her face.

"Marion?"

"I should have known," she muttered. "I should have known you wouldn't be honest with me. That I couldn't depend on you any more than I could depend on my father or anyone else. I should have taken care of this myself from the beginning, but I let myself get drawn in by friendship and... and..." Her eyes came up to briefly meet his. "Kisses."

He shook his head. "What are you talking about?"

She took a few steps closer to him, her brown eyes flitting to the door before they refocused on his face. "I must tell you the truth."

He frowned as the premonition of a trap returned to him, this time much stronger. "The truth about what Marion?"

"The reason why I need your help so badly." She took a short breath and blinked back the tears that had suddenly filled her eyes. "I wanted to tell you the day I first asked for your help, but I was embarrassed. Then, as we grew closer, I didn't want you to know that he-"

She stopped, clearing her throat as if what she was going to say was distasteful to her. Although Noah still felt cornered by her strange behavior, he also was compelled to comfort her in her obvious distress. He touched her arm, but the instant he did so he recognized his mistake. Her body heat seared through his skin, while her scent filled his nostrils and dizzied his mind.

"Slow down," he said, more to himself than to her. "Tell me from the beginning what happened."

She nodded, but didn't pull away from him. He didn't seem to have the strength to draw back from her, so he continued to hold her arm in a gentle grip, feeling the electricity between them pulse through his hand, his blood, and his entire body.

"Noah, when I came to you and told you my father had traded a promise to wed me for the debts Lucas holds over him, I didn't tell you everything." Marion's composure slowly returned to her, no thanks to Noah's hands on her.

His eyes narrowed, the blue going from the dark color of desire to a brighter, more cautious hue. "What did you leave out, Marion?"

As the coldness crept back into his voice, she swallowed hard. What she was about to say would surely spark his anger. "My father didn't just sell my hand in marriage." She took a deep breath. "He sold my… body, as well."

Closing her eyes, she waited for his rage. Instead, he released her arm as if it burned him and took a step back. "I don't understand."

"I said, he sold my body to Lucas." How she hated repeating the words.

"Look at me." He put a firm finger beneath her chin to raise her face toward his. "What does that mean?"

She couldn't stop the flow of the tears as she took in the look of pure rage on Noah's face. He hated her for her deception, just as she knew he would.

"Lucas wants an heir, but Georgina couldn't give him one." She choked the words out. "He told my father he had to *insure* I would breed for him, so he plans to take a husband's rights before we're married."

He made a sound of disgust in his throat.

Marion whispered, "The end of the month wasn't when he planned to become engaged to me, it was the time he planned to take me to his bed, whether I agreed to that or not."

She turned her face away and braced herself for the tirade surely to come. Noah's rage emanated from his body in long waves and he hadn't even spoken yet.

To her surprise, instead of beginning a diatribe against her, he turned away to stalk to the fire. His back faced her and for a long time he neither spoke, nor moved.

"You don't have any liquor in here, do you?" he asked after what seemed like an eternity had passed.

"N-no," she stammered. "I'm sorry, it isn't exactly the kind of thing I keep in my bedroom."

"No."

He spun on his heel to face her, but the only indication she had of his anger were his stormy eyes. The rest of his face and his body were the vision of a calm and collected man. He could have been chatting with her in a salon, rather than speaking about the sale of her virtue while she stood in her bedroom clad only in her dressing gown.

"Aren't you going to shout at me for lying to you?" The waiting seemed worse than the bellowing she knew would come.

"If I start telling you how *reckless*--" his voice finally rose as emphasis on the word. "--you were for keeping the entire truth from me, I'm afraid I'll bring down the house."

Her bottom lip quivered, but she forced herself to remain calm. She couldn't fall apart, not in the face of his total composure. It would only seem more manipulative than she had already been.

"I didn't want you to think less of me, Noah. I *liked* being your friend and I didn't want to lose that because of my father's vile plans."

He snorted out a curse under his breath. It was a word she'd never heard before, but she didn't have to guess the meaning.

"So to maintain our friendship, you *lied* to me?"

"It sounds so terrible when you put it that way," she said quietly as she turned away. This unruffled reaction was far worse than anything she'd imagined. Before she got two steps away from him, he caught her arm and spun her back.

"Don't turn your back on me while you talk. I want to know what's a lie and what's the truth, I can only do that when you look at me," he growled.

Another sob escaped her lips, but she did as she was told and stared into his face. "I deserve that, but…"

"But what?" His eyes narrowed. "But you think I'm the kind of man who would judge you on your so-called father's actions? That I would think less of you because he sold you?"

Her pent up emotions finally overflowed. "I didn't know what you would think! I'm not like you. I cannot just analyze a person within a few moments and decide if they're trustworthy or not."

"But you did." His voice rose up another notch before he took a deep breath. "You did exactly that when you decided to lie. My God, do you know what you've done?"

She wanted to beg for his forgiveness, but it was far too late for that. Instead she dipped her head in defeat. "I've hurt your case, I've ruined our friendship, and I've made you hate me."

"Hate you?" He wrinkled his face as if that was a foreign notion. "None of those things! You've put yourself in terrible, terrible danger." With one step, he had both her arms in his hands. "Any night, Josiah Lucas could have come through that door and taken you, and I would have known nothing about it. He would have hurt you, and I couldn't have protected you. That's what makes me so furious with you that I want to shake some sense into your head."

Her heart, which had already been pounding, now doubled its time. "I realized that today when he attacked me in the library, and that's why I sent for you," she whispered.

"He attacked you?" Noah's face twisted into a terrifying mask for a moment, then returned to normal. "Did he touch you?"

His eyes narrowed and malice entered his tone. In that

moment Marion understood the dangerous man behind Noah's façade. God help the man who crossed his path. He would live to regret his mistake.

"No," she whispered. "But he made it clear to me that you would never take me from him."

"My God."

With a shiver, Noah folded her into his arms, crushing her against his chest until she could barely breathe. His heart pounded against her cheek, and suddenly she realized he wasn't angry, he was afraid for her.

"I could have spared you all that fear," he said. He drew back and stared down at her. "I could have ended this nightmare you've been living for the past month, if only you'd told me the whole truth from the start."

"I'm sorry." He was so close she felt her own breath reverberate hot against her lips.

He tilted her chin up a fraction. "Don't be sorry, just promise me you'll never lie to me again. Trust me to help you."

She nodded, held willing captive by his arms and his eyes. For a brief moment, she forgot everything around her as he filled her vision and kept her warm with the heat of his body. But even as she nodded, the faint flickering of guilt in her mind reminded her of her plan for Noah that night.

Would she really be able to force his hand after all the kindnesses he'd done for her? After all the feelings he inspired in her? No. She couldn't lie to him once again. No matter what, she would find a way to escape her father without using Noah.

"Yes, I promise, but…"

Before she could finish her sentence, Noah brought his lips down to consume her with a kiss that turned all her bones to water and her blood to fire.

Instantly, Noah felt Marion collapse into the kiss, giving up freely what he demanded with his mouth and with his hands as they roamed down to her waist. His fingertips dug into the cotton of her wrapper and around her hips, dragging her up against him until their bodies touched intimately and

Marion let out a quiet sigh of surrender. The rage and fear that had coursed through him when she told him the truth eased from his body, replaced by a pulsing desire he couldn't control. Truth be told, he didn't even want to control it any longer. He needed Marion. He needed to feel her in his arms and keep her safe by making her his.

By the way she returned his kiss, she wanted the same thing, though he doubted in her innocence that she knew what that want inside her was. He smiled against her mouth. He would teach her. He would teach her what that ache deep within her belly was, and how easy it was for him to release her from its pleasurable grip.

"Noah," she sighed against his mouth, clutching him closer.

"I want you," he whispered, pressing hot, swift kisses against her cheek, her jaw line and up to the shell of her ear. He teased the outer rim with the tip of his tongue. "Let me love you tonight."

She nodded, her only answer a deep, throaty moan of pleasure. With that permission asked for and granted, he guided her backward until her backside bumped against the mattress edge. There he was surprised when her hands came up to loosen his jacket buttons. She shoved the heavier fabric aside and slid her hands down his chest and across his ribcage. He sucked in his breath as his need threatened to burn out of control.

But this would be her first time, and he wanted to make it special, an experience she would look back on with a blush of pleasure, not a grimace of discomfort. Tamping his need down, he cupped her chin to kiss her once more. She shivered under the touch and the soft half-moons of her fingernails grazed his muscles as she clutched at his shirt.

Noah eased his mouth down to Marion's throat, taking a deep breath of her scent as he continued to kiss her. Funny how he'd never really noticed the uniqueness of each woman's scent before. Until Marion, he hadn't noticed a great many things about women.

Marion moaned when Noah's mouth trailed across her collarbone. He shoved aside the top of her wrap while he moved lower, revealing more and more of her skin. But instead of being shy, Marion shifted to aid him, wanting to be free of the confines of her clothes. She wanted to press her body against his in the intimate dance of sex she knew so little about. Fear was the last thing that crossed her mind.

She lifted trembling hands to Noah's shirt and began to work at the buttons there. One by one she opened them until she could free the fabric from his shoulders to pool in a heap by his feet. In the firelight he was truly magnificent. His blue eyes held hers with an intensity that made her quake with anticipation. His broad shoulders and toned chest and stomach put off enough heat to warm her even without the fire. In fact, she was almost too hot and squirmed nearer to him.

Noah smiled at her eagerness. Her emotions were probably all too clear to the insightful man before her, but she didn't care. She needed him and she wanted him to know that. And if he also guessed how deeply she had fallen in love with him, then so be it.

Her trembling hands glided down his chest. His muscles contracted under her fingertips, and he sucked his breath in as she learned the curves and hollows of his upper body. She only hesitated for a moment before she pressed a soft kiss against his chest, her fingers tangling in the wiry hair there as she tasted his skin.

"Marion-"

When she lifted her eyes, she could see how much he struggled for control and felt an immense power. She had made his eyes glaze over like that. *She* had made him tremble.

But if she felt power, it was soon pushed away when Noah gripped her hips and lifted her up to sit on the bed. He nudged her legs far apart and stepped between them, wrapping her thighs around his hips until their bodies met. She gasped at the new contact, but when he shifted his hips closer and his hard manhood brushed against the apex of her thighs, she shivered in response. The pleasure at that spot was instant and powerful, sending a rush of new sensation through her.

Now Noah's hands fumbled at her robe tie, catching the ends and yanking them until the knot released itself and the wrapper fell open. He gasped to find that Marion didn't wear a nightshift beneath the cotton wrapper. She was entirely naked, from her small, warm breasts, to her flat stomach, to the wispy brown curls that rested where her thighs met.

She blushed at his parted-lipped appraisal of her body. Clutching at her robe, she pushed it partly closed again.

"No, you're perfect." He shoved the fabric down to bunch at her hips, then lifting her up the slightest bit to take it off completely. "I was surprised, that's all."

She nodded as the tension in her eyes faded a fraction. He had the strongest urge to feel her pressed against him. Grabbing her hands, he wrapped them around his neck and pulled her up off the bed and against his chest. Her breasts flattened as her skin glided across his like silk.

With a quick pivot, he laid her back down on the bed, this time with her hair spread across the pillows like a fan. Her breath came in short bursts as she stared up at him. He met her eyes as he crawled up beside her and stroked his hand along her belly.

She stiffened under his hands now that they caressed her bare skin, but when he slid his fingers up to brush her pink nipples, she relaxed again with a soft, "Oh my."

Marion had never realized how good being touched could feel. Her own life had been devoid of affection since her mother had died, but she'd convinced herself she didn't crave physical touch. She'd never dared to imagine a feeling like this, though her body rose up when Noah's hands caressed her. Even though the sensations rushing through her at blinding speed were foreign, they were intensely pleasurable and filled her with a burning ache in every nerve of her body.

"Kiss me." Noah's order was thick and husky as his

mouth came back down to cover hers. Her body relaxed as he slowly made love to her mouth, his tongue gently tracing her lips, then dipping inside her for slow, languid thrusts.

In the sensual haze he created, she almost didn't realize his hands were moving down her body. When his thumb grazed her nipple a second time, she gave a moan at the flash of pleasure that started where he'd touched her and then shot down to the throbbing ache between her thighs.

Then his mouth moved away from hers, following the path his hand had made with slow, humid heat. Marion blinked up at the canopy over her bed as her nerves crackled with new awareness. She'd never known someone could or would want to kiss her all over, or that she would rise up to meet those kisses with the breathy moans she heard herself utter.

When Noah placed his lips on her breast and darted his tongue out to tease the hard bud, her whole body convulsed with pleasure.

He smiled up at her, loving how a thin line of sweat made her brow shine in the firelight. Her eyes were cloudy with desire and surprise. "Relax, Marion. I promise you, what I'm about to do won't hurt you."

She nodded, and her eyes closed with another moan when he returned his lips to her breast. When he felt her surrender completely, he slid his hand down to the heated, slick place where her legs met. She was already wet with desire, ready for him to make love to her, but he practiced the self-control he'd been taught as a spy and waited. As much as he wanted to bury himself deep within her core and feel her body contract around him, he also wanted her to beg him to do just that. It would make her experience better and he wanted this to be perfect.

He glided one teasing finger across the outside of her nether lips, feeling her body shudder with anticipation of the invasion about to come. He continued to suckle from one breast to the other while he slid the same finger inside of her, uttering his own groan when her body flexed around him. She would be a most responsive lover once her nervousness subsided. He could tell already she would enjoy every moment, not simply endure his touch while she waited for the experience to be over.

She rolled her head from side to side as he began to slowly advance and withdraw in and out of her with his fingers. "Noah…"

"Yes, love," he whispered back, inching lower and lower with his mouth.

"I feel… I'm-" She gasped, sinking her teeth into her lower lip.

"Do you want me to stop?" He looked at her innocently as he stilled his hand's movement.

"No!" she said, eyes opening wide.

"Then perhaps you'll enjoy this more?" he asked as his mouth met his hand.

Marion arched up, her surprise at the invasion of his mouth fading in an instant when he spread her legs a little further and began kissing her with tenderness. Every time his tongue grazed the little hidden bud of pleasure she bucked up, seemingly unable to control the way her body ground against him.

If she had her wits, she would have been embarrassed by her wanton display, but her wits had left her the moment Noah had touched her in that secret place where she only dared to wash and not think about. All that was left was the throbbing need for him to release her from the prison he'd locked her in with hot kisses and shocking touches.

The strange, pleasurable pressure inside her began to grow, becoming more persistent, more urgent as the speed of his mouth increased. Finally, just when she thought she'd explode if she endured one more moment of sweet torture, Noah slipped his hand between her legs again and ground his thumb against the spot where she ached the most. Pleasure exploded in every part of her body, blinding her while she let out a long cry of release. Her body thrashed wildly as her hips rose off the bed, eagerly searching out the source of the gratification.

With a gasp, she collapsed back down, flopping one arm over her eyes as she panted to regain her breath. She heard Noah's husky chuckle and moved her arm to peek at him. Slowly he got to his knees and slid off the bed. With one smooth motion, he kicked off his boots and shrugged out of his trousers.

Her eyes grew wide at the long, thick thrust of his erection, but her body twitched again as if it knew he wouldn't hurt her, but bring her even more pleasure.

"I take it you enjoyed that?" he asked with a wicked grin as he stalked back toward the bed.

"I've never felt anything so exquisite in my life," she said with a nod. She sounded like a woman of easy virtue and didn't care. She wanted to know what was coming next.

He lay down. "If you'll allow me, I'd like to make you feel that good again. Perhaps even better."

She bit her lip as she glanced down his body to the hard length of him. "Better?"

How could anything feel better?

"After a little pain at the beginning," he promised as he rolled over on top of her, though he supported his weight on his elbows. The feel of his entire body pressed against her was wonderful. She felt warm and safe, as if she belonged to him even though she didn't.

She parted her legs a little further as she nodded her head. "Show me."

Noah closed his eyes at the innocent invitation. The refrain in his head repeated over and over, *slowly, slowly,* but he was losing his famous control.

He positioned himself between her legs, the tip of his erection just nudging her sheath. Then he leaned down and kissed her deeply. Just as he began to advance into the welcoming heat of her body, there came a loud pounding at the door.

CHAPTER SIXTEEN

Noah didn't fully comprehend the banging on the chamber door until Marion clutched both his arms and her eyes went wide with terror. "Papa!"

Noah shook his head to clear his addled mind.

"Marion!" Walter Hawthorne's loud, angry voice pierced through from the hallway. "Marion, what that maid told me better not be true. I'm going to kick this door in if you don't answer me!"

"What the hell?" In one smooth motion, Noah kicked off the bedclothes and scrambled around for his trousers.

"No," Marion whispered. "Please!"

Noah paused midway to reaching his pants and turned to look at her. Her brown hair was tangled from his fingers, her skin flushed from pleasure and anticipation. She looked beautiful. She looked guilty as hell.

"Wait…" His mind slowly came clear. How had she known the person at her door was her father? She had proclaimed it was him before Hawthorne spoke. She couldn't have known unless…

"You planned this, didn't you?"

The pounding picked up again in earnest, as well as Hawthorne's angry hollers, but Noah ignored both as he took a step toward the bed where Marion stared up at him.

"Didn't you?"

"Yes." She nodded with teary eyes. "Most of it. I didn't think things would go this far, but I *did* plan for my father to find you here."

"Damn." Noah raised a hand to his spinning head. "You told me you wouldn't lie to me again and then you did exactly that!"

"No." She reached out to him, but he backed away from her. "Please, we don't have much time. Allow him to find you. Let him believe…"

He shook his head. "That you're ruined. My God, you presented yourself to me not because you wanted me, but because you wanted an illusion."

That wasn't true, at least not completely. But he said it to hurt her because he felt strangely hurt that she would use the passionate experience between them to achieve her own end.

"Fine." He climbed back into the bed to pull the sheet over his lower body as he lay back down on top of her. "Kiss me."

He ground his mouth against hers, meaning for it to be a punishment, but his body leapt to life when she responded. Even though Noah knew he was bruising her soft lips, she clutched him closer and returned his angry kiss.

Behind him, the door crashed open. It bounced off the wall and Hawthorne uttered a loud, lewd curse. Noah rolled over and put on his best rakish face.

"Oh, hello, Hawthorne." He pushed the blankets over so Marion could cover herself.

"Papa!" she whispered.

Noah could see her humiliation was real, though the surprise at being caught wasn't.

"You whore!" Hawthorne burst out, taking a step into the room before he slammed the door behind him.

Noah reeled back in shock. The man had just found him in his daughter's bed and his first reaction was to call *her* a whore? Not even bother to confront Noah or threaten to call him out?

"See here," he began, but Marion had already wrapped the sheet around her and leapt out of the bed.

"Papa-"

"Just like your mother, I always said it." Hawthorne continued his tirade with flashing eyes as he looked his daughter up and down with a disgusted sneer. "And now you've ruined everything!"

Noah pulled his trousers up over his hips and buttoned the lower two buttons before he spoke again. "Don't blame your daughter, Hawthorne. I came here with the full intention of seducing her. I make it a habit to collect virgins."

Marion's eyes darted over to him. For a brief moment he saw the hurt flash in their brown depths before she returned her gaze to her father. "Papa, I don't know what to say."

As Noah pulled his mangled shirt back over his shoulders, he stifled a grimace. He had an idea Marion knew exactly what she planned to say to her father. She'd certainly known what to say to *him* to convince him to participate in her deception.

"You..." Hawthorne turned on Noah with a glare. "Get out. And Marion... get dressed and meet me in the Green Salon in three minutes."

Hawthorne spun on his heel and stalked out of the room, shutting the door behind him with a loud bang.

Noah's eyebrow went up. Hawthorne had reacted fairly calmly considering he'd just found his only daughter in bed with a man who claimed he'd been using her, but Noah felt the fury coming off the man.

"I'm not leaving you alone with him." Noah had his back to her as he buttoned his shirt.

When he turned, he was surprised to find Marion had dropped her protective sheet and was standing at her armoire throwing a shift over her head. Unlike many women who feigned embarrassment after they'd made love, she didn't seem bothered by the fact that Noah was staring at her. He felt his loins contract with unfilled need when his eyes moved over the soft curve of her hips, the round fullness of her breasts. He knew almost every inch of that incredible body, and yet it wasn't enough. Despite her deception, he wanted to finish what they'd started.

"Please go, Noah."

Her voice was only the shadow of the lively woman he'd come to care for so much. She took a gown from the closet and pulled it over the shift. When she reached around the back to fasten the buttons she let out a quiet grunt of frustration.

In a few steps, Noah crossed the room. With fingers deft from years of practice, he fastened the back of her gown, then turned her to face him. He searched her eyes for some sign of her reasons for tricking him. He found none.

"*Why* did you do this?"

Her eyes filled with tears, which she blinked away. "I'm short of time. Please, go. I'll find a way to talk to you again, to explain-"

Noah opened his mouth to protest, but shut it again. He was too frustrated to deal with Marion's explanations at present. "I can't leave you with your father. He looked ready to kill, Marion."

She shook her head. "He won't hurt me. Trust I'll be safe."

"I don't trust your father for one moment."

Her eyes softened. "You saved me from something terrible and I thank you. And you gave me something…"

Her small shiver sent another jolt of desire through Noah.

"You gave me something unexpected, but a gift nonetheless," she finished. "I can't ask you to save me more than you already have."

"I won't leave." He caught her arm and spun her back around to face him.

She shook her head in exasperation. "You'll only make things worse if you stay. You don't know him. He'll bluster himself out. I can take care of myself."

Noah dropped her arm and stepped back. "You just can't trust me at all, can you? You can't let me help you, only use me."

With a sigh, she dipped her head. "People use people. That's what you told me."

A shot of pain edged through Noah like a knife through his heart.

"Very well," he said, barely tamping down the urge to punch the wall.

She refused to meet his gaze, but turned away toward the door. "Good night. And thank you." Then she was gone.

Uttering a curse, Noah stalked to the window and swung out on the ledge. He had been used and it made him feel things he'd never felt before. Helpless, foolish. Had he made others feel this way? He'd certainly manipulated his fair share of people, though his intent had never been unkind.

With a shake of his head, he began crawling down the tree trunk. When he hit the ground, he hurried to Phantom and rode. The wind on his face did nothing to cool his anger. How the hell had he let things go so far with Marion? And why had she felt so compelled to lie and entrap him?

He'd thought they were growing closer, but perhaps that was part of her lie, as well. From her reactions there was no doubt she desired him, but that wasn't the same as trust. That wasn't he same as…

He slowed his horse with a startling though he couldn't help but voice. "Wasn't the same as what… love?"

Ridiculous. He needed a drink. Probably several. Hell, the whole bottle. Tomorrow he'd go back to Toppleton Square and make the arrangements for Marion's future. He'd buy her freedom and send her to her aunts. Once she was gone and safe from her father's cruelty and Lucas's crude attentions, he wouldn't have those troublesome questions in his head. He could go back to London and the life he'd planned there without so much as a backwards glance.

Marion was shaking. Her hands were shaking, her shoulders were shaking, even her hair was shaking. No matter how confidently she'd told Noah she would be safe with her father, now that she stood in the doorway of the Green Salon looking at the man, she wasn't sure her prediction would prove correct. She'd never seen Walter Hawthorne so angry.

Her father's face, which was nearly always red, had darkened to a plum purple. His eyes flashed with an anger and hatred she'd never felt the full force of before. She'd had always known her father didn't like her, but she'd never known he despised her until that moment.

"Come in and shut the door."

The fury in his voice made her hesitate. Too afraid not to, she did as she was told. She edged over to a seat by the fire to wait for her father's tirade to come. There was nothing she could say to explain herself. She didn't want to explain herself. She wanted nothing more than for her father to disinherit her and allow her to escape to a happier life.

"Just like your mother." He rose to his full height and shook his head as he poured himself what looked to be a second or third drink. "She ruined everything and now you have, too."

Her anger moved to the surface at his accusation. "I'm not the one who sold my child. If you put yourself into a bad situation, you certainly used me in the worst way possible to get yourself out."

Her father's eyes narrowed. "What do you know about that, girl?"

"I heard you." She jumped to her feet. "I heard you sell not just my hand in marriage to Lucas, but my body. Well, my body belongs to Noah Jordan now, and even I know that transaction cannot be made twice."

Her father's hand swung before she could react and

smacked across her cheek, sending her sprawling to the floor. For a moment, Marion lay still in shock. Even through all the cold years between them, Walter Hawthorne had never struck her. He'd ignored her, yes. Screamed at her, yes. But never touched her.

Her face stung at his hard blow. Slowly, she eased up to a sitting position to peer up at him from the floor.

"Shut your mouth, you worthless child!" He downed his drink as if she were nothing more than a dog needing a disciplinary kick.

"I'm ruined, Papa." Using the arm of the settee, she pulled herself back to her feet. "You can beat me all you like, but you cannot recapture what I've given away tonight."

For a moment her father only glared at her, but then his face softened and he began to laugh. Marion winced at the hollow, humorless sound. It didn't bode well.

"You stupid girl," he said. "You think you've saved yourself from Josiah Lucas's hands by giving that body of yours to another man?"

She remained silent. By God, she would keep her tongue and some shred of her dignity through this trial.

"Well, you're wrong." He clapped his hands together. "Only three people in this world know what a moll you've made of yourself tonight. There's me, and I'll certainly not tell a soul. There's Noah Jordan. Now that he's had a taste of you, he'll certainly not come back a second time. He admitted he collects virgins. He'll probably be glad that you marry another and I don't call him out."

Marion's heart skipped as she saw what her father was leading up to.

"And then there's you." His eyes narrowed as he turned them on her with a grin.

"And I'll tell Josiah Lucas everything," she promised. "I'll tell him that any child I bore could be Noah Jordan's."

Her father crossed the room faster than she'd ever seen his heavy frame move. He lifted her up and backed her into the wall, knocking the breath from her lungs with the force of the push. "If you say one thing, you'll join your rotting mother in the afterlife, do you understand me, girly?"

A tear slipped from Marion's eye and rolled down her cheek before she could hold it back. She searched her father's eyes for any affection, any love he might have once felt for her and saw nothing. No feeling. Nothing but anger. Hatred.

"Why? Why are you doing this?" she begged. "You're my father, doesn't that mean anything to you?"

"Nothing." He let go of her arms, and she hit the floor with both feet and stumbled before catching herself on the edge of a table nearby. "I've raised you, I've supported you, and you *will* repay me now by fulfilling this bargain."

"No!" She couldn't find air, like she was drowning.

"In fact," he continued, taking yet another drink. "Your little performance tonight has only earned you an accelerated destiny. When Lucas returns from his business, I'll send him to you. Before the dawn, you'll lay in that bed of yours and pretend to lose your maidenhead to him."

He leaned down with a sneer. "It shouldn't be hard to pretend, surely you remember how painful it was when Woodbury ran you through."

She turned her face away from his putrid breath and lewd words. "I won't do it. I won't."

With a bark of anger, he grabbed her by her tangled hair and dragged her from the room. Marion squealed at the rush of pain through her scalp as he pulled her up the stairs and down the hall. Once in her room, he let her go, but only to hit her again. This time the blow was with a closed fist that sent her careening toward her bed. She remained laying on the floor, too shocked and frightened to move for fear she'd provoke more of her father's drunken, infuriated battering.

"Good night, daughter."

He turned and stormed from the room, slamming the door behind her. With horror, she heard him insert the key in the lock. She leapt to her feet and flew across the room, throwing herself against the door. But the lock was already bolted and she was trapped.

"No!" she screamed against the wooden barrier. "Please, Papa let me out! Don't do this to me!"

Her only answer was her father's footsteps fading farther and farther away down the hall. Marion slid to the floor in a pool, too shocked and in pain to cry or scream or even think.

CHAPTER SEVENTEEN

How long had she been lying there? An hour? Two? Or perhaps only a few moments. Marion couldn't say, but it seemed as if an eternity had passed since her father had bolted her into her room... her destiny.

With effort, she pulled herself to her feet and crossed to the mirror at her dressing table. Already her face was red from the two blows her father had dealt her. In an hour or two they would be nasty bruises, reminders of what had been said and done that night.

Tears collected in her eyes, but she blinked them back. She wouldn't cry. The best thing she could do for herself now was get out and quickly. At any moment Josiah Lucas could barge through her door and all would be lost.

With deft movements, she put on her boots. As she pushed her hair back into a bun, she surveyed her options. The door was locked, there would be no escape that way this night. Her only other choice was the window. If Noah had come and gone that way, that meant she could do the same.

Noah. The thought of him made the pain in her heart even greater. He had been so furious when he left her bed, the anger in his eyes had made them a piercing blue that had stabbed into her soul. But even though he was furious, he would surely help her now if she went to him.

And there was nowhere else to go.

With a shiver, she pushed the window wide open and looked down. She was three dizzying floors above the hard ground below with not even a bush or hedge to break her fall. If she couldn't manage to get down by way of the tree, she would probably kill herself in the process.

"What other choice do I have?" Staying and waiting for Lucas to return home and rape her seemed a fate worse than death.

With her head pounding from her father's blows, she slung her foot on to the outside window ledge. It was much narrower than she'd estimated and it felt as if her foot could slip off at any moment. She gripped the shutters and yanked her other foot out.

"Don't look down, Marion," she whispered.

Focusing on the nearby tree limb, she shivered. Noah made this exercise look easy, even fun, but she could see now just how difficult it was. The limb was a good body length away from the ledge. She had no choice but to jump for it.

She fidgeted on the ledge, trying to get up the nerve to make the leap. It seemed almost impossible. She had almost decided to give up and go back inside when she thought of Josiah Lucas putting his hands on her, kissing her the way Noah had kissed her just hours before. Her determination returned threefold.

"One." She let go of the shutter. "Two." She measured the distance in her mind. "Three."

Marion leapt and hit the tree limb with the entire length of her middle. The impact knocked the air out of her for a painful moment. She scrambled to get a hold on the surprisingly slippery branch and managed only after she'd torn three fingernails on her left hand.

With her fingertips stinging and her lungs burning, she somehow managed to pull her body up further on the branch. Finally, after several failed attempts, she was able to hook a leg over and found herself sitting precariously, looking down at the earth far below.

She was trembling as she inched her way toward the main trunk of the enormous tree. Though half her work was done, she still had to get to the ground, and the old trunk didn't appear to have many foot or handholds.

She clawed at the trunk for a handhold first, digging her ravaged nails into the wood and hanging on for dear life. Then she dropped a foot down and began the frightening task of finding a place for her boot to rest. Inch by terrifying inch, she worked her way down the tree, pausing when the sweat on her brow dripped down her forehead and into her eyes. But she never stopped for long because at any moment her father or Lucas's face could appear in the window above and all her plans would be dashed.

Halfway down, exhaustion began to set in. Her arms grew weak and trembled whenever she paused for a breath and her legs threatened to give.

"Just ten feet more, Marion."

She heard the catch in her voice and hated the weakness that made her so afraid. Firming her right arm's grip on a branch, she wiped her forehead and nose on the arm of her gown. She was long past behaving like a lady. Just as she was about to continue her flight, her foot slipped. With only one arm supporting her, her fingers lost their grip.

And she fell.

She scrambled to grab the tree, but couldn't get a firm hold. With a twist, a grunt, and a painful crunch, she landed on her left side on the cool grass.

For a long moment, she was too afraid to move. Too afraid that she wouldn't be able to, or that a pool of her own blood would seep out if she breathed. With her mind racing, she began to test each limb. Her legs moved and though they ached from the fall, they didn't hurt like they were injured. The same with her back. Her right arm moved fine and her left…

"Ouch!" she barked out, biting back a loud curse. A sharp sting of pain through her left arm told her she'd been hurt.

With effort, she rose to her feet and glanced down at her arm. Though it wasn't twisted and no bone had pierced her skin, it hurt as though it had been pulled from the socket, then replaced none too gently. But despite that, Marion smiled. She was free.

With a quick glance at the window high above and the life she was leaving behind, Marion hobbled into the woods toward Noah's estate.

Night was beginning to fade. The moon had already drifted down over the horizon and the sky in the East was turning a soft purple in preparation for the dawn's approach. Marion had been walking for hours. Normally it wouldn't have taken so long to cross the three or four miles to Noah's estate, but between the cold of the night and her arm hurting so much, Marion stumbled more than walked. And at one point her sleep-deprived mind had become cloudy and she'd been lost for half an hour.

But now she could see Linton Green rising up like a savior in the distance over the treetops. In just a few moments she would be there. Noah would be there. He would help her.

Shivering and cursing herself for not wearing a heavier gown, she continued forward.

Thoughts of Noah drove her. She would explain everything to him. She'd make him understand she hadn't meant to trick him the way he thought. Yes, she'd told Sally to fetch her father to come to her room. But it hadn't been to catch them in bed, but with the lie that Marion was running away with the Marquis.

Marion thought her father would open the door and find Noah in her room, at worst kissing her. She'd never thought they would come together so passionately. That Noah would open her body to him with the same gentleness with which he'd captured her heart. And she wanted more. She wanted to feel them joined as they nearly had been when her father had burst in.

If she confessed all that to Noah, he'd understand that desperation alone had driven her to such an act. He *would* understand. He had to.

Her thoughts scattered as she passed through the gate and into the main part of the estate. It was strange that the gate was open, as if the house were expecting an early morning visitor. But it couldn't be her.

With a shake of her foggy head, Marion continued forward. Each step seemed more difficult than the last and the door felt like it was moving further away rather than nearer. Finally, her foot hit the first step of the marble stairs and she scrambled up.

With tears of happiness and exhaustion falling from her eyes, Marion pounded against the hard wood until her right fist ached. To her joy, she heard a flurry of movement from behind and the lock clicked open.

On the other side stood Basil York, Noah's kind butler. He was dressed completely unlike a servant in a long dressing gown and a nightcap. In his hand he held a long club, ready to strike.

"Noah," Marion whispered to the wide-eyed man.

"Miss Marion?"

Before she could answer, the world began to spin and she sank down to the ground in a heap.

Noah dug his heels into Phantom's sides, hoping the wind rushing against his face would do something to improve his mood. The hours he'd spent at a rundown pub just outside of Woodbury surely hadn't. Even the buxom serving wench who'd plopped herself into his lap and made him promises of a night to remember had done nothing for him. He'd shoved her aside in favor of another round. It had been a long time since he'd been able to resist temptation like that.

But it had also been a long time since he really cared for anyone else. He didn't think he'd ever cared for anyone the way he did for Marion. He was consumed by her. He thought of her every day and all night. And it wasn't just that he wanted her in his bed. When he saw her it was as if someone had lit a candle in his life.

But she *had* lied to him. Not once, but over and over again. Even if he understood her motives, he hated her lack of trust in him.

He rounded the bend in the road at a hard trot. Up ahead he saw Linton Green in the gathering dawn. Except instead of being dark and still, it was lit up like a beacon calling him home. Light streamed out of most of the windows and he could see shadows of servants bustling around in the chambers above and below. By the position of the sun he knew it was far too early for so much commotion. Something had happened.

With a few soft words of encouragement, Phantom leapt to full speed, whisking Noah ever closer to home. His heart pounded as all the possibilities rushed through his head. The last time he'd found his home like this his father had died. Could his mother have fallen ill? Or perhaps there had been an accident and one of his sisters was hurt?

As he rushed through the gate and moved up the drive, he saw a carriage parked in front. He swung himself down before Phantom came to a full halt and ran toward the door just as it opened and the shire's physician, Dr. Fielding, came down the staircase with Noah's butler and housekeeper, Basil and Myrna York at his heels.

"Keep that arm in a sling for a few days and don't allow her to use it. It's not a break that I can tell, just a bad sprain," he said.

"Oh, yes, doctor," Mrs. York said with a nod.

"My Lord!" Basil's face relaxed with relief as he peered over Dr. Fielding's head to see Noah running toward the group.

"Is it my Mother?" He panted for breath, anxiety taking his air more than as physical exertion.

"No, my lord." Basil shook his head. "Lady Woodbury is still at her party and is not expected back until late this morning or early afternoon. No, it was Miss Hawthorne who scared us nearly to death just an hour ago."

"Marion!" Noah stumbled back a few steps as he shifted his gaze to the doctor. "What happened to her?"

Dr. Fielding smiled at finally being recognized. "Oh, she had a spill from a tree and a very long, cold walk in the night. But she'll be fine after a bit of rest. And those bruises on her face should heal in a week or so. I should run along. Don't hesitate to call on me if there should be any further complications."

Noah nodded mutely as he stared at his two servants. Surely they could explain what had happened while he'd been drinking the night away to forget.

Mrs. York nodded at his pained expression. "She just showed up here, my lord. When she collapsed on the stairs, Basil had one of the footmen carry her up to Lady Audrey's old room. I felt it would be most comfortable for her."

Noah was already pushing past them on a course for his sister's old bedroom. He climbed the stairs two at a time, driven to find Marion, to see with his own eyes what her injuries were. What the hell had happened? By God, he needed an explanation. One only she could give.

He burst through the door and came to an abrupt halt when he saw her. She lay on Audrey's bed, covered by a thick blanket and coverlet to warm her cold skin. She looked small in the massive pile of blankets.

With stealth, he moved ever closer. When he reached the bed, he sat beside her and stared at her face. The beautiful face he'd been taken with since the first moment he saw her in the woods was now puffy and bruised. Her arm was in a sling, huddled at her side. She was in deep sleep, probably from opium Dr. Fielding had given her. Noah silently thanked the man. He wouldn't have been able to stand her being in pain.

Being careful not to wake her, Noah reached out to run his fingertips down her unbruised cheek. She turned her head into his hand. In her sleep she whispered, "Noah."

His entire body clenched. Despite everything she'd been though that night, despite all the anger she'd faced from him and probably from her father, she still said his name as if she trusted him to save her.

"I'm so sorry, Marion."

He leaned down to place a gentle kiss on her cheek. As much as he wanted to stay, he rose to allow her the rest she needed. Later, he would ask her all his questions. Until then, he'd have to piece together what had happened from the accounts of his butler and other servants.

He shut the door silently, then turned in the dark hallway. Now that he was sure Marion was alive, all his attentions turned to her father. The rage he'd tamped down in her bedroom roared to life. Hawthorne would pay.

"Basil?"

"I'm here, sir." The other man stepped from the shadows with a grim nod. "I thought you'd want my account of tonight's events after you'd assured yourself Miss Marion is unharmed… for the most part."

"Yes. What happened?" Noah's voice cracked with emotion before he could calm himself.

Basil looked at him with a sad smile. Noah knew what he saw. The butler had been with his family for years. He'd watched Noah and his sisters grow up. He was sure Basil saw a weak idiot before him.

"Sir, you look exhausted. Perhaps some strong coffee will do you good. Would you like to speak in the Morning Room? Mrs. York is already preparing some food and drink to warm you."

Noah couldn't help but smile. The kindness of his servants was overwhelming. If Marion couldn't have found him home, he thanked God she'd found Basil and Mrs. York. Without even asking, he knew they'd treated her with the respect and affection she deserved after whatever ordeal she'd endured. Now he just had to find out what that ordeal was, so he could dole out the proper punishment to her father and to Josiah Lucas.

CHAPTER EIGHTEEN

"Drink that up, my lord." Myrna York topped off Noah's coffee and gave him a look more befitting a worrying mother than a housekeeper. He smiled at her order then turned his attention back to Basil.

"Sit down, both of you and tell me what you know."

His butler nodded as his wife took a place beside him and began speaking first. "It was about four this morning when I heard a terrible pounding on the front door. I worried something had happened or that we were under siege, so I grabbed my club and told Myrna to wake a few of the bigger footmen. Imagine my surprise when I opened the door to find Miss Marion standing there."

"How did she look?" Noah leaned forward, gripping his cup in both hands. He flashed to that image of her lying on the bed, dark hair hanging around her bruised face. The picture in his head made him wince.

"Not very well," Mrs. York interrupted with a frown. "Her face was already bruised and it was clear her arm was causing her pain. She whispered your name and then fainted dead away."

Noah turned his head so his servants wouldn't see how much he'd begun to care for Marion. She had come to the house looking for his help, his protection, and he hadn't even been there.

"Continue."

Basil nodded. "I had Rothschild carry her up to Lady Audrey's old room, then run for the doctor. I realized summoning him would bring more attention to her being here, but we had no idea what was wrong with her."

Again, Noah winced. He hadn't even begun to think about the ramifications for Marion's reputation. Of course, Dr. Fielding, who wasn't known for his discretion, would spread the word that a bedraggled Marion had come to his door in the middle of the night and had spent many unescorted hours in his company. She would be ruined, and not just in the eyes of her father and Lucas.

"You did the right thing." He choked out the words. "If she was injured, she needed a doctor, not to have her reputation protected."

Basil sighed with relief. "She was in and out of consciousness."

"Yes. She said your name very often." Mrs. York smiled, ever the hopeless romantic. "And she cried out for her father to stop a few times as if she were having a vision."

He closed his eyes and measured his breaths. Anger wouldn't solve this problem. Not yet.

"And her injuries?"

"Her arm was weak and hurt her when we were forced to move it." Mrs. York frowned. "And of course the bruises on her face."

"Was she able to tell you how she was injured?"

His housekeeper's face fell. "She was lucid from time to time. She mumbled something about falling out of a tree when the doctor asked about her arm."

Noah pursed his lips. After years of practice, he was able to scurry in and out of rooms like Marion's with ease. But the oak outside her window was tall and difficult to manage. She was lucky she hadn't gotten killed.

"So, her bruises were from the fall."

"No, my lord." Mrs. York's whispered reply shocked

him back to reality.

"No?"

"No. One of the few times she was cognizant, she said…" Mrs. York lifted her face. "She said her father hit her."

Noah stood up so quickly that the chair beneath him flipped over and skidded backward across the room. "What?"

Basil nodded. "Yes, sir. I also heard her. We were shocked as you are, but we couldn't get any more details because that's when the doctor's pain medicine finally took hold and the young lady fell into a deep sleep." He frowned. "We tried to find you, I swear we did. But with no indication…"

"No, it's not your fault."

Noah took several deep breaths. When he saw Hawthorne, he was going to kill him with his bare hands. That bastard would pay in full for each time he'd dared lay a hand on his daughter's beautiful face. For the torture he'd put her through wondering if at any moment Josiah Lucas would rape her.

The thought drew him up sharp. If Hawthorne had beaten Marion, did that also mean he'd allowed Lucas his 'husbandly rights'?

"Basil," he choked out. "Will you leave me with Mrs. York for a moment?"

"Yes, sir."

When the butler had gone, Noah turned to the other man's wife. She looked up at him with clear, kind eyes full of curiosity.

"Is there something else you wanted to know?"

Noah nodded. "Were there any… other injuries?"

"None that I know of, my lord." She cocked her head. "Why?"

He squirmed uncomfortably. It wasn't every day he had such a delicate conversation with a woman who'd helped raise him. "Did it look as though she'd been-" he paused, seeking the right words. "Touched in any other way?" He dropped his voice a level. "Ravished?"

Myrna's eyes grew wide. "No, sir. Not that I could tell. And she certainly didn't mention anything in her ramblings. I believe she was frightened out of her wits and beaten by a coward. Otherwise she seems unhurt."

Noah shut his eyes and let the air in his lungs out in a long whoosh. "Thank God."

Myrna stood with a kind smile. "If that will be all, I'll go back to my duties. You needn't worry about the servants, sir. Basil and I will be sure they keep their gossiping to a minimum."

"I know you will. Thank you again."

When she'd gone, Noah sagged back into a chair at the table. Hearing only part of Marion's troubles was bad enough. In a few hours, she would awaken and he would hear the rest, the whole tale from beginning to end. He only prayed she wouldn't look at him with accusation in her eyes. He was already well aware of how he had allowed her to come to harm.

Noah hadn't even been aware he was dozing until the knock came on his private study door a third time. He'd chosen that room because it was across from Marion's bedroom door and he wanted to be there when she woke up. Now his body screamed awake. He sat up with a start and barked, "Enter."

Smoothing his hair and rubbing his eyes, he did his best to look like a Marquis as his butler entered the room. Basil, who usually looked benign enough, had a fiery gleam in his eyes and his face was pinched.

"What is it?"

"*He* is here, my lord." Basil could barely contain the utter disgust in his voice. Noah didn't think he'd ever heard such a tone come from the gentle man in all his years of service.

"He, who?" Noah was still confused from sleep.

"Miss Marion's father has come demanding her return. I put him in the Blue Parlor with Rothschild at the door as guard. Should I send him away? I didn't realize you were… er, working." Noah followed Basil's hawkish eyes to the mess on his desk where he'd been resting his head.

"I'm fine." He was fully awake now, his mind turning on all the things he'd do to the man downstairs. "Give me a moment to prepare and I'll be right down."

The butler gave a smart nod.

"Oh, Basil."

"Yes?"

Noah gave him a grim smile. "Let Rothschild know if Mr. Hawthorne makes any attempt to leave that room, he has my full permission to break both the bastard's legs."

Basil's wrinkled face broke into a wide smile before he smoothed his expression back to a stern, unaffected butler. "Yes, sir. I'll make sure Rothschild knows, sir."

When he'd gone, Noah passed through the adjoining door to his chamber. He splashed a bit of cool water on his face while he took a glimpse of himself in the mirror. He looked like hell. Definitely not the cool, collected image he needed to portray when he met with Hawthorne. But the man could wait. In fact, it would do him good to pass the time with the large, intimidating Rothschild breathing down over him. And who knew, maybe his servant would get a chance to break a few bones before Noah made it downstairs.

Hawthorne jumped to his feet when Noah entered the room. "Just who do you think you are making me wait for half an hour while this footman refuses to let me out of this room to collect my daughter?"

Noah strode across the room past Rothschild and

grabbed Hawthorne by his lapels. He slammed the other man into the wall with all the force he could muster and watched with pleasure as Walter turned from pink-faced to red with fear.

"I am the Marquis of Woodbury and you will leave this house with your daughter only if you kill me first." He shook the man once then dropped him, allowing him to hit the floor in a heap.

Hawthorne gaped up at him with wide, frightened eyes. "M-my lord! Surely you don't mean to deprive me of my property. I could call this kidnapping. The magistrate-"

Noah chuckled as he leaned one elbow against the mantle, though the laughter was empty and meant to intimidate. He certainly didn't find anything amusing in Walter Hawthorne's shameful disregard for his own child.

"The magistrate will side with me."

"She's *my* daughter!" Hawthorne seemed to regain some of his bluster when he finally managed to raise his fat frame back on his feet. "I'll say where she stays."

Noah's smile fell. "You think of her as property, not a person. You've said it yourself, not that I hadn't already guessed."

The man stared at him with a blank face. "Surely you understand what a woman can bring in trade. With a proper marriage, I could gain wealth, power. You can't take that away."

"But you already did try to trade her, didn't you?" Noah took a step toward the other man. Hawthorne scrambled back. "You bartered her away to one disgusting, old man in return for what? The debt of a few thousand pounds?"

Hawthorne gasped. It was clear he hadn't thought Noah would investigate his debt, but Noah knew the amount down to the last shilling.

"Then you understand why I need her back." The other man smiled warily. "We're both business men. We know the value of protecting ourselves. Surely you know if I don't pay my debt to Lucas I could lose everything I have. My mills, my home…"

Noah glared at Walter. "Do you really think I'd allow you to take her out of my protection only to return her to the place where she risked her life to escape? Do you really think I'd return her to *you*, a man who would prostitute her in exchange for a debt?"

Hawthorne's face fell. "Wh-what do you know of my plans? What did that bitch tell you?"

Noah balled up his fist and swung, connecting directly with Hawthorne's square jaw. The other man squealed like a stuck pig as he careened backward and hit the wall.

"Try again." Noah leaned down to speak into Walter's face. "But this time ask nicely."

Rubbing his face, Marion's father looked up at him with fear and hatred-filled eyes. "What did she tell you?"

Noah's smile was thin and emotionless. "That's better. She told me you sold her off to Lucas like he was the highest bidder in some auction for her virtue. You disgusting pig. How could you do that to her?"

Hawthorne bit his lip as if contemplating his best course of action. "You were interested in buying her yourself not that long ago. I'm sure we could work out an arrangement—"

"You mean my offer during our picnic?" Noah shook his head. "That deal is off the table. You lost all privileges regarding Marion when you raised your hand to her."

Hawthorne balked. "What if I give her to you instead?"

Noah drew back in disgust, though the idea of Marion belonging to him hit him in the gut with a blast of emotion. But he wouldn't buy her from her father. No, if she was to be his, it would be because she came to him of her own will.

The other man continued to ramble. "You've expressed interest in her before, and you can have her. I won't even demand you marry her after you ruined her. Just give me enough to pay part of my debt to Lucas and she'll be yours. I'm sure we can work out an arrangement for the rest later."

Noah considered punching the man again, but he doubted Marion would want her father dead, despite everything he'd done to her. "I can't believe you're offering to sell her to me now. You're disgusting."

"You don't know!" Hawthorne held out his arms for understanding. "Lucas tricked me into the debt and then he bought the rest of my notes besides. He's furious enough that Marion's gone that I don't know what he'll do to me. You've got to help me, my lord. You must help me."

Narrowing his eyes, Noah looked at the weak, piggish man in front of him. He despised the bastard with everything in him and he had no intention of saving him from the hole he'd put himself in. Especially since the man had done his best to drag Marion into that hole with him.

"Get out of my house. And never come back here." He nodded to Rothschild who had stood by impassively during the entire exchange. "If you ever go near Marion again, I'll see you rot with the devil. Go back to whatever it is that Josiah Lucas plans to do to you. You've earned whatever punishment you'll receive."

When he waved the man away, Rothschild picked him up unceremoniously and hauled him from the room. Hawthorne squealed and flailed his legs the entire time. When the front door had slammed and the disgusting man was gone, Noah sat down by the fire and rubbed his eyes. More and more, what he would have to do was coming clear.

In a short time his mother would return. After he talked to her about everything that had happened, he and Marion would have to have a serious discussion. He only hoped she could accept what fate had handed them.

Marion's eyes fluttered open, but the room around her

was a blur. When she'd blinked a few times, her vision cleared and she took in the magnificent chamber. The walls were richly painted and papered in shades of blue that reminded her of Noah's eyes. The space around her was big, filled with furniture that was classic and lovely.

"Where am I?" she asked no one in particular as she sat up. Everything seemed foggy, like she was still in a dream… or a nightmare. Her head throbbed and her arm stung like the devil.

It all came back to her in a rush. Noah nearly making love to her. Her father's savage attack. Climbing out the window. And the long, cold walk to Linton Green.

"Linton Green."

Now she was fully awake and stared around her.

Slowly, she pushed the covers from her body and dangled her bare feet off the edge of the bed. She was no longer in her own gown, but in a nightshift that was a little too big for her. Who had put her in it? She vaguely remembered Noah's butler saying her name and then a female voice that had spoken to her very kindly. But not Noah. She didn't remember his presence in the shadow that was the night before.

A long robe lay across the dressing table chair. Marion hobbled over to it and with one arm draped it over her shoulders. A shot of pain ripped through her when she tried to slide her arms through the sleeves, so she left it hanging instead.

Before she turned to the door, she caught a glimpse of herself in the mirror attached to the table. Collapsing into the chair with a gasp, she took a second look. Her face was bruised and puffy around her left eye. Her hair was a mess of tangles and knots. But worse than that, her eyes held a look of defeat in them that she hadn't felt since her mother's death.

Blinking back tears, she skirted away from the mirror and the self she didn't want to face. Later she would take the time to consider all that had happened, but for now she had to concentrate on one thing: finding Noah.

She cracked the door open a fraction. In her shift and the robe that hardly covered her, she felt naked. She didn't want someone to see her. In fact, she hoped she'd find a maid who could tell her where Noah was and perhaps send him a message.

Instead, at the sound of the door's creaking hinges, Noah's head popped out of his private study a few steps down the hall. When he saw her, his eyes lit up with relief and he hurried out of the office to meet her in the hallway.

"Marion." He breathed her name like it was a prayer and the tender look in his eyes was enough to make her go weak in the knees.

"I-I don't have anything to wear."

With a sigh, she shut her eyes. Here she was standing across from the man who she'd nearly made love to, a man who had saved her by allowing her to stay in his home, and the best she could think to say was, 'I don't have anything to wear'?

He motioned to the partly open door with an expression she couldn't read. "Come back into Audrey's room."

With a nod, she followed him. So this was once his sister's room. That explained why it was so feminine, so personal. But she wondered why she'd been put there and not in another guestroom. Surely the massive estate had many such rooms to choose from.

He opened the armoire in the corner to reveal a few older dresses. Though they were two or three seasons out of date, they all looked serviceable and were made of expensive silks and beautiful fabrics.

He turned back to hold up a gown. "You can choose one of these. I'll have a maid come up to help you get ready. You won't be able to dress yourself or fix your hair with your arm in that sling."

Noah's words unconsciously forced him to look at Marion's body. The dressing gown she wore didn't give her even a modicum of protection since it was only slung over her shoulders. And the nightshift, which was a bit large for her, revealed the soft curves of her arms and shoulders more than the most scandalous gown would have done. The thin muslin clung to her curves and made Noah long to touch her.

Clearing his throat, he turned back to the armoire to re-gather his senses. Marion didn't need to be ravished, she needed to be treated with respect.

The logic in that did nothing to tamp down the desire that had begun to throb in Noah's veins.

"Thank you."

He turned back to see her staring at the floor, not him. It killed him to see her so meek, not the fighter he'd butted heads with or teased over the past few weeks. Her father had beaten that spark out of her, and Noah only prayed he could nurture it back to life. Marion without her vitality was like Marion without her soul. And that vitality and soul was what drew him to her.

Somehow he'd taken a few short steps toward her without even realizing it. But now she was inches from him, yet she still hadn't lifted her eyes. With a trembling hand, he cupped her chin and raised her face toward his. She blinked back tears of humiliation and sadness, but held his gaze.

"Marion…"

He didn't know what he wanted to say to her. Perhaps that what had happened wasn't her fault. Or that he was sorry for letting her down. Or maybe that he cared for her. But before he could say any of those things, she turned her face away from his touch and put a few feet of distance between them.

Her voice wasn't more than a whisper when she said, "I want to dress. After that, I know we must speak to each other about-about many things."

He fought against conflicting urges. One was to take her in his arms and have it out with her right then and there. The other was to respect the space she requested and let her regain some level of dignity before he told her everything he needed to say. Finally, the latter won out.

"Yes. I'll send someone up right away." At the door, he turned back.

"I'll join you when I'm finished," she promised.

But he could see from the innocence in her eyes that she understood nothing of the shock he was about to give her. With a sigh, he turned away. If only he knew what her response would be.

CHAPTER NINETEEN

When she came downstairs an hour later, Marion felt refreshed and ready to face whatever Noah would say to her. A pleasant maid had helped her bathe, then dressed her in one of Audrey Berenger's gowns. She'd even fixed Marion's dark hair until even she had to admit it looked lovely. The only thing the girl couldn't hide were the ugly bruises that marred Marion's face. And the sting in her heart related to more than just her father's betrayal.

The light she'd always seen in Noah's eyes when he looked at her had gone out. When he came into her room that afternoon to help her find the clothes she now wore, she'd seen his desire, but not his affection. It was almost as if he dreaded seeing her.

That was what she'd done by lying to him. By barging into his life uninvited and ruining his case and his plans. Now all she could do was slip away. Allow him to return to his life without her interference.

He rose from the table when she entered the small dining hall. It was a place for family dinners with its cozy table and few chairs. A place where love and laughter were shared. Why had he brought her here?

"You look much better." He held out a chair for her with a false smile. Her hand automatically went up to touch the bruises on her face. His smile fell. "The doctor said those would heal in a few days. There will be no permanent marks."

She nodded. Suddenly her throat felt dry. Never had she felt so uncomfortable with the man across from her, but now she could think of nothing to say. Nothing could bring them back to the friendship they'd once shared and she valued so much.

"I-I didn't have anywhere else to go." She shut her eyes when the words spilled from her lips.

His face softened. "I know that."

Before he could go further, the door opened and Mrs. York entered. The second Marion saw the woman, a rush of memories returned to her. This was the person who had tended to her, spoken to her in soft, warm tones. Her eyes filled with tears at the thought.

Mrs. York smiled at her as she set a plate of food before her. The smell of warm beef and hearty potatoes gave her stomach a twist of hunger.

"I'm glad to see you up and around, Miss Marion," the woman whispered before she backed from the room.

Marion stared at the closed door. "She helped me."

"Yes." He watched as she picked at her food. "Eat. You need your strength to heal."

She nodded and took a few bites. Within moments, her appetite roared to life and she finished the meal without speaking. Noah said nothing, only leaned back in his chair and watched her intently. Finally, when she'd wiped her mouth and taken a last bracing sip of wine, he spoke.

"Would you like to tell me what happened?"

She stiffened, not that Noah had expected anything less. The memories of her ordeal would be difficult for her, but he needed to hear the entire story to decide what punishment Hawthorne and Lucas would ultimately face.

She dipped her head with a sigh. "You've probably guessed most of it."

"I don't want to guess, I want to know." With trembling hands, he leaned forward to brush her hair away from her face.

"You can trust me."

Marion winced. If she had trusted him at the beginning, none of this would have happened. Yet she'd withheld the truth at every opportunity, too filled with girlish embarrassment to protect herself. Even now, she found her trust a hard gift to give. And she knew he wouldn't give her his in return. She'd done little to earn it.

"Please."

His soft voice drew her gaze to him. His expression pleaded with her to share her trauma. She found herself doing so in quiet tones, strangely lacking any emotion about the entire situation. He, on the other hand, had enough emotion for them both, cursing at certain points and shutting his eyes at others.

Finally, she said, "And then I came here. After that, I don't remember much. It's like a dream."

"A nightmare." He stood to mix himself a strong drink.

She dropped her stare back to the tablecloth. "Yes. But it's over now. At least I'm free."

Noah brought the decanter of scotch down on the table with a loud clatter. Her eyes flew to his face. He looked sick as he stood staring at her. Apology was in his eyes and his body language.

"What is it?" She rose to her feet with a gasp. "You aren't returning me to my father, are you?"

He turned his face as if she'd slapped him, but not before she saw the hurt glitter in his eyes.

"No. Your father came here this morning, and I made it more than clear to him that he would never see you again. Don't lump me into whatever category you've put him in. I've only let you down once." His face clouded with emotion. "Last night."

Her heart leapt into her throat and she took three long strides across the room toward him. "No!"

He ignored her outburst. "I should have trusted my instinct, not let my anger get the better of me. I let you down.

That vile, disgusting Lucas could have raped you. You could have been killed during your escape attempt." The heat left his voice as his clenched fists dropped to his sides in defeat. "I'm sorry."

She shook her head though she didn't speak. There was nothing she could say to assuage his guilt, that was clear. But she wanted to let him know that she didn't blame him. Not for what had happened to her. If anything, he'd been her one light of hope since she'd arrived at Woodbury. He had given her companionship and laughter, something that had been lacking in her life for a long time.

When she reached his side, she lifted her hand to touch his cheek. He shut his eyes with a sigh at her gentle caress, though he seemed to be fighting internal demons. By the way he trembled under her touch, she knew he wanted her, but still he distanced himself.

Finally, with aching slowness, he looked down at her. Their eyes locked and Marion lost all thoughts.

"Nothing that happened to me was your fault." She wasn't sure how she got the words past her tight throat. "I told you to go. I thought I would be safe with my father, of all people."

His eyes darkened. "But I knew you wouldn't be. And I still left because I was angry."

She dropped her hand, the spell between them broken. "I'm free of him now. I can go on with my plans." Her eyes met his again. "And that's thanks to you."

Once again pain twisted his face. With a short step he was inches from her. His hand came up to touch her unbruised cheek with a tenderness that was as sweet as any kiss. "I'm sorry, Marion. Your plans must change now."

Her eyes grew wide, though she didn't back away from him. It seemed she couldn't. "Why?"

Behind them, the door opened. Both turned, and when they saw Lady Woodbury staring at them with concerned eyes, Marion blushed like a schoolgirl who'd been caught.

"Because you've been terribly compromised by coming here and staying in Noah's home with no escort." Lady Woodbury said the words slowly as Noah backed a step away from Marion. "And now we must find a way to redress the situation."

Noah winced when Marion's cheeks colored dark red at his mother's intrusion and her plain words. How he hated that she was embarrassed, but it would only get worse. When she heard their plans for her, her world would come down around her.

"Lady Woodbury?" Marion glanced from Noah back to his mother.

His mother's face softened at her distress. Noah had to smile. He hadn't been so lucky as to receive her kindness when his mother heard his tale. But she wouldn't be as harsh with Marion.

"My dear, I doubt I know the entire story." Her eyes darted to Noah. He felt a flush darken his skin. No, his mother didn't know the entire tale. She didn't know he'd nearly made love to Marion, only that her father had caught them in a compromising position. "But I've heard enough to know you've been ruined."

Marion's eyes widened, and she stumbled toward Tabitha. "No. Only in my father's eyes." Her gaze slipped to Noah. "That was our bargain. Only in my father's eyes."

His mother grimaced. "I don't think I want to know what you're talking about. In any case, this situation has moved far beyond your father's eyes now. When you fled here in your distress, the entire situation changed."

"I'm sorry." Marion moved closer to the woman as if her proximity would somehow convince Tabitha to agree with her stance. "I never meant to intrude in your home. If I'd had any other choice…"

His mother held up a hand to silence her, then the hand came down on Marion's uninjured arm for a gentle squeeze.

"My dear, I wouldn't consider your coming here an

intrusion. From what I've seen of you this morning..." Her eyes drifted to Marion's bruises with a shiver. "And what I've heard of your untenable situation at Josiah Lucas's, you should have come much earlier. If I had but known what your troubles were, I would have happily welcomed you here with open arms."

Marion's face softened with a smile at Tabitha's kindness. Noah was stricken by how glad he was that they were friends. That Marion wanted his mother to like her, and that Tabitha did, despite her disapproval over the arrangement Marion and Noah had made.

His mother sighed and her arm dropped. "But when you came here last night asking for Noah, people saw you."

"No!" Marion shook her head. "No, it was so late there was no one on the path I took to get here."

"The doctor, Marion," Noah interjected.

His mother shot him a warning look and he shut his mouth. Apparently his participation in her discussion wasn't welcome.

Marion's eyes flitted to him and some of the hope faded from them. "The doctor. I'd forgotten there was a doctor. If only I hadn't fallen from that bloody tree." She covered her mouth with a gasp. "I'm sorry, my lady. I should mind my tongue."

Tabitha smiled. "Under the circumstances, I would have used a much stronger word." Her smile faded. "Dr. Fielding is an excellent physician, but he isn't known for his discretion. He discovered I wasn't at home and that Noah had arrived while you were still alone. More to the point, he saw Noah go to your room when there was no one to make sure nothing happened between you."

"I was nearly unconscious!"

"That won't make a difference." Tabitha shook her head. "The rumor will grow. The tale of how you crept out your window and came to my son in the middle of the night will spread like wildfire. And not just here. It will go to

London and anywhere else you live. A rumor like this one will fester and grow, not die out."

Marion spun to face Noah with wide eyes. "I'm sorry. I never meant to damage your reputation."

Tabitha let out a little burst of laughter. "*His* reputation? My dear, though my son doesn't think I know it, his reputation will only be further solidified by this little story. It's *your* reputation I worry about. When word of this scandal leaks out, you shall be damaged beyond repair. Your ability to marry well will vanish."

Desperation shot through Marion. "But I don't care about that!" she insisted with a shake of her head. "I never planned to marry, I planned…"

"You may say that now, but Noah and I can't stand by in good stead while a young woman gives up her future because of a mistake she had no choice but to make." Tabitha shook her head and in her eyes Marion saw a flicker of understanding for her plight. "We *must* fix this."

Marion stepped back and came in contact with the dining table. She was trapped in more ways than one. "How?"

The room was deathly silent for a time and the air was thick with anticipation and even dread. Finally, Noah stepped forward. His eyes held hers, merciless and unwavering, telling her she wouldn't refuse what he was about to say no matter how she felt about it.

"You will marry me," he said softly.

Marion's world shattered around her as Noah's words echoed in her head. Marry Noah? It was like a dream and nightmare all at once. Long ago she'd realized how much she loved him. But she had also accepted that he was promised to another. A woman who would give him the home he expected and the respectability he'd earned. He would never love Marion in return, and she guessed even his lust for her would fade in time.

"No." The whisper was her own but she barely recognized her rough voice. She sounded very far away. "I'll go to my aunts. That was our plan. That was our bargain, Noah."

He winced at her betrayed expression. Here she had tacked all her hopes on leaving Woodbury and going to live with the family she'd never known. And he was ripping those hopes out from under her.

His mother sent a pointed glare in his direction. "If Noah made that arrangement with you, Marion, it was unfair. He should have done the honorable thing and removed you from that situation immediately. Or at least left you alone."

Noah turned his head at his mother's sharp accusation. She might as well have added 'like your father would have', for he heard the silent addition in his head. Wasn't that what his whole life had become in the past year? A race to earn the name his father had possessed. A battle to fight his own adventurous, passionate spirit and ease into the calm, staid life his father had led.

But even with all his vows to marry the right woman, to do the right things, he had failed and failed miserably.

"My mother is right." He choked the words out as he kept his head down. "I never should have made an agreement with you. It was unfair to drag you into my case and use you as a pawn to catch Josiah Lucas."

Yet why had he? He certainly hadn't needed Marion's help. His informants could have gleaned most of the information he'd acquired from her. He could have broken into Lucas's home without her open window. But he'd struck an agreement with her instead.

Because he wanted to be near her.

The realization struck him like a thunderbolt. With a jolt, he stared at her. She was so beautiful, but it was more than mere beauty that had drawn him to her. She had a quality about her. A wit, a zeal for life even though hers hadn't always been a happy one. With every moment they'd spent together, she had slowly wound her way into his soul.

"It's not your fault." Her whisper pulled him from his

thoughts. "But I can't believe this is the only way."

He nodded. "Unfortunately, it is."

Tabitha patted Marion's hand. "It is, my dear."

She stared from one to the other, her eyes pleading with them both to reconsider. When both returned her stare with unwavering eyes, she let out a little sob and hurried from the room.

Noah covered his eyes with his hand. What a mess.

"She'll come around." Tabitha crossed the room to rest her hand on his arm. "It's obvious she cares for you a great deal."

"Yes." He scrubbed his hand over his face. Exhaustion was beginning to set in. "But she lied to me more than once, which makes me wonder about the strength of a future together. And worse yet, I've been forced to take a dream from her that's she's cherished for years. I don't know if she'll recover from that."

His mother's face became amused. "Oh, Noah. For all your years as a rake, you still understand so little about women. You believe you've taken her dreams?"

He nodded.

"Then give her new ones. And as for her lies, that's something you two will have to work out. But don't forget that the lies she told you were to protect herself. If she doesn't feel she has to protect herself anymore, she won't lie."

Noah's eyes widened at her observant statement. Somehow he'd thought his mother wouldn't understand. How wrong he was. "I should speak to her."

"Give her an hour or so," Tabitha advised. "Give her time to adjust to her new position before you press her further."

He stared at the open door where Marion had just fled. "I don't know, Mother. I don't know if she'll ever be able to adjust to what has happened."

CHAPTER TWENTY

Marion sat on a wide bench in Noah's opulent rose garden. The scent of the petals hung heavily in the air around her, soothing, yet stifling her at the same time.

Like Noah.

Part of her yearned to be with him. To share her life with him would be like living a fantasy. But a prison, no matter how pretty, was still a prison. She had fled her father for forcing her marry. But in doing so, she'd walked unwittingly into a situation where she would, again, be forced to take vows that would bind her for a lifetime. She covered her face with both hands and a sigh escaped her lips.

"May I join you or would I be intruding?"

Marion kept her head down at the gentle sound of Noah's voice. Slowly, she eased her gaze up until she looked at him. As always, she was taken aback by how handsome he was with his sparkling blue eyes and tall, strong body. And she knew that body intimately, had felt it pressed against her. God help her, she still wanted to feel his touch, to finish what they'd begun the night before.

"Marion?"

She shook off her thoughts. "Please sit."

He eased his large frame down on the bench and sat silent, merely staring at her for a while in the soft summer air. "I wanted to talk to you."

Shrugging one shoulder, she dropped her gaze to the grass below her feet. "What is there to talk about? Everything is ruined now."

Noah winced at that assessment. The sting worked through him until he had a bitter taste in his mouth. "That's a bit dramatic, don't you think?" His voice was harsher than he'd intended it to be.

"For you perhaps." Her eyes came up to meet his a second time. "Whether you marry me or marry Charlotte Ives is meaningless, you'll be allowed to continue your life just as it was before."

He contemplated that point. There was no way Marion and Charlotte were interchangeable in his mind. Charlotte he'd chosen for pure connection. Her good name and breeding would make her the perfect Marchioness. She would keep a good home, raise him well-behaved children.

But Marion was a completely different story. He'd been drawn to her of her own accord, without thought to what she would bring to his future. Except her smile. Her laugh. Her intoxicating touch. And now a future filled with those things seemed much brighter than his first choice had been.

She sighed. "The only difference to you between marrying me and marrying her is that you'll have a much keener sense of disappointment when you look at me across the breakfast table. After all, I'll bring nothing to a marriage except myself."

His eyes narrowed at her self-deprecation. "Which is more than enough."

A sad shake of her head was her reply. "If I ask you a question, will you answer me honestly?"

"I believe honesty is key to a good relationship." He arched an eyebrow at her.

Marion blushed. Did he have to bring up her lies? She hadn't had time to explain to him why. She would later, but now the future between them was much more pressing than the past.

"Do you love her?" She held her breath.

"Who, Charlotte?"

She nodded. Noah drew back with a look of surprise on his face as if he'd never even considered that question before. For a long time, he seemed to struggle with an answer. Her heart sank with each passing moment.

"No," he finally stammered out. "I don't love her. I don't even know her."

She soared with relief. If he didn't love Charlotte, perhaps they had a chance after all. "Why are you marrying her then?"

"I *was* marrying her for her background," he admitted with a sheepish look in her direction.

Her relief faded. "Then you *will* be disappointed in any union we make, no matter what pretty words you say to deny it."

"No!"

She cut him off with a shake of her head. "Yes. Can you honestly tell me you aren't desperate to create a certain image?"

Noah drew back in surprise. Here she'd touched on the very fact that had been plaguing him for months. Yet if he demanded honesty from her, there was no way he could be a hypocrite and give her less.

"You're right."

Her face fell with distress at his short answer. For a moment she didn't speak, but finally raised her gaze back to his. Her face was full of sadness and loss and other things he couldn't identify.

"Whose image are you trying to recreate, Noah?"

"My father's." He was surprised at how quickly he answered her. This wasn't a subject he'd discussed even with his family, yet he easily revealed the truth to a woman he hadn't even known a month before.

Marion's face softened. "What was he like?"

A knot formed in Noah's throat at her question. He

tried not to think of his father in terms of a person, just a goal he had to reach. When he dared to think of the flesh and blood man, it invariably hurt him to his very core.

"His name was James. He was actually a second son, but when his older brother died, my father took over the title." He glanced down at his fisted hands. "And did more with it than even he would have wagered in the beginning. He had studied shipping and trade and in two years time he doubled the wealth of Woodbury. He instituted changes in how business was done with our tenants and our servants. He made them partners in our successes as well as the shire's woes. He even learned their names and found out at least one personal thing about them so he always had a connection."

Marion tilted her head with a small smile. "But what was he like, Noah?"

"He was…" Noah shook his head as he searched for the right words. "Everything. He loved with all his heart. He worshipped my mother, did all he could to protect my sisters, no matter how misguided that protection might have been. He taught me to be a man, not just a lord of a manor."

"You loved him." Marion's eyes grew distant and pained. "You're lucky you were so close to him."

For the first time since he'd come to sit beside her, Noah touched her. Heat rushed through him even though he only brushed her hand. She jumped at the caress, but didn't move her fingertips from beneath his.

"I *was* lucky. But I took him and his lessons for granted." His heart sank. "Though he never said it, in the end, I let him down."

Marion looked at the man who now sat with his fingers laced with hers as if they'd been together for years, not weeks. His normally jovial exterior was gone, replaced by the true emotional pain of a man who craved to live up to a dead man. Yet, in her eyes, Noah was already everything anyone could possibly admire.

"Why would he ever have been disappointed in you as a

son?" She squeezed his fingertips. "You worked to protect your country while he lived. And since he's been gone, you've driven yourself to meet some expectation that perhaps he never had."

His brow wrinkled in consideration, but he still didn't look convinced. "I chose the path of a rake, Marion. A path he never looked down, let alone traveled."

"Why did you?"

He shrugged one shoulder. "I was young. I liked the pleasures of the world." His gaze came up to hers with heat. "Of the flesh."

She drew in a short breath at the desire in his eyes, but kept herself focused on their conversation. Noah wouldn't distract her from it with amorous diversions.

"Many men choose that path and eventually come back to one more admirable. But from what I've seen in you, Noah, you've never been dishonorable. If you played, it was for a purpose. You may have gleaned some pleasure from it, yes, but you also used that reputation to help your country."

For the second time, Noah was stunned and touched by the observations of the woman beside him. How did she know what he needed to hear? How did she see exactly how to ease the ache in his heart?

He lifted her hand to his lips to place a soft kiss along her knuckles. A visible shiver moved through her at the action and some of his tenderness turned to lust at her responsiveness.

"I'm sure your father was proud of you, Noah."

"Perhaps." At the reminder of his father and his choices, his lust faded. "But when he died, I realized I'd have to give that life up in order to be a good Marquis. In order to be a good man, I must become more like him."

She withdrew her hand from his to touch his face. "Noah, what's wrong with just being you? Being who you are and leading your shire in your own way? No man can take another's path."

"You don't understand what it's like to live up to

someone else's image." The oppressive weight of desperation pressed on his heart. "Especially someone who was so good."

Her eyes saddened. "But you shouldn't have to. You may believe you're still some kind of rogue, but you aren't. By the way you've treated me alone, I know you've never been anything but a good man. And you'll never be anything else. Perhaps you aren't an exact replica of your father, but you are... perfect."

Marion looked up into the eyes of the man she loved and saw a vulnerability there she wouldn't have believed existed even a few hours before. Not when he'd stared at her with the steely resolution of a man not to be questioned and told her he would marry her.

She never would have guessed how driven she would find herself to take his pain away. Inching closer, she flattened her palms against his chest, then slid them up to wrap around his neck. His breath came shorter, warming her face as she leaned up to press her lips against his.

For a moment the kiss was only giving, the gentle healing of a friend to another. But then giving turned to possessing as she parted her lips. Noah's hands came around to grasp her waist and she found herself pressed against him, her blood rushing hot and fast in her veins as she tangled her fingers into his hair.

Noah smiled against her lips, and she felt the tension ease from his body. "Do you remember how good I made you feel last night? Before your father burst in?"

Blood rushed to Marion's face at his reminder of their intimate moments together. She'd been able to think of little else since her whole world had exploded in a dazzling, pleasurable flame. He'd kissed her in the most intimate way possible, had brought her to the edge of a place she'd never dreamed existed, then promptly taken her over the edge. And she craved more.

"Ye-yes," she whispered, darting her tongue along his lower lip and reveling in the taste of his skin.

"If we were married, I'd make you feel that good every night. Better," he promised in a low growl that warmed her blood.

"Better?"

His answer was to deepen the kiss, drawing her closer to him until she could feel every inch of him against her. He feathered kisses along her jaw, down her throat until she burned and every nerve crackled with awareness and desire. Yet there was still a niggling doubt in her mind. He'd obviously shared these kinds of pleasures with many other women. Eventually he'd tired of every one of them. If this were all they shared, he would tire of her, too.

With desire still pulsing through her, she whispered, "I have no choice, do I?"

His mouth stilled on her throat and she felt the tension return to the muscles in his shoulders. With a frown, he pulled back.

"No."

Noah watched her face closely, waiting for her anger. Waiting for her to return to arguing with him about the need for such a drastic step. Instead, the desire in her eyes was replaced by defeat. Her shoulders rolled forward as she slowly shook her head.

"I'll do this without fighting you any longer. But I'd like for you to do something for me as well."

Disappointment coursed hard through his veins. She still felt she had to bargain with him. That would be the first thing he'd teach her as his wife. She didn't need to trade to get what she wanted. If she asked, he'd do his best to give her whatever she requested.

His eyes drifted over the curves that had been pressed against him so intimately not a few moments before. Well, perhaps not the *first* thing he'd teach her.

The corner of his mouth quirked into a smile. "Yes?"

"I want to retain Sally as my maid. She did her best to assist me while I was at Toppleton Square and asked that I help her get out of Lucas's employ in return."

He narrowed his eyes. Though Marion viewed Sally as a friend, he had to wonder if the woman's motives were so pure. Obviously she was using Marion, if only to get away from Lucas. It was something he couldn't completely blame her for. But he still had to wonder at the maid's swift surrender of information.

"I'll do that for you, if it's what you desire," he said slowly. There would be time for investigation and argument later. For now, giving her what she wanted seemed best. "We'll make a happy life, Marion."

Her expression was incredulous. "Happy or not, Noah, a prison is still a prison."

Again, pain shot through him with a power that was frightening. "And that's what you see life with me as being."

Marion could sense his anger, but pressed on. He'd already said he wanted honesty. Even if it hurt, or made him furious, she could do no less. Especially if they were to be married.

"As much as I…" Was she going to admit she loved him? No. Not now. Not when he had an angry fire in his eyes that told her how frustrated he was with her continued resistance. "As much as I care for you, this isn't what either of us wants. Not this way. Eventually I fear you'll resent me."

His eyes met hers with a spark of denial and fury. She continued speaking to prevent the interruption she knew was coming.

"You'll resent me for what's happened," she said with her voice trembling. "You'll begin to reinvent our history until you'll remember me, a country chit, trapping you, a Marquis, into marriage."

He opened his mouth with an outraged growl. "I'm sorry you feel that way, Marion. Unfortunately circumstances have left neither of us with a choice. Resentful or not, you *will* marry me. Get used to it."

With that, he abruptly stood and walked away, leaving

Marion to stare at his rigid back as he crossed the lawn toward the house.

CHAPTER TWENTY-ONE

Noah heard Marion call his name as he strode away from her across the lawn, but didn't stop. He didn't even glance over his shoulder, though his heart and body screamed at him to look at her. He already knew what he'd see. Not a woman happy to be his forever, but one torn apart by her lack of choices.

It infuriated him. But why was he so damn angry? Her analysis was perfectly correct. This wasn't what either of them had planned for or wanted, but having her put those feelings so plainly hurt.

What did he want anyway? A blushing bride totally in love with him? He had never planned on that when he intended to offer for Charlotte.

But he hadn't *wanted* love with Charlotte.

"Damn it," he barked to no one in particular.

"Sir?" Basil looked up as Noah stormed into the house and slammed the door behind him.

"Ready the household to depart for London tomorrow," he called over his shoulder as he continued down the hall in long, purposeful strides.

At least in London he wouldn't have to share a roof with Marion. Perhaps that distance would clear his head and make him remember his place, not the need for her that coursed through him like a constant drumbeat.

Marion twisted her gloves in her hand as she returned to the house and closed the door behind her. Her head was spinning from the encounter with Noah nearly an hour ago. He had aroused her, angered her and confused her with his reaction to her reticence to marry. Along with the fact that he'd refused to turn back when she called his name.

That had stung the worst. How she'd wanted him to return and allow her to explain that her feelings confused her, but that she would try her hardest to make a marriage between them work because she loved him and wanted to make him proud. But he'd not turned back, and she'd been too much of a coward to follow him.

No, she sat like a ninny and watched. And contemplated how ridiculous the entire situation had become.

"Would you like some tea, miss?"

Marion cleared her thoughts with a shake of her head and smiled at Mrs. York who had appeared from the dining room with a gentle smile for her guest.

"No, Mrs. York. I think I'm going to go up to my room to rest for a little while. My arm is still quite tender and I'm tired." Through her sadness she found a weak smile for the housekeeper.

"To your chambers, miss?" Mrs. York's eyes widened a fraction.

"Yes. I'll be down in time for supper though."

With a nod for the older woman, she climbed the stairs to her room. To her surprise, her chamber door was open and two maids were inside going through the closet where Audrey's old gowns still hung.

"These two will do for a while," whispered the blonde to the red head. "She'll have more made when she arrives, so it won't make no difference anyway."

"Excuse me." Marion took two steps into the room.

The pair spun around to look at her with polite smiles. "Oh, hello Miss." The blonde draped the gown in her hand over one arm. "Did you need to use the room, then? Lord Woodbury told us to finish up in the other rooms if you needed the chamber."

"Finish up what?" Marion surveyed a small trunk on the floor beside the armoire. Certainly Audrey Berenger wouldn't have asked for her out-of-date gowns now that she was a countess.

The redhead gave her a patient smile. "The packing, miss. You and the master and Lady Woodbury will be leaving for London tomorrow morning at first light."

Marion's mouth dropped open. Noah hadn't mentioned anything about a move to London. "I beg your pardon?"

"Very last minute arrangements miss." The redhead nodded, but her eyes widened with interest as she realized Marion hadn't been informed of the plans. "But we can scurry away if you'd like to rest."

Marion's eyes narrowed. "No. But can you tell me where his lordship is? I have a few things to discuss with him."

"His lordship has gone for a long ride, at my order."

Marion spun around. Lady Woodbury stood in the doorway with her arms crossed, staring at her. "And I think you'd better calm your nerves, as well, before you speak to him again."

"My lady…" Marion's embarrassment filled her and she trailed off in utter misery.

"Come with me. If you aren't too tired, perhaps we can share a cup of tea in my private salon down the hall."

The older woman beckoned to Marion as she strolled from the doorway and down the hall. At her cloaked order, Marion hurried to keep up.

Tea was already laid out on a service in the salon. It was a small room but elegant and befitting the woman before her. The interior was done in soft shades of blue and green with comfortable furniture spread about.

"Sit." Lady Woodbury motioned to the chair opposite her as she sat down in the other. "I'll pour."

With a nod, Marion did as she was asked and stared with trepidation at the woman who would soon be her mother-in-law. Though Tabitha Jordan's eyes were kind when they met hers, it was also obvious the older woman had much to say on the subject of Marion's upcoming wedding, and her conduct so far. She had a feeling not all of those sentiments would be joyful or approving.

Once the tea had been poured and scones put on plates, Tabitha leaned back in her chair and gave Marion a long, appraising glance.

"You are very upset about this entire arrangement, aren't you?" Tabitha asked before she took a long sip from her cup.

Marion hesitated. The last thing she wanted to do was offend Lady Woodbury, but she didn't want to lie, either. "My reticence isn't a slight on your family, I assure you. I simply never intended to marry… not this way."

"Of course you didn't. What woman would?" Tabitha's understanding smile fell. "But this choice is what you and Noah created for yourselves. I'd hate to see you destroy any chance you have at happiness before you even start."

"You must allow me some period of adjustment." Marion set her teacup down.

"Of course. But you must also admit that you had a hand in creating this situation." Tabitha's eyes narrowed. "After all, you made a bargain with my son that wasn't appropriate. That it didn't go as you planned is as much your own fault as it is his. I do place added blame on him as the more experienced of the two of you."

Marion threw her hands in the air. "You don't understand my situation. What I would have been forced to… *do* if I didn't find an alternative."

Tabitha arched an eyebrow. "Of course I understand. You were facing a life with Josiah Lucas, and worse, a very uncouth entry into the physical aspects of marriage. And now I've found out Mr. Lucas may even be suspect in his late wife's death, so I can see why you were desperate." She leaned closer. "But none of those things make you any less responsible for your own actions."

"Of course not." Marion shook her head. She was willing to take some of the blame for what had happened. "But I still believe there must be another way for us to resolve this situation beyond dragging me to London for a forced marriage."

One of Tabitha's eyebrows arched up in warning. "No. You've compromised yourself, and you'll continue to be until you are no longer under Noah's roof."

"But you're my chaperone here."

"The damage is already done." Tabitha shook her head at Marion's continued arguments. "Noah is right to take you to London. There you can stay with Lord and Lady Berenger, my daughter Audrey and her husband Griffin. Audrey and I can introduce you into Society for a month or so until the scandal begins to fades. Your marriage to Noah will erase it completely."

All Marion's hopes dropped to the pit of her stomach. There seemed to be no way out of this mess. "I-I worry about losing control. Noah is making my choices just as my father did."

At that, Tabitha set her teacup back on its saucer with a clatter. "Noah is nothing like your father."

Marion shook her head. Noah had been just as angry when she'd said something similar, but neither of them seemed to understand her true meaning. Noah had none of the coldness, the cruelty her father possessed. It was more the situations she was comparing, not the men.

"Of course he isn't. I couldn't bear to be near him if he was, let alone marry him. I only meant that I looked forward to controlling my own destiny and now that dream looks out of reach once again." She sighed.

Tabitha's demeanor softened. "Control is a tricky thing, Marion. We never have it, even when we think we do. And constantly striving for it only seems to put it further from reach."

Marion frowned. She hadn't ever thought of it in those terms before. Her father had made sure she never had any control, so she'd never contemplated that it might not be a good thing.

"Still, I had so many hopes. I fear they're lost forever now." She stared at her tea, picturing the little life she'd planned with her estranged aunts. But now that picture seemed cloudier, less perfect. Instead, an image of Noah kept intruding.

Tabitha sighed before she reached out to touch Marion's hand. She looked up to find Lady Woodbury's eyes filled with compassion. "I know my son. He'll give you new hopes if you meet him halfway." She paused, but her gaze kept Marion hostage. "It should be easy when you love him as much as you do."

Marion yanked her hand away as if Tabitha's touch burned her. She rose to her feet in shock, overturning the empty plate on her lap and depositing crumbs all over Lady Woodbury's oriental carpet. She hardly noticed the mess as she stumbled back a few steps.

"That-that's ridiculous, my lady. I barely know Noah, Lord Woodbury." Her cheeks flamed with heat. Her denial sounded lame even to her own ears.

Tabitha looked up at her with a bemused smile. "If it helps you to deny it to me, by all means, continue to do so. But don't make the mistake of denying it to yourself."

The hot sting of tears pricked Marion's eyes as she crossed to the window. A faint breeze stirred the leaves on the trees and made the well-tended lawn wave. Marion wished she were outside, away from the pointed accusation of a woman who knew what she spoke of all too well. Marion didn't have the strength to deny her statements.

"He doesn't love me."

She didn't dare face Tabitha. She didn't want to see the agreement in her eyes. She didn't want to see that Tabitha thought she was a silly girl for loving her son, a self-proclaimed rake and a man so far above her station that he might as well have fallen from heaven.

Tabitha rose to her feet and cocked her head as she contemplated that statement. "Hmmm. Noah has never been easy to read when it came to the feelings in his heart. Even when his father died, I could see his grief, but no other emotions. But he certainly cares for you more than he did for Charlotte."

That was cold comfort. Marion turned to look at her future mother-in-law. "He told me he felt nothing for Charlotte."

"No." Tabitha's face softened and a sadness came into her eyes. "And in a way, I'm glad he won't enter a loveless, if 'suitable' marriage. One of my children already took that course at my urging and it cost her, and our family, dearly."

Marion frowned. "But won't our marriage be just as loveless? And it won't be suitable, or at least as suitable as the other match would have been."

Snapping herself from her reverie, Tabitha gazed at her. "You love him. He cares for you. Already you have more than half the marriages in the *ton*." In two steps she was standing in front of Marion. She took both her hands and smiled. "My dear, since you have no choice, I suggest you make the best of what you have."

Marion turned back to the window with a sigh, wondering what she *did* have exactly, and if Noah would ever look at her with the same love in his eyes that she felt for him.

Marion had already taken down half her hair when she remembered Tabitha's order to her. The older woman had told her since she was to be a Marchioness she'd have to get used to having servants hovering around her, dressing and undressing her. This night, especially, Marion would have much rather been alone, but she'd vowed to do as her hostess had asked and try to make the best of the situation she now found herself in.

She rang the bell by her door with a sigh, then returned to her dressing table to wait. As she gazed at her reflection, her mind wandered, taking her to a predictable place.

Noah.

She hadn't seen him since he'd left her in the garden. He hadn't come home even for supper. Was he angry? Or was he simply avoiding her while he prepared to go to London? Back to the place where he wanted to be. To the people he wanted to see. His friends, his family, perhaps even a mistress.

She lurched at that thought. Of course a man like him probably had a mistress, maybe even several. Especially since he'd already told her he didn't love his fiancée.

The door opened behind her, mercifully pulling her from any more thoughts of Noah tangled with another woman.

"I was hoping you'd help me with my hair and to undress," she said as she turned to face the maid who'd come in. She stopped, her mouth gaping open when she saw who had come at her call. "Sally!"

The maid grinned. "Oh miss, I'm so glad you're all right. I was worried when you showed up missing and the master went into such a rage."

Marion raced over to her friend's side and hugged her, glad to see a familiar face after the past few days of turmoil and confusion. "How on earth did you come to be here?"

"It was all Lord Woodbury's doing, Miss Marion." Sally motioned to the dressing table for Marion to sit. "He appeared this afternoon. He and your father and Mr. Lucas had a huge row. There was screaming and breaking of glass, especially after Mr. Hawthorne realized Lord Woodbury hadn't come to bargain for your return."

Marion felt bile rise in her throat at the mere thought.

"Papa thought he'd come to sell me back?"

Sally nodded as she picked up the brush on the table and began to work Marion's locks down from their twists and curls. She shut her eyes as Sally continued her work. Marion had never had much pampering, but she could see how easy it would be to grow accustomed to it.

"Yes, your father said something about Lord Woodbury coming to his senses. But his lordship refused to even speak to your father and demanded that I be allowed to come with him. I had to stop listening after that because that nasty butler of Mr. Lucas's caught me peeping, but they had an argument that went on for hours."

Marion looked at her friend's reflection in the mirror. Noah had gone to Lucas's and endured a nasty encounter with her father just because she'd asked for Sally, a woman Noah didn't even trust.

He'd done it for her.

"Did he say anything to you once he got you out of the house?"

Sally shrugged. "He sat with me in the carriage on the way home and said I'd be responsible for taking care of you now. That I was to treat you right and be a good girl or I'd answer to him. Then he took me here, and I spent rest of the afternoon and evening with one of them chambermaids learning the ways of the house and what would be expected of me. It's been a long while since I took care of a lady's needs. Not since Mrs. Lucas died."

Marion's eyes darted to her new maid. "You never told me you were Georgina's lady's maid."

She thought she caught a twinkle of fear in Sally's eyes for a moment before she ducked her head to concentrate on her brushstrokes. "Didn't I? Well, at any rate, that man surely thinks much of you. He says he's going to marry you."

Whatever doubts Marion had in her head washed away with that reminder. "Yes. That seems to be his plan."

"Lucky girl." Sally sighed as if lost in thought as she

continued to work at Marion's hair.

Marion shivered at Sally's observation. Noah had done so much to try to make her happy.

"And where is his lordship?" she asked, suddenly overcome with a need to talk to him. "You said he brought you back this afternoon, but he wasn't at supper this evening."

"He seemed a mite distracted," Sally admitted. "And said something about needing air to clear his head. I don't think he's come back yet. I heard his valet muttering about it in the hallway when I was coming up to you."

Disappointment rushed through Marion at that revelation. Tomorrow they would be on the road with Lady Woodbury as a chaperone. She wouldn't have much chance to sit with Noah privately, only share moments with him in the carriage with his mother watching the whole time.

As Sally began unfastening her gown, Marion looked once more at the reflection in the mirror. Whatever it took, she and Noah *would* meet in private before they were married. She would thank him for all he'd done for her, and apologize for anything she'd done to him.

CHAPTER TWENTY-TWO

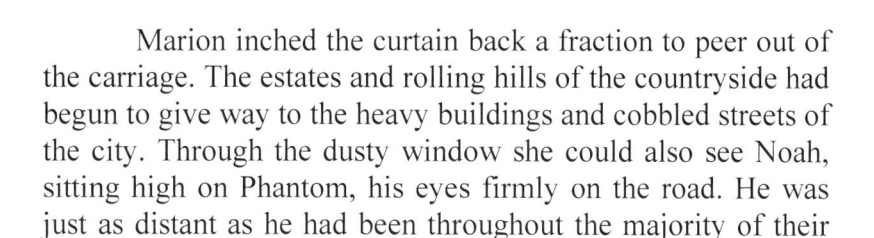

Marion inched the curtain back a fraction to peer out of the carriage. The estates and rolling hills of the countryside had begun to give way to the heavy buildings and cobbled streets of the city. Through the dusty window she could also see Noah, sitting high on Phantom, his eyes firmly on the road. He was just as distant as he had been throughout the majority of their three-day trip to London.

Leaning back in her seat with a sigh, she allowed the curtain to swish closed. Though he'd had shared meals with them and been nothing less than cordial, the rift that had formed between them during their confrontation in the garden so many days ago still existed. And the distance seemed to grow with each day.

Most frustrating was that she could do nothing to close it. Lady Woodbury always accompanied the couple when they were together. It didn't exactly allow Marion to say anything of an intimate nature. Worse, Noah didn't seem to mind their lack of privacy.

Tabitha looked up from her needlework with a bemused half smile. "He's still there, is he?"

The color flooded to Marion's cheeks. "I don't know what you mean, my lady. I was simply taking in the view. I've been to London only a few times."

"We'll arrive at Griffin and Audrey's soon and then

you'll have your fill of the city, I'm sure." Lady Woodbury set aside her work as she discreetly stretched her neck. "There's so much for us to do. Not the least of which, is to have gowns made for you."

Marion shook her head. "No, I don't want you to go to that kind of expense and trouble."

"Don't be ridiculous." Tabitha's voice was sharp with the argument she'd been having with Marion for days. "We can't have the future Marchioness of Woodbury running around London in two out-of-date hand-me-downs. It isn't proper. You'll need a few ball gowns, morning gowns, several pelisses…"

Marion shut her eyes as Tabitha continued to list what she considered the bare necessities of life. It was only a reminder to Marion of how little she knew of the *ton* and their ways. In Northumberland she'd only owned six or seven gowns in total. They were always in fashion, at least for the country, and no one had ever seemed to ponder them overlong. Now the slightest mistake in the turn of her ankle and it seemed she would bring shame upon Noah's family and herself.

"Then we'll immediately have to arrange for vouchers to Almacks and for tea with several of the most important women in our social circle." Tabitha seemed to have entered her own world where she cared very little if Marion agreed or disagreed with her assessment of their needs. "*That* should quiet the gossip, especially when they see what a lovely young woman you are."

Marion winced. "I still find it hard to believe a harmless piece of country gossip started by a doctor could be all that important to the members of the *ton*."

Tabitha's laugh was immediate. "It wouldn't be if that harmless gossip weren't about one of the most eligible and sought after members of the *ton*. I'm sure everyone knows the circumstances of this marriage by now."

Dropping her eyes to the floorboards of the carriage, Marion contemplated that. "Even Charlotte?"

Lady Woodbury's eyes flashed up to her. Her answer came slowly. "Yes, I suppose even Charlotte."

Another stab of guilt worked its way through Marion. She could only imagine what Charlotte Ives felt about the entire situation. Though Noah claimed not to love the young woman he'd planned to wed, Marion couldn't imagine any woman not loving Noah as she did. The humiliation would be secondary only to the pain of losing him.

"Poor Charlotte," she whispered.

When she dared to look at Tabitha again, the other woman's face had softened. "Many people would consider her a rival, not one to be pitied. But then, that isn't you, is it?"

Marion shook her head. It hadn't really occurred to her to think of Charlotte as someone to compete with, though thoughts of her with Noah didn't please Marion in the least.

"Ah, the carriage is stopping. We've arrived at Audrey and Griffin's."

Tabitha's face lit up in anticipation as she drew the curtains back and looked outside. Over her shoulder, Marion could see a lovely city estate rising above the high gate that protected it from the street. Already the front door was opening and a man and woman stepped from the house together, their arms locked.

The footman opened the carriage door, but Noah was the one standing outside to help his mother and Marion out. Tabitha went first. When her feet hit the ground, she immediately rushed forward and took the couple on the steps into her arms.

Noah smiled as he offered Marion his hand. She took it and the shock of awareness flashed through her like lightening.

"Look at them," he murmured as his grin widened. "Who would guess that just a few short years ago my mother and Audrey didn't interact at all? And now they're closer than ever."

Marion stepped to the ground as she examined the three people on the step. She could see the similarity between Noah,

Tabitha and Audrey in their bright blue eyes, but aside from that, Audrey looked very little like her family. Unlike Tabitha and Noah, who had thick, dark hair, Audrey's was an auburn that complimented her fair skin.

Her husband, Griffin Berenger, had hair the color of dark gold and warm brown eyes that swept first over Noah with a grin and then over her with a questioning glance. She blushed as she dropped her stare away from the handsome man.

"Oh, Noah!" Audrey hurried down the stairs to give him a fierce hug. When she stepped back, Noah felt her eyes boring into his, searching them for any sign of what was going on in his heart. Yet, the unspoken communication they'd once shared so easily as spies had faded away now.

"Audrey, Griffin." Noah grinned up at his best friend who was just now extracting himself from Tabitha's chatter and coming down to stand beside his wife. "May I present Miss Marion Hawthorne."

His sister slid a bit closer and held out a hand in welcome. "Miss Marion, I'm so pleased you could join us here at Bentley Square. We've heard so much about you in Noah and mother's letters."

Although Noah knew his sister only meant her greeting in the kindest way possible, Marion stiffened with a blush that darkened her cheeks to a cherry red.

"Thank you, my lady," she mumbled with a short curtsey more befitting a maid than a future Marchioness.

Audrey frowned at her reaction, but took her hand with a genuine friendliness that even Marion seemed to recognize as her eyes slowly lifted.

"Marion, we're very pleased you'll be joining our family." Audrey stepped back to wrap a slender arm around her husband's waist.

"Both of us are," Griffin added with a smile for Marion though his gaze shot over to Noah.

"Thank you," Marion replied, this time with more

sparkle and less fear. "I appreciate you taking me into your home under such unusual circumstances."

Tabitha shook her head as she came back down the steps with a frown. "No, no, no. From now on there are no unusual circumstances. You are an old friend of the family who we've reacquainted ourselves with. If anyone has the gall to say otherwise, that is the story you will tell and then you will immediately inform me and I'll make certain any other version vanishes."

She linked her arm with Marion's. Audrey joined her on the opposite side and the three of them began to walk into the house together.

With a grin, Noah embraced Griffin. "My sister looks radiant as always. I'm glad to see you're continuing to keep her happy."

Griffin laughed. "And she me. But I'm more concerned about *you* in the midst of all of this mess."

Noah looked away. After being friends with Griffin for over thirty years, the two were like brothers, and not just because of the marriage to Audrey. Still, he wasn't sure he could explain the entire situation he found himself in, even to his best friend.

"I'm fine. It's a change of plans, that's all." He motioned his head toward the house. Griffin took his lead with an unreadable glance.

"I think it's more than that, but perhaps now isn't the time to get into it after all." Griffin tilted his head. "From the spark in your eyes when you look at Marion, it appears to be a conversation best shared over good port and a roaring fire."

As they entered the parlor where the three women were chatting, Noah took a long look at Marion. Though he could still see the remnants of embarrassment by the blush on her cheeks, he could also see how much she liked both his mother and his sister. And the feeling was mutual. Though he'd never looked to his family for approval, having it made his heart lighter.

"Perhaps later," he murmured as he plunked his large frame into one of the chairs across from Marion.

She glanced up and their eyes met. Hers sparkled with happiness that he was once again in the room. As if he would protect her. He smiled back, but inwardly winced. He couldn't keep her from being sized up and gossiped about. Not until he married her. And he wouldn't be able to do that until he spoke to Charlotte Ives, a prospect he wasn't looking forward to.

"The first thing we must do is get a mantua maker and have you fitted for your gowns." Audrey looked at Marion with a friendly smile. "I loved that dress, but it's helplessly out of style now. I'll send for Miss Fox today. I'm a good customer."

She shot a wink toward Griffin, who rolled his eyes theatrically. "Yes, her best I'd wager."

Audrey giggled. "As if you mind, my love."

"No, I'm proud to say I have the most beautiful wife in all of England and that other women swoon when she comes by in silk and chicken feathers."

Audrey's blue eyes widened. "They were *ostrich* feathers, you naughty man. And they were all the rage."

Noah watched the couple exchange playful barbs. All the while their eyes danced. For the first time in his life, he envied their loving relationship and how certain they were that they would be happy for the rest of their lives. He envied how Griffin could place his palm on the small of Audrey's back and that she would lean into his hand.

He took a quick glance at Marion. Would they ever reach that point? Because Audrey and Griffin were deeply in love and had been for a long time. Marion, on the other hand, blamed Noah for a forced marriage. She'd made that point perfectly clear and it still stung.

"I have a few things I must tend to this afternoon."

He rose to his feet. The rest of the group did so as well, Marion's eyes went wide. He suddenly felt a strange urge to fold her into his arms and reassure her that in a year she would barely remember her fears. That they would be happy and she would be the toast of London Society. But he wasn't sure if that was a promise he could keep.

"Will you be back later?" she whispered.

He nodded as he held out a hand to her. The rest of the room and its inhabitants faded into the background. There was only them. "I will be. In the meantime, you'll have a wonderful time with my sister and mother. They'll take excellent care of you."

She nodded, but he could still see the doubt glittering in her eyes.

"You'll have a marvelous time, Marion." Audrey's voice shattered the dream world around him. "Miss Fox is the most sought after dressmaker in London. You'll end up feeling like a princess by the time she's done with you."

Marion nodded and Noah could see that she, too, had been caught in the same web as he'd been. "I'm sure."

Noah's grip on her fingers tightened, sending warm flashes up her spine. "Will you walk me to the door?"

Marion glanced around her at the other people in the room, but none of them seemed to object to his request. With a nod, she followed him to the hallway. Once they were alone, she was sure she caught a look of dread in his eyes.

"Will you really be all right here?" he asked while he rubbed a fingertip across her cheek.

"Yes." She put all her focus into speaking rather than the delicious slide of his skin against hers. "But what about you? Are you going to see Charlotte?"

His eyes widened at her observation, then he nodded. "Yes, how did you know?"

She shrugged one shoulder. "Just a good guess. I suppose I'm beginning to know you. Good luck."

With a nod, he released her fingers. "I'll see you in a short while."

Then he was gone. After he'd closed the door behind him, she whispered, "I'm sorry."

THE TEMPTATION OF A GENTLEMAN

The Ives house was almost unbearably quiet. It seemed as if even the room was waiting for the encounter about to come. The servants ducked their eyes from Noah's gaze, and all talk had ceased when he'd come into the foyer with his card. Then there was the agonizing wait as Charlotte determined whether or not she would receive him. But his superior title... or perhaps her desire to dress him down... seemed to have won out, for he was now seated in her parlor.

Though he'd run the scenario over and again in his mind, Noah still wasn't exactly sure how he would tell her what he'd come to say. After all, they hadn't exactly been engaged... yet. Despite that, he owed her an explanation. And an apology.

The door opened and Noah immediately clamored to his feet to greet her. As she pushed the door shut, he examined her. She looked pale, even paler than usual. Worse, she looked upset.

"Sit my lord," she said softly.

"Lady Charlotte," he choked out, truly unsure of what to say now that she was standing before him with accusation in her eyes.

"Sit," she repeated as she did the same. "Would you like some tea?"

He started. How could she be so polite?

"No. I think you know why I'm here."

Her serene expression blanched for a moment, revealing the anger beneath her icy exterior. "Yes. I've heard the whisperings about your activities at Woodbury. Some little country girl, wasn't she? And now she is to be your..." She paused for effect. "Marchioness."

He shut his eyes briefly at the disgust in her voice. Though he'd never cared for Charlotte the way he cared for Marion, the last thing he'd wanted to do was hurt her. When he

215

left for Woodbury he had fully intended to keep the vow he'd made to her about no public dalliances. How was he to know he would meet Marion?

"Yes, I'm afraid what you've heard is true." His eyes opened to face her when he confessed. "I assure you, I never planned for this mess to happen and I'm sorry you've been embarrassed by my actions."

With a twist of one slender wrist she waved off his words. "It doesn't signify. What *does* signify is you made a promise to me and you didn't keep it. I don't like being lied to, my lord."

Guilt stabbed directly in to Noah's heart, gnawing at his every nerve. How he would have liked to spare everyone involved the pain his decisions had caused. Then his mind strayed to Marion and the way she'd responded to his touch, to his mouth. The way she'd looked after her father had beaten her. No, there had been no choice, and he would never again regret it.

"There were circumstances."

She barked out a sharp burst of humorless laughter. "Circumstances? I can imagine what those were." She shook her blonde head. "A man like you will never settle for one woman. I only hope your newest obsession realizes that."

Noah winced at her harsh words and the ring of truth they held. Yes, in the past he'd bored of his conquests. But Marion was different somehow. He wanted to be true to her.

"Charlotte…"

"I never should have trusted a rake." With a soft sigh, the heat left her voice and for a brief moment her shoulders sagged. "Please leave."

Noah rose to his feet and held out his arms in surrender. "I'm sorry."

She didn't look up, but her face had returned to its normal calm and unflappable mask. Noah far preferred Marion's passionate expression of the emotions in her heart.

"Just go," she whispered.

He did as she asked with a short bow. In the foyer, the butler opened the door with a sniff, and Noah found himself once again in the muggy late summer air of London. He shook his head as he swung up on his mount to head back to his estate.

As he rode away, he was wracked by conflicted feelings. Yes, he did care for Marion, but he still doubted his own ability to do the right thing where she was concerned. Perhaps his own true self would never be stifled to conform to the man his father had been. Marion professed not to care about that fact. In fact it had been she who'd urged him to remain his own self instead of trying to be his father.

Yet, did she really understand what that real self was? A womanizer. A spy. A man who lived for pleasure. At least, that's what he'd been for so long that he hardly remembered anything else.

Suddenly he longed for a private moment with the woman who would be his wife. A moment without a chaperone where he might look into her eyes and see if he could find any goodness in himself reflected there. He would have that moment. Tonight, after supper was over.

Proper or not.

CHAPTER TWENTY-THREE

Marion twirled a lock of hair around and around her fingertip as she stared out her chamber window at the flickering lights of London. Where was Noah?

He'd shared supper with his family, but had left before ten, saying he had other business to attend to. From his somber expression and quiet demeanor, Marion guessed his meeting with Charlotte hadn't gone well, but there had been no opportunity to ask him privately.

But now he was long gone, perhaps at home in his own bed. Or perhaps off at a club gaming. Or somewhere else. Somewhere she couldn't and didn't want to imagine.

She rubbed her bare arms with a shiver. Her dressing gown remained draped across the bed where she'd left it, but she doubted putting it on would help. It wasn't the room temperature that made her quake. It was the idea of Noah in the arms of some other woman. A woman who wasn't nervous about giving him her body. A woman who knew how to return the intense pleasure he'd shared with Marion back in Woodbury.

Her body reacted at that thought, softening and aching as she remembered the touch of Noah's mouth on her skin. His hands caressing her in ways she'd never imagined, arousing reactions she couldn't control.

She leapt at the quiet tap on her door. Spinning around,

she stared guiltily at the barrier between her and the hall. Here she'd been thinking the most intimate, scandalous thoughts and a visitor was right outside.

"Co-come in," she stammered, for she feared her legs wouldn't hold her up if she tried to walk.

With a quiet click, the door swung open and the very man she'd been fantasizing about leaned on the doorjamb, occasionally glancing over his shoulder as if he were afraid he'd be caught.

"Noah." Without hesitation, she hurried across the room to him. Here was the opportunity she'd been longing for. To be alone with him. Before she thought of the prudence behind her action, she threw her arms around his neck to hug him.

For a moment he stood stunned, but as Marion's warmth seeped through his coat and into his skin, Noah brought his arms around her in a crushing embrace. It felt so right to hold her. Despite

"Marion," he breathed into her hair.

When he said her name, it seemed to snap her back to reality. With a gentle shove, she pulled from his arms and scurried back a few steps. An enticing pale pink blush spread from her cheeks to her chest.

"You shouldn't be here."

Noah couldn't have agreed with her more. She stood just feet away from him in a thin shift that barely covered the smooth, velvety curves of her skin. He hadn't snuck back in to Griffin and Audrey's estate to make love to Marion, but now that he was standing in her bedroom with her warmth still on his skin, he was having a difficult time thinking of anything else.

She cocked her head. "Noah?"

He shook away his thoughts as he slipped into her chamber to shut the door behind him. The last thing either one of them needed was to be caught. Again.

"I was worried about you. I came to see if you were

doing well here." He took another small step toward her, reveling in the way she swayed in his direction.

She snapped herself back to full attention as she turned away. "I'm fine. Your family is very kind."

"They like you."

"I'm glad of that, I like them, too." She looked at him slowly. "How did things go with Charlotte? I wanted to ask at supper, but it didn't seem the time."

Noah's expression transformed from one of desire to sadness and guilt.

"It went as well as could be expected. She's angry, but she's accepted the change. And no one called me out over it, so I won't be dueling with her father at dawn at least."

Marion sank her teeth into her lower lip. "I wonder if she'll make things difficult for me as a form of revenge."

It had been something she'd not worried about until that day. Audrey and Tabitha seemed so focused on making her appearance in Society perfect. She would hate to see them, or Noah, disappointed.

He brushed her arm. His touch heated her skin even as it sent goose pimples across the flesh.

"No, she wouldn't do that. It isn't in her nature. She'll avoid you before she'll try to hurt you." His eyes darkened to a midnight blue that drew Marion in and didn't allow her any room for escape. "I don't want to talk about her any longer."

"No?" She heard the tremble in her voice as she stared up into Noah's eyes, the eyes that told her so clearly how much he desired her at that moment. And she hoped hers gave him the same message. That she ached for his touch. "What do you want to talk about?"

In answer, he dipped his head and caught her lips with his own. Their pressure was firm, yet gentle as he drew her into his embrace. When the tip of his tongue nudged her mouth, Marion melted. Her limbs became water and Noah her only support as she opened herself to an even deeper kiss. She arched against his hands as he slid them down her spine, their heat piercing through the thin cotton of her shift.

"I'm sorry," he whispered against her mouth before he pulled away to run a hand through his hair. She smiled as little pieces stood up on end, giving him a disheveled, utterly rakish look.

"Why?"

Before he could respond, she rose to her tiptoes and placed another heated kiss on his lips. Noah surrendered to his desire and pulled her against him a second time, loving her taste and her smell and the way her chestnut hair curled around his shoulders.

"Because," he panted, grasping her arms to push her back a fraction. "I know this marriage isn't what you want."

Her eyes flickered with brief sadness, but it was quickly replaced by the desire he'd kindled there. With a shrug of one shoulder and a soft smile, she whispered, "I'd like to make the best of it."

To Noah's surprise, she shrugged out of his hold to glide her palms across his chest. Looping her fingers under the lapels of his jacket, she pushed it from his shoulders and down to the floor in a heap. Her eyes never left his as she began to work the buttons of his linen shirt.

"Wait." He caught her roving hands with both his own. "Are you sure you want this? Because once it's done, there will be no turning back."

"I've wanted this since Woodbury. I've hardly thought of anything else."

She blushed, but there was no hesitation in her eyes when she pushed his hands aside to continue her exploration of his body. Her fingers nudged his buttons open, pulling his shirt aside until finally it, too had fallen to the floor.

"You're so perfect," she breathed, running soft fingertips along the contours of muscle and tangling them in the wiry chest hair that peppered his chest.

Noah sucked in his breath through his teeth, all the while reminding himself of the control he'd been taught as a spy. He needed all of it to keep from throwing Marion on her bed right then and there and taking her. No, for this first time he would give. There would be plenty of time for taking in the future.

With a dip of his head, he placed a hot kiss on her throat, easing his lips down the curve of her shoulder until his mouth met the thin strap of her chemise. He caught it with his lips to lift it away from her skin. She whispered her pleasure as his teeth grazed her shoulder.

"Noah…" Her hand gripped his bicep as he slid the strap from her shoulder to droop around her elbow.

"Yes?" he asked with a smile.

Marion shook her head. She wanted something but didn't know how to ask. She wanted him to ease the ache he'd begun by touching her. "I don't know."

His mouth returned to her sensitive shoulder, his tongue probing her soft skin as he slowly eased her back toward the bed. The gentle touch sent moist heat from his mouth directly through her body. Every nerve crackled with even the slightest touch, and between her legs she throbbed with need for him to give her the same powerful release she'd experienced before.

His fingers caught the second strap of her gown and with aching slowness he pulled it down. The soft fabric slid over her breasts, down her hips to pool at her feet. Though she should have been embarrassed to be so revealed to him, she wasn't. In fact, she was proud of how his eyes widened as they moved over her skin.

"And you say I'm perfect," he murmured as he stepped nearer to her to cup the base of her neck for another soft kiss. "You're more beautiful than any woman I've ever seen in my life."

Tears welled up in her eyes at his compliment. "Then make me yours. Tonight. Now."

He nodded as he brought her up against the full, hard length of him. The warmth of his body took away her chill from earlier in the evening, leaving her almost too hot. His hands did nothing to ease the fire in her. When he made a slow slide up her stomach to cup the smooth flesh of her breast, that fire was only stoked. His thumb strummed over her nipple in a rhythmic way that had her wriggling closer while sensation rushed through her.

They knelt on the bed and for the first time Marion felt bold enough to touch Noah the same way he had her. She slid her hands over his muscles, smiling when they bunched under her palms, and he closed his eyes at the pleasure of even the slightest stroke of her fingers.

With hesitation, she pressed her lips against the hollow at the base of his throat and felt his pulse throb beneath her with a wild cadence. Feeling even more adventurous with this newfound power, she darted her tongue along his collarbone as her hands kneaded the cut muscles of his stomach.

When she wrapped her lips around the tight ridge of Noah's nipple, he let out a low groan and his fingers dragged around her shoulders.

"Did I hurt you?" she whispered as she continued to place wet kisses on his chest and neck.

"Far from it," he choked out before he grasped her in animal desire and brought his mouth down on hers to devour and claim. "But I think you've played long enough for now."

She squirmed as he laid her back on the bed. "But I want to know your body as well as you know mine."

Again, his eyes closed and he muttered something unintelligible under his breath before he brought his hand up to cup her chin. "And you will. You'll have years to find every spot that makes me moan, every way I like to be touched." He grinned. "And there are many of those. But tonight I'm going to pleasure *you*."

She shivered as his voice dropped to the husky tone she instinctively knew meant that the time for talking was over. Silently she took his hand to place it on her breast and with a smile he followed her lead. He dropped his dark head to her chest and began to suckle one nipple as his fingers teased the other. The sensations he created there seemed to go straight to the core of her womanhood, the place where she grew wetter from every brush of his hand, every sweep of his lips.

With a slow slide, Noah brought his hand down her body to rest it on her thigh. Immediately her legs fell open, inviting him to touch her in the most intimate ways possible. He took the invitation willingly. He took a teasing sweep of his fingers across the cleft between her thighs and found the telltale dampness amongst the dark curls that told him she was more than ready to join with him. With a second sweep, he parted the soft lips there and grazed his thumb across the tight bead of pleasure that had her rising from the bed with a little cry.

Her eyes were dilated with anticipation, fear and desire. They met his with a wild intensity that both flamed his need and inspired a deeper protectiveness in him.

"Don't be afraid."

He continued his slow massage of her womanhood as he kissed her deep and slow. She eased her head back against the pillow with a sigh as she arched against his finger. In response, he slid the long, thick digit inside her, mimicking the way he would move when they finally made love.

Her face filled with heat, her eyes shut as he brought her closer and closer to the brink. He'd brought many women to the edge of where she now balanced, so close to release, but he'd never paid much attention to their reactions. Marion's breath was short and shallow, and a soft flush tinged her neck and chest. She arched up with a little cry and her inner muscles throbbed around him in release.

As the blinding colors faded around her, Marion opened her eyes to give Noah a shy smile. The delicious feeling of him touching her was incredible, but not enough for her to forget that he hadn't taken his own pleasure, not either time they'd lain together in a bed. Tonight she wanted to remedy that. She wanted to experience the full joining of a man and a woman. She wanted to hear Noah cry out her name the way she cried out his.

When he began to rise from the bed, her hand shot out to grip his arm. "Don't go!"

"I'm not going anywhere," he reassured her. "God, I couldn't leave now."

He peeled her fingers from his wrist and stood up to shrug out of the remainder of his clothes. Marion's eyes widened as he turned back to her. He seemed carved in granite, larger than life, from his broad shoulders, to the hard thrust of his erection that jutted out proudly from between his legs.

He returned to lie beside her. "Slow and easy, I promise."

"Slow and easy," she murmured, drawn to touch him as intimately as he'd touched her moments before. With trembling fingers, she slid her hand down his body, over his stomach until her fingertip glided over the curve of his penis. Noah groaned out his breath.

"The skin is so velvety." She wondered how he could be so hard and strong and yet tender at the same time.

With a grunt, he rolled over to lie on top of her. He pushed her legs apart with a gentle nudge until the tip of his shaft pressed against the moist opening there.

"Slowly," he said softly before he pushed forward, claiming her inch-by-inch.

The feeling wasn't unpleasant, just strange to be filled in such a way. Marion felt as if she were being stretched, but her body seemed made for the task and her nerve endings crackled with the heavy, hard weight of Noah atop and within her.

"Here is where it will hurt for just a moment," he whispered as he darted his tongue along the shell of her ear.

Marion shut her eyes at the dizzying sensations created by his mouth and body. At that moment, Noah drove into her, pushing past the barrier of her untried body and sent a shot of pain through her.

As she caught her breath, Marion realized the pain had

subsided and now she could feel Noah sheathed entirely within her quivering body. She wiggled a bit to test how it felt and was surprised when the pleasure that had built in her before returned, only this time with more intensity.

Noah groaned and brought his mouth down against hers for a hard, consuming kiss as he began to move his hips in a slow, circular motion. Every part of Marion felt alive as his steady, even thrusts brought her nearer and nearer to release, to the end of the throbbing pressure that was once again building inside her.

Noah felt himself approaching the edge of a precipice from where he wouldn't be able to keep himself from taking all the pleasure Marion's responsive body inspired in him. But he wanted to make her cry out one more time. With shaking hands, he reached between their two bodies and found that little hidden spot within the curls that made her arch even harder against him with a little cry.

"Now," he whispered. "Let go now."

She did, clasping her arms around his neck with all her might as she let out a primal scream against his damp neck. He caught her cry with his mouth and merged it with his own as he clutched her hips against him hard and poured himself into her.

For a long time he stayed where he was, only relieving her of his weight by balancing on his elbows. He should roll away and leave her to return home, but somehow he couldn't tear himself away from her arms. She felt too right laying beneath him, running her fingertips up and down the line of his spine while she looked up into his face with a smile of contentment.

"I should move." He placed a gentle peck on the tip of her nose. "I'm crushing you."

"I like your weight," she said, massaging across the expanse of the muscles of his back. "It lets me know you're really here and I didn't dream this night. I didn't dream *you*."

"I would wager you've never dreamt something so wicked in your life." He smiled to relieve some of the emotion she inspired in him with her statement.

A grin quirked one side of her mouth and the sly look made Noah aware he was becoming aroused by her yet again. It wasn't as if he were some green young man. God, he wasn't even in his prime anymore. But this woman with her sparkling brown eyes and giving nature made him react in ways he hadn't for a long time.

"No," she whispered as she lifted her hips a little and placed a hot kiss on his jaw. "But I know what I'll be dreaming about the rest of tonight."

"Only tonight?" Gathering her closer in his arms, Noah surged forward into her again. With a low, possessive laugh he said, "If my goal is to make sure you dream of my touch every night of your life, I'd best work some more on that."

CHAPTER TWENTY-FOUR

Noah strummed his fingertips across the tabletop and stared at the breakfast room door. A night of lovemaking with Marion should have left him tired, especially since it was before noon and he hadn't crept from her bed until the very wee hours of the morning. Instead, he felt rejuvenated in ways he hadn't since he worked on cases in the War Department.

In those days, everything had seemed possible and interesting. Around every corner danger and intrigue lay in wait. But in the time since his discharge, that feeling had faded, leaving him bored and restless.

Until Marion.

Although she wasn't dangerous, and aside from a few key omissions on her part, she didn't bring him intrigue, she made him feel *alive*.

"Noah!"

His eyes came up to the door in a flash, but dropped again in disappointment when only his sister entered the room with a wide smile on her pretty face. Griffin followed close behind. He arched an eyebrow at the dark shadows that lingered beneath Noah's eyes.

"Good morning Audrey, Griffin." With a sigh, he rose from his seat.

"Good morning." His sister sank into a chair as she smiled at the maid who poured her tea. Once the young woman had done the same for the two men and left the room, her smile turned wicked. "Marion isn't home this morning."

Noah's heart sank into his stomach and the world that had looked so glorious a few moments before suddenly turned bleak. He shook his head at his swift, maudlin reaction. When had he turned into such a romantic fool?

"Oh?" He did his best to keep his voice smooth and free of emotion. "Where is she?"

"Mother took her for another fitting with Miss Fox. Then they're off for a bit of socializing. She thinks it would be best to introduce her quickly to people in our circle who'll be her allies. That way when we begin to make the rounds at parties in a week or so, she'll already have friends on her side."

Audrey took a sip of her tea, but Noah could feel her eyes boring into him even over the edge of her cup.

"A good plan." He took a side-glance at Griffin in the hopes that his best friend would distract his wife from her singular purpose, but Griffin looked amused rather than poised to play savior.

"Yes, we thought so." Griffin grinned. "But it seems you came here for nothing."

Noah shook his head, determined to pretend his fiancée's absence didn't affect him in the least. "No, no. I'm happy to share my breakfast with my family."

Audrey let out a burst of unladylike laughter. "Noah Jordan, London has been your primary residence since we were released from our duties at the War Department last year. In that time, I believe you've shared your breakfast with us a total of three times. One of them was Christmas Day last year, and that was only because you hadn't gone to bed after carousing the night before."

Noah pursed his lips. "I wasn't carousing."

Now it was Griffin's turn to laugh. "Would you rather we call it reveling?"

Audrey winked at her husband. "And now you wish me to believe that you came all the way across town out of some desire to break your fast with Griffin and me?"

Noah shook his head as he stirred his tea with vicious speed. His sister and brother-in-law were teasing him as they loved to do, but they were dancing very close to the edge of a truth he wasn't ready to face himself, let alone share with anyone else.

"I will admit I wished to see Marion," he ground out.

"Didn't you see enough of her last night?" Griffin asked with a half smile.

"I'd hardly say a staid supper with my entire family was spending quality time with my future wife," Noah countered with a superior glare.

"And you didn't see enough of her after you snuck back into our home and into her room?" Though Audrey's voice still held the teasing in it, her eyes had become serious as she searched her brother's face.

Noah froze at her accusation. "How did you know about that?"

"She was once a spy, too." Griffin had a quiet gravity that brought the room's tone back to one of seriousness.

"You haven't said anything to her, have you?"

Noah held his breath as he waited for an answer. Marion would be humiliated if she knew his sister had discovered their tryst. It would shake her already lowered confidence about coming out in Society and taking her place as his wife.

"Of course not." Audrey frowned. "I would never embarrass her in such a way. And as far as I know, Mother knows nothing about it either."

"Good." Noah leaned back with relief. The last thing he needed was yet another lecture from his mother.

Audrey moved a chair closer to her brother and looked at him with sincere, caring eyes. "I have very little room to judge the behavior of two people about to be married." She tossed a quick look at Griffin, who smiled at her. "But I'd like to offer you a small bit of advice."

Noah cocked his head with a shrug. Audrey had offered very little unasked-for counsel even during the years they'd worked together. The words of wisdom she had imparted to him had always been good, even if he hadn't heeded them. And Audrey had gone through her own trials in love. She and Griffin hadn't always been able to be happy together as they were now.

"What is it?"

She smiled to soften her words. "Be wary. Marion is still uncertain about the future and could easily be hurt, even if that isn't your intention."

Noah nodded slowly. He was painfully aware of that fact. "I've already taken so much from her."

Griffin cocked his head. "Then give her something back."

Audrey's attention moved from Noah to Griffin and her smile widened as a look of complete love sparkled into her eyes. For a brief moment, Noah was shut out of their world and was desperately jealous of what they shared.

When Audrey returned her gaze to him, her face was lit up. "My husband is not only handsome, but he's brilliant."

Despite his own tangled emotions, Noah felt his mouth turn up in a grin.

"But what?" His eyes moved to Griffin who was watching him with an unreadable expression. "What can I give to her?"

Griffin shook his head with a short laugh. "Even after all your years of playing the rake, you don't know a damn thing about women. Think Noah. What does she *want*?"

Noah searched his mind, grasping for the things Marion had told him with words and with actions in the time he'd known her. Marion wanted independence. He could give her that, but not in the way she had wanted for so many years under her father's thumb. And independence wasn't a grand enough gesture.

Marion wanted family and love. The love her father had

withheld from her since her mother's death. The love she had once hoped to find with…

His eyes widened as he rose to his feet. "Thank you both." He set his teacup back on its saucer and hurried toward the door. "When Mother and Marion come back let them know I'll return in a few days. I have an errand I must perform. Take care of her while I'm away."

He was halfway out the door when Audrey called out, "Wait!"

He turned back with impatience. If he wanted to reach Dover before midday the following day he'd have to leave now and ride hard all afternoon and most of the night.

"What is it?"

Audrey reached his side. "Where on earth are you going?"

Noah shot her a cocky grin before he bent to kiss her cheek. "It's a secret."

With a wink for Griffin, he hurried away.

Audrey turned to her husband with a shrug as she trudged across the room to sit back down. "Besotted."

Griffin narrowed his eyes as the man he'd called friend for as long as he'd been alive rode past the morning room window and down the street as if he were being pursued by the devil himself.

"Yes, Audrey. I think you're right. And now we'll just have to see if Noah can conquer love as easily as he's conquered everything else in his life."

Marion fidgeted in her chair, twisting the fingertip of her glove in her hand under the table. This was the third luncheon she'd attended in as many days, and she still fretted about using the wrong fork or saying the wrong thing to the wrong person. The fact that Noah had vanished a few days before left her feeling even more alone. Her greatest ally had disappeared into the night without explanation or even a goodbye.

She was left with little but memories. Memories that made her hot in the middle of the night and long for him the rest of the day. Certainly not the kind of reminiscences one should have been having in the middle of an important engagement with some of the most influential women of the *ton*.

"Well, Miss Marion." A voice shook her from her daydreams. She turned to find one of the women at their table staring at her with hawkish gray eyes. "You seem to have left us entirely. I wonder where you could have gone that was more important than here?"

Marion bit her tongue to withhold the retort balancing on it. She could think of a hundred places more important than the room she was in now, but she wouldn't give in to the nasty woman's picking.

"I'm so sorry Lady Latimer." She sighed with relief as she remembered the woman's name with only mild difficulty. "I became distracted by the beautiful painting on the wall above your head. I wonder who the artist was?"

This sent the table into ohhs and ahhs over the artwork and made Lady Oswood, their hostess, beam with pleasure at the attention she'd garnered from Marion's remark. When Marion looked at Tabitha, the older woman gave her a nod of support and pride.

"I'm surprised a lady such as yourself would even notice the artwork," Lady Latimer said, refusing to be put off. "After all, you were raised in the country by a *tradesman*, weren't you?"

She sniffed and sent a rush of protective anger through Marion. Though she spared no love for her father, she knew full well that a man who earned his living was no better or worse than one born into it.

Before she could say any of the sharp words that came

to her mind, Tabitha arched a well-defined eyebrow and glared at Lady Latimer. "Why Giselle, a tradesman is only a few steps below a Knight, isn't he? Your own father would probably agree."

The other woman choked on her sip of tea as the ladies at the table all swiveled their eyes to her for her response. When she'd regained her composure, she nodded her head once.

"Yes, my father might very well agree, Lady Woodbury. I'm lucky to have married an Earl."

Tabitha had won and her smile was one of quiet triumph as Lady Latimer dropped her eyes back to her plate. The tension in Marion's chest began to loosen and her shoulders relaxed as it became apparent no one else at the table intended to challenge her presence there.

Just as they had at some of the other events they'd taken her to, the Jordan women had scooped her up under their wing and given her the protection of their name and their reputation. It was becoming increasingly clear that those protections would continue until the *ton* forgot or chose to ignore any remaining scandal associated with her.

She couldn't help but smile softly as the remainder of their luncheon came to an end and the ladies around them began to leave. Tabitha chatted with their hostess for a moment before she returned to Audrey and Marion's side and ushered them toward the door.

"You made a very good impression on Lady Oswood," Tabitha whispered as they climbed into their coach.

Marion gave her a nervous smile. "But probably not on Lady Latimer."

"Pish posh." Audrey waved off her comment as if it were meaningless. "Lady Oswood is far more important."

"I appreciated your coming to my defense, Lady Woodbury." She smiled at her future mother-in-law.

"You're family now," Tabitha reassured her with a gentle tap of her fan across Marion's gloved knuckles. "We'll never allow someone to hurt our family."

Audrey nodded her silent agreement. Marion felt a rush of love that she hadn't felt in years. Here she'd spent a lifetime without allies or sisters to call her own. But with a few twists of fate, she was now in the midst of a family who would bring down the entire city if it caused a threat to her. The feeling was indescribable.

"If this is how the Jordan family operates, I cannot wait to meet the rest of the clan," she said with a laugh before she gazed out the window.

Audrey's smile fell as she exchanged a quick glance with her mother. "I'm afraid that may never happen. Virginia doesn't speak to our family often. She may not even make it to your wedding."

Marion frowned. "Why?"

The color drained from Tabitha's cheeks. "I arranged her marriage and it is a very unhappy one. She still blames me and the family."

She said the words in such a way that it was clear the subject was closed. But Marion didn't wish to speak about it any longer as it was. Just the idea of an unhappy arranged marriage made her ill. Were she and Noah much better? After all, they'd shared a few beautiful hours together a handful of nights before, but he had disappeared just as soon as he could after.

Audrey assured her that Noah wasn't angry with her or unhappy about their situation, but Marion had to wonder. Had he run for some purpose other than the secret he'd claimed to his sister?

Marion could only judge her own emotions, not Noah's. The night they'd spent in each other's arms had only solidified the love she felt for him. His mouth on hers, his body pressed against and in her, that explosion of pleasure so intense it was almost painful. All those things only made her love for him grow.

Perhaps it was different for him. Making love to her

could have bored him. She'd heard of the joy of the chase before, how a man would pursue until he had what he wanted and then grow tired of it and move on to the next challenge. Perhaps that's what had happened with Noah. She prayed not.

"Here we are." Audrey smiled at her as they pulled through the gates of Bentley Square, and Marion shook away her troubling thoughts to smile back.

She was the first to escape the confines of the carriage and welcomed the cooler air outside. But as she gazed around her, she noticed a second carriage was parked on the drive. The carriage with a special seal on the door that identified it as…

"Noah," she breathed as she took an involuntary step toward the door. He was inside. He was waiting for her. And something told her that what he said to her that day would let her know if he still wanted her.

CHAPTER TWENTY-FIVE

Noah paced the sitting room and hated how tense he felt… and probably looked. Concealing his emotions had always been easy for him, but he couldn't do it now. Not when he knew that at any time Marion would walk in that door and he'd be forced to change her life forever.

Going to Dover to find her aunts seemed like such a simple gift. But what he found there changed everything. Now he feared he'd be giving his future bride a curse rather than a blessing.

He heard the front door open and the three women come giggling and talking into the foyer. Taking a deep breath, he stepped into the hallway with a false smile.

Marion noticed his presence first. Her eyes lit up and her face filled with pleasure. For a brief moment, Noah forgot his twisted emotions and fought against the need to cross the room and take her into his arms in front of his mother, his sister, and the butler.

"Noah!" she said with a grin and took three quick steps toward him before she skidded to a halt with a guilty glance back over her shoulder. Her face filled with hot color.

"Noah?" Audrey tilted her head as she removed her hat. "What's wrong?"

Trust Audrey to notice his inner turmoil. Years of working together had sharpened her ability to see his emotions even when he was trying to hide them. Marion had seemed to have gained that same ability in only a few weeks.

"I need to speak to my fiancée alone." He locked eyes with Marion. Her face paled.

"Something has happened?" she asked.

He nodded slowly.

"What is going on, Noah?" his mother asked with concern. "Where's Griffin?"

"In the Green Parlor. He has a guest there, and I'm sure they'll explain everything to you. But for now I need to speak to Marion." He reached out and she took his arm without waiting to hear if his proposition was appropriate.

He led her to a sitting room and shut the door behind him. Marion took a seat by the small fire and smoothed her skirt reflexively all while she watched him pace around the room. The tension rolled off of him in waves. But why? Had he changed his mind about their upcoming union and was now trying to find a kind way to tell her? And who was the guest he'd brought with him from whatever mystery destination he'd gone?

She cleared her throat uncomfortably. "Please tell me what's going on. This tension is too much."

He stopped pacing to look at her. His blue eyes held hers with such tenderness that she wanted to weep, but she controlled her reaction and gave him a weak smile.

"I'm sorry. I don't know how to start," he muttered as he shook his head. Finally, he crossed the room to stand before her. He looked down at her for a moment, then, to her complete shock, dropped down to kneel in front of her. He took both her hands in his and squeezed gently. "How did your father tell you your mother died?"

She pulled back at the question, but he held her fast and didn't let her move away. They hadn't said much on the topic of her deceased mother, and she was surprised at how the subject stung.

Taking a measured breath, she answered, "She had a

sudden illness."

His face hardened. "Did you see her during her illness?"

Tears she couldn't control pricked at her as she remembered the events surrounding her mother's death. She'd been out playing with friends, when she'd returned... "No. It was all so sudden. She was just... gone."

"What of her funeral, her grave?"

She winced again. Why would he be so cruel as to press her for the details of a time that was the worst in her life? Without her mother, her life had gone from generally happy to barely tolerable. All the love Marion had felt had evaporated, replaced by her father's resentment.

"I don't wish to speak further on this topic." She yanked her hands away. Noah blocked her escape, so she turned her head and stared into the fire instead.

But he didn't take her not-so-subtle hint. Instead, he turned her face back toward his with a gentle finger on her chin. "I realize this is a painful subject and I would not force you to relive it if it wasn't very important. Please, Marion."

Her anger faded slightly at his earnestness. It seemed to pain him to ask her these questions as much as it pained her to answer.

"My father wouldn't allow me to attend any services in her honor," she explained. "And he never parted with enough money to give her grave a proper marker. A blank slab of stone is where I put my flowers each year on her birthday."

The tears in her eyes finally began their slow slide down her cheeks, no matter how she blinked and fought to keep them at bay. She'd done her best to keep her feelings about her mother to herself. First it had been because her father became angry when she mourned. He'd only let her wear black for a few scant days after her mother's passing.

Later, her privacy in her grief had become more personal. There was no one in her life that she felt close enough to share her private pain. Until now. Now, sitting before the man who she'd soon marry, she wasn't ashamed by her tears. In fact, sharing her anguish seemed right.

And he took that pain exactly as she would have wished. He raised a hand and gently brushed the tears from her eyes.

"Hold my hand, Marion," he whispered as he leaned up and kissed her temple.

She did as he asked and slipped her fingers to intertwine with his. The warm cocoon of his palm soothed her, but she still felt an enormous trepidation. Though he smiled as he comforted her, she saw the worry in his eyes. The worry about whatever he'd brought her into this room to reveal.

"I don't think you brought me here to ask about my mother." She gazed into his face. "What is it?"

He swallowed as if what he had to tell her was difficult for him. "You probably wonder where I've been these past few days."

She nodded slowly. "Yes. But you've no need to report your activities to me, Noah. We aren't married. And even when we are, a man must have a certain freedom to…"

He cut her off with a frown. "I wasn't off gallivanting with other women, Marion."

The pain in his eyes made her wish she hadn't said anything. Noah actually seemed hurt by her implication. "Then wh-where were you?"

He sighed. "I went to Dover to collect your aunts and bring them here to you as a surprise."

Marion's shock was quickly replaced by joy. Her aunts here! At this very moment? She could talk to them, ask them questions about her mother, bond with them as a family. But why did Noah still look so upset?

He answered as if she'd spoken out loud. "What I found there was shocking and I've been tormented by it ever since. What I know may hurt you and God, but I hate to do that again."

Her heart rate increased two-fold and her eyes widened.

"What is it?"

His grip on her hand tightened as if he were afraid of her reaction to what he said next. "Your mother didn't die as your father told you."

"Wh-what?" Marion had heard him perfectly well, but she didn't understand. Perhaps she was becoming daft from all the things that had happened in the past few weeks.

His eyes softened. "She didn't die, Marion. Your father sent your mother away." His grip on her tightened again. Though he didn't squeeze her painfully, she felt his support. "She's alive."

"What?" She couldn't seem to think of anything else to say.

"One of the 'aunts' who've corresponded with you all these years was actually your mother."

Marion's tears were gone now, replaced by a cold shock that crept through her blood until she actually shivered in the warm room.

"I. Don't. Understand," she managed to croak out as she searched his face for a better explanation.

Perhaps he was jesting. Because it couldn't be true. It couldn't. If her mother were really alive, she would have come for her long ago. Wouldn't she?

"I wish there were a better way to tell you this." He released her hand to run it through his thick hair. "She's here right now. I brought her to London. If you don't want to see her, we both understand."

Her eyes widened. "No!" She took a deep breath to calm her raging nerves. "No. I want to see her."

Noah closed his eyes, rocked by the inner strength the woman before him possessed. Most of the young ladies he knew would have swooned when they heard such shocking news. And once they'd come back to consciousness they would have gone into hysterics. But Marion, though pale and shocked, handled his revelation with the calm serenity of a woman, not a foolish girl.

"Very well," he said with a soft smile he hoped would comfort her. He brushed the back of his hand across her soft cheek before he pushed off his knees to stand upright. Before he could turn to the door, he felt Marion grip his hand. He turned back and looked down at her.

She stared up at him with brown eyes that were wide and clear and full of trust, trust in him. Even in her shaken state, her beauty and good soul were as evident as her worry and fear. And Noah realized, with the strength of a thunderbolt, that he loved her. Not loved her as a friend, but an all-consuming, earth-shaking love that rocked him to the very center of his soul. He loved her and had loved her from the very first moment she'd stormed around the lake and given him… and his horse… a tongue-lashing.

He staggered back from the force of the realization and stared gape-mouthed at her.

"You aren't going to leave me, are you?" she asked, so wrapped up in her own tangled emotions that she didn't notice the passion in his eyes.

He shook off the reactions that made his body tremble and put his focus back on Marion. There would be plenty of time later to analyze and over-analyze the feelings that had just changed him irrevocably. At this moment, the woman he loved, the woman he'd soon marry, needed him, and he would be there for her.

"I won't leave if that's your wish." How he managed to make the words come, he wasn't sure.

She nodded slowly. "I *need* you to stay."

A great swell of pride and love filled Noah's heart at those words. Marion needed him. She wanted him to be a part of this, the most important moment of her life so far. And if that was what she wanted, than he would do all he could to help her.

Marion shifted in her place, trying to find a comfortable position while she waited the eternal moments for her mother to walk through the door. When she couldn't relax, she stood with a sigh and paced over to the fireplace.

Noah sat in the chair in the corner of the room as he had since he'd told a footman to fetch Ingrid Hawthorne. To fetch her *mother*.

She caught his eye and his smile soothed her. "Don't worry."

She felt the strangest urge to go to him and kiss him, to pull him up against her just to prove that something in her life still existed as it had before she'd learned her mother was alive. Everything but Noah seemed different now, changed irreversibly. Her life, her feelings had all been lies. She had no idea how to carry on.

The door creaked softly as it began to open, but to Marion it sounded like a gunshot, and she leapt in her place as she spun to face the intruder.

"Mrs. Hawthorne," the footman announced before he stepped back and allowed the woman behind him to come into the room.

Marion wrapped a hand around the mantelpiece and gripped it with all her might as the woman stopped and looked directly at her. If Marion had been harboring any suspicions this wasn't real, they evaporated in an instant. Her mother stood not six feet away from her, looking much as she had when Marion had last seen her fourteen years before.

Her hair was still the same chestnut brown Marion herself saw in the mirror each morning, only her mother's had a few streaks of gray running through hers. Her eyes sparkled with kindness, though the humor that had always made her look like she was laughing was now gone, replaced by a depth of sadness Marion often felt herself.

"Marion," she breathed as she took a step into the room. She seemed to think better of it and halted abruptly. "My, how beautiful you've grown."

Though Marion hadn't noticed him move, she felt Noah's strong hand on her shoulder. She leaned back against his chest, needing his warmth and his dependability. Both seeped into her skin, and she suddenly felt strong enough to speak.

"I-I'm not sure what to say." She straightened, though she lifted her hand to cover Noah's for a brief moment.

Her mother let out a short, nervous laugh. "Nor am I." Ingrid edged forward a few steps, and Marion found herself meeting her mother halfway until they were just inches apart. "I'm so sorry."

Without thinking, Marion fell into her mother's arms and the two women held each other tightly. She wasn't sure if she spoke, but she knew they communicated, sharing apologies and forgiveness, as well as the tears that flowed freely.

"Come and sit down," Marion finally said when she found her voice and could bear to separate herself from her mother's warm embrace. "We have so much to talk about."

As the two women sat, Marion found herself looking toward Noah. He had settled back into a quiet corner of the room. Like the man she knew him to be, he didn't interfere or make himself a part of her reunion, but stayed close by in case she needed him. Her love for him swelled as she threw him a fleeting smile then returned her attention to her mother.

"Tell me what happened."

Her mother dropped her eyes to the floor with a sigh. Her cheeks colored to a dark red. "You have a right to know, but it's a long story."

Marion brushed her hand across her mother's. "Mama, I've waited fourteen years to hear it."

Ingrid nodded and slowly lifted her eyes to her daughter. "My marriage was never a happy one. Your father and I had an arranged union. He wanted me for my family connections and our money. Once he damaged my family's associations and spent my generous dowry, he tired of me." Her mother's eyes clouded with painful memory. "The things he'd say to me…"

Marion nodded wordlessly. She vaguely remembered her father's tirades against her mother, and had been a victim of them since. She knew how deeply his words could cut.

"I decided to leave," her mother continued. "I asked my sisters to take us both in. But he caught me as I was preparing our things. He threw me out into the street and told me I would never see you again, let alone take you with me."

Marion shook her head. "Why? He never wanted me."

How true that statement was. Her father treated her like free labor or a burden, not a child he loved.

Her mother shrugged. "He didn't want me to have you because he knew how much I loved you. You became his pawn. I stayed in Northumberland for as long as I could, trying to change his mind, trying to get anyone to help me. But the law sees children as the property of their fathers. Walter stayed firm that you were no longer a part of my life."

Tears stung Marion's eyes again, but she refused to let them fall. "So you left."

Her mother nodded. "I had no choice. I'd been cast out of the Society in Holyworth and had nowhere to go. I watched you play one last time to burn an image of you in my heart. Then I went to my family in the hopes your father would become bored with using you and let you go, or change his mind."

Marion laughed bitterly. "When Papa gets something into his head, he rarely lets it go. Especially if he gains something from it."

She thought of him selling her to Josiah Lucas with a shiver. Only this time someone more powerful than her father had finally put a stop to him. Noah.

"I pleaded with him through letters to allow me to see you. He took great pleasure in informing me that you believed I was dead. I knew then I would never convince him to let me into your life. Not as your mother."

Marion's mother sighed and a tear wove its way down

her soft cheek. She didn't bother to wipe it away but continued her tale. It was almost as if she didn't even notice tears any longer.

"After a long while, I wrote to him again and told him if he would allow me to write to you, I would pretend to be your aunt. For years I wrote to him, begging for his permission. Then I wrote to you, playing the part of Hester, in the hopes he might change his mind and allow you to see the letter. When you wrote back, I was shocked. I never thought he would allow such a day."

"He didn't." Marion swallowed back the sharp taste of bile in her throat. "He saved your notes, probably to enjoy the pain he caused us both. I found them and later I enlisted the help of our cook to sneak my letters out and yours in."

"My goodness, but you were bold." Her mother smiled. "There were so many times I nearly told you the truth about who I was, but I feared the consequences for both of us."

Marion nodded and her hand stole up to her arm. It was only just out of the sling and no longer painful. Feeling her father's full fury made her painfully aware of just what those consequences would have been.

Her mother's face twisted and Marion realized Noah had told Ingrid about the beating her father had given her.

"I'm so sorry," her mother whispered. "I never thought he would harm you. He only raised his hand to me once, when I was leaving."

With a sigh, Marion shook her head. "Mama, it isn't your fault. And this is a chance to start again." Her eyes went to Noah. He was staring at her with an intensity that made her heart flutter and her hands tremble. "For all of us."

CHAPTER TWENTY-SIX

Marion smoothed her trembling hands over her icy blue gown for what must have been the tenth time. She couldn't seem to control the achy sensation her nervousness created in the pit of her stomach. Tonight was her first appearance in Society with Noah at her side.

She'd been to luncheons and teas with only ladies in attendance, but tonight she was to attend a ball, one of the last of the Season. According to Tabitha, the place would be a crush of people and the perfect place to make it clear that Marion would soon be the new Marchioness of Woodbury.

"The perfect place to make a complete fool of myself," Marion muttered as she turned away from her mirror to look out the window.

What if she forgot the steps to all the dances she'd been taught over the past few weeks? What if she said the wrong thing to the wrong person and offended them? What if Charlotte Ives was there and made a scene?

Any one of those things would embarrass the Jordan family and force Marion to work all the harder to be accepted by the *ton*.

Another wave of anxiety rocked her before she faced the mirror again and gave herself an appraising glance. She looked the part of a Marchioness in her fashionable gown with its high waist and expensive silk fabric. No detail had been ignored, from the soft edging on the navy ribbon below her breasts to the delicate brocade along the thin skirt. Sally had twisted and curled and piled her hair until it crowned her head in a shimmering, chestnut mass.

Yes, she looked the part. But could she truly play it?

The door behind her opened and Sally entered. "Lady Berenger says it's time to go. Lord Woodbury and his mother are downstairs waiting for you."

Marion nodded wordlessly before she turned. "Is my mother downstairs, as well?"

"Yes. Waiting to see you off."

She bent her head slightly. "I wish she could come, too, but I understand why Lady Woodbury doesn't wish for too many questions about me all at once."

Sally nodded. "You look absolutely beautiful, miss. Lord Woodbury will be knocked from his stallion the moment he sees you come down the stairs."

Marion's mouth quirked into a half smile at Sally's colorful description. She hoped her maid was right. The only thing she wanted was to look and feel right for Noah. She wanted him to look at her the way he had when he came into her room and made love to her. If she could kindle that flash of desire in his eyes, she would consider the evening a triumph. Especially since they'd had so little time alone between Noah leaving and her mother's surprise return to her life.

"Are you ready to meet the rest of your party then?"

Sally's voice brought Marion back to the present time, away from her wandering thoughts of Noah. It was just as well. Whenever she thought of them making love, her body tingled and grew hot almost like he was touching her again. As pleasant as that sensation was, tonight she needed her wits about her.

"Yes."

As she swept out her chamber door and into the brightly lit hallway she heard voices. The women, including her own mother, chattered away while the occasional male voice of

Griffin piped in. But it was Noah's rich baritone that stood out from the rest, rising up to her ears and giving her the same thrill the sight or scent of him gave her. As always, she was astonished by the power of her reaction to the man. And soon he would be hers, at least in name. And perhaps, in time, he'd come to feel for her in the same way she did about him.

She shook away the thought as she began a slow descent down the staircase into the foyer. At the bottom of the stairs, Noah leaned against the handrail, his elbow draped casually over the end. He was talking to Griffin, but suddenly he stopped and turned as if he sensed her presence. She was pleased when his eyes widened and his voice trailed off.

Marion felt the others' eyes on her as the room grew silent, but she couldn't tear her gaze away from Noah. She was drawn to him and him alone.

"You look magnificent." He said the words softly as if they were a prayer or if he said them too loudly the moment would pass.

A hot blush of pleasure warmed her cheeks and she hoped she didn't seem like this was her first compliment. Every one from Noah made her behave as if it was.

Noah held out his hand to Marion and prayed it wouldn't tremble as much as his knees were. He'd known many beautiful women, but the one he was to marry shook him in ways he hadn't believed were possible. It was terrifying and exhilarating at the same time.

He heard his sister's voice, but didn't comprehend what she was saying for a long moment. Finally, he broke the intense gaze he was sharing with Marion and focused.

"You really do look lovely." Audrey spoke to Marion, but her blue eyes were locked on him and an expression he couldn't place was on her face. "That shade of blue compliments you perfectly."

Ingrid Hawthorne stepped forward. "Yes, you're going to make quite an impression."

Noah felt Marion slipping away toward her mother and

reluctantly let her go. Though he was happy she was getting to know Ingrid after all their years apart, he desperately wished to take her away from their families and spend a week or two or three worshipping her body and getting to know her better and better. Their marriage date was going to have to be moved up, there was nothing else to be said about it.

Tabitha glanced at him quickly, then back to Marion. "We should be off. We want to be fashionably late, not overtly rude. Come along."

Noah saw Marion's smile tighten as servants appeared with wraps and opened the front door. Although she was putting on a brave face for his family, she was frightened and worried about making a good impression. What she didn't know was that it didn't matter two whits to him whether Society liked her or not. He'd fallen too much in love with her to turn away from marrying her now. He just had to find the right time to tell her that. And hope she'd feel the same.

Noah gave Marion a sideways glance as the carriage rocked around a corner. She hardly seemed to notice the movement as she continued to gush to his mother about the ball. Her first night in Society had been a smashing success, better than anyone could have hoped for. People had been wary at first, but Marion's disarming charm quickly had them whispering that she was the new 'original'.

Griffin leaned over to him, careful not to alert the women to his words. "You seem worried. Anything I can do to help?"

Noah shook his head, amazed as always at how well his best friend could read him. "I received word from Golding about Marion's father at the ball tonight."

Griffin's eyebrow came up in concern as he glanced at the young woman who'd so thoroughly disrupted all their lives.

"What of him?"

"He's left Woodbury, but no one knows where he's gone." Noah sighed as he watched Marion laugh.

The thought of Walter Hawthorne coming near enough to Marion to harm her was enough to make his blood boil, but Noah tamped down the emotion when his fiancée briefly turned her eyes toward him. The laughter faded from her lips, replaced by a brief blush and a dip of her head.

Noah's body clenched with desire. Even after he'd made love to Marion, her quiet shyness still made him weak for her. If his entire family hadn't surrounded them, he would have drawn her into his lap and taken her right there in the carriage. The thought of her writhing in pleasure above him made him shift uncomfortably in his position as he forced his mind to think of something else. Anything else.

Marion allowed her gaze to move to Noah a second time and was surprised to see hot desire glittering in his eyes. She couldn't control her body's reaction to his stare. Her limbs grew heavy as she imagined him kissing her, touching her, claiming her.

"That success will make our next step all the easier."

Marion shook off her desire and looked at Tabitha. "I'm sorry, I was woolgathering. What did you say?"

Tabitha shot a knowing glance between Marion and her son. "I feel it may be best for all of us to have you two married as soon as possible. I'd like to set a date in just a month, if that's agreeable to you both."

Heat filled Marion's cheeks at the thought. Though it had been made clear that she would marry Noah, now that they were talking about dates, the full reality hit her. In a month she could be the Marchioness of Woodbury. She would be Noah's by law and by the bed they lay in together. Every night.

Her mouth was suddenly dry and she licked her lips. "Since my mother is now here, I see no reason to object to a month. If that's agreeable to you, my lord?"

She glanced at Noah and prayed she wouldn't see

desperation or need for escape in his eyes. She was pleased to see neither, though his look was unreadable beyond that.

"Fine."

He turned away to look out the window and Marion's heart sank. Though Noah cared for and desired her, she still wasn't certain he could ever love her. And though they had no choice but to marry, she somehow hoped she would know his heart felt the same as hers before they exchanged vows before God.

"Very good. Then we have much to plan. Tomorrow I'll have Miss Fox come to fit you for your gown, and for gowns for your mother."

Tabitha and Audrey began to discuss the virtue of a gray gown versus a silver gown for a wedding and Marion shut them out. Her only focus was Noah. He seemed very far away at the other end of the carriage and she wondered what she would have to do, to say, to bring him close to her. To bring him into her heart as she had taken him into her body. How they could find a way to love each other?

"I'm so glad the ball went well," Ingrid Hawthorne said as she brushed her daughter's hair. Marion shut her eyes at the feel of it, each brush stroke bringing back happy childhood memories.

"It did go very well. People seemed to warm to me within the first hour. Charlotte wasn't there, and I was allowed to dance with Noah twice."

She smiled at the thought of Noah's strong arms around her, holding her and claiming her in front of hundreds of people. Surely the world had seen they were to be together.

"And other men, as well."

Marion opened her eyes to meet her mother's stare. "Yes. But I don't remember them. They're all the same. Noah is the only one who stands out in my mind. The only one who holds my interest."

Ingrid sighed as she rose to her feet and paced to the window to stare outside. Marion could tell her mother had something on her mind, something she was reticent to share.

"That will work out well for you since you two are to be married so soon."

Marion rose from her seat and gathered her swishing blue skirt into her hand. She'd been too busy chattering with her mother to remove her gown.

"Why do you sound worried when you talk about me marrying the man I love?"

Ingrid bit her lips as she turned. "I worry more that you're *required* to marry him. A forced life together can be a hardship as easily as it can be a blessing."

She dipped her head. "You mean like what happened with you and Papa."

"Yes, that's part of my reluctance. I loved another person when your father and I wed. It didn't matter to my father or to Walter that I didn't desire the marriage. Ultimately it led to so much pain for all of us. I don't want to see that happen to you and Noah." She brushed Marion's hand gently before returning to her watch over the street.

The hairs on the back of Marion's neck bristled. "I know Noah cares for me, Mama. Perhaps he doesn't love me the same way I love him, but he can learn, can't he? We can still build a happy life together."

"I don't want to hurt you. It's the very last thing I would ever do on purpose, but I never had a chance to shield you from pain as a child." Her mother's head dipped. "Perhaps I'm only overcompensating now. I believe Noah will make a go of it in good faith, but if he doesn't really want a marriage with you, eventually he'll resent your union."

The blood slowly drained from Marion's face. That was the last thing she wanted to hear, but she also recognized the truth in her mother's statement.

"What do you think I should do, then?"

Her mother shook her head. "I'm probably not the best one to ask, but perhaps you should share with Noah how you feel about him if you haven't already. You'll certainly see where he stands and come away with a better understanding about what your life with him will be like. Have you told him you love him?"

"No." Marion shook her head. "I've been too much of a coward. I was afraid he'd laugh at me or turn me away. But perhaps it would be better to know that now than in a few years when it will hurt all the more." She gathered her hair back into a clumsy bun at the nape of her neck and thanked the heavens she hadn't changed.

"Where are you going?"

She paused at the doorway and glanced back at her mother. "Downstairs to tell him right now. If I don't, I'll never sleep, and tomorrow I may convince myself that I don't want to know if he could ever grow to love me."

Her mother stared at her. "Marion, you are so brave. I admire that. I admire you. I wish have could have been more like you." Marion blushed and her mother blinked at tears. "He would be a fool not to love you. Now good luck."

Marion nodded, then slipped into the hallway. As she shut the door and leaned back against it, Marion drew in a long breath. She needed more than luck to face the handsome man downstairs.

"You look as though you could use a drink."

Noah looked up from the fire burning brightly and met his best friend's dark eyes. He hadn't realized he'd been lost in thought for so long, but from Griffin's expression he had been.

"Perhaps two," he chuckled, though he had to force the laughter.

"We'll start slowly." Griffin handed him a glass of brandy as he motioned to the two chairs before the fire. Noah followed his friend's silent order and sat. "Things seemed to have gone well tonight."

Noah nodded. "Yes, mother and Audrey were pleased, and after a few moments of terror, Marion seemed to relax as well." His eyes returned to the fire as he recalled how beautiful she was that night. "I'm glad. I only want her to be happy and the sooner she feels at ease with Society, the happier she'll be."

A small smirk lifted one corner of Griffin's lip as he took a sip of his drink. "Her happiness is important to you."

Noah froze as the trap Griffin wished to set closed around him. Though he trusted his best friend with his life and with his sister, he wasn't certain he was ready to reveal his feelings for Marion just yet.

"We are to be married. I suppose my job is to insure her happiness the best I can, isn't it?" He sighed. He sounded defensive.

Griffin shook his head. "Seems to me to be more than that. I've never seen you so focused on one woman before. You breathe, eat and sleep Marion Hawthorne." His friend grinned again. "And you blush like a schoolboy when the subject is broached. Sort of like you are now."

Noah's hands came up to his face and he did feel the telltale heat of a blush warming his cheeks. Damn Griffin for taking so much pleasure in his discomfort.

"You're a bastard, you know that?" He gave his friend a half-teasing frown. "You poke your nose where it doesn't belong."

Rising to his feet, he paced across the room to refill his drink. Though Griffin laughed, he could feel the other man's eyes following him, concerned and intrigued.

"I think you need a friend to talk to. And since I'm the only one left in our circle who can stand you, I'll have to do. Do you want to talk about what's going on? Or shall I just wheedle it out of you the deeper in drink you sink?"

Noah spun back around for a biting retort, but found he could think of nothing to say. Griffin was right. He needed to talk about his confused emotions. At least sober he could control the way he said what was on his mind.

"I had a plan, you know."

Griffin laughed. "You always do."

"And this was not the plan." He set his drink down on the mantel and folded his arms. "This wasn't supposed to happen. I wasn't supposed to go down to Woodbury and get tangled up in this mess."

His friend arched a brow. "Why *did* you go to Woodbury?"

"Investigation." He waved off the question with a shake of his head. "It was only to be a bit of an adventure before I settled down and got married like I was supposed to do. To a respected young woman in the *ton*. To Charlotte." He frowned as he thought of the pain he'd caused Charlotte, of the promise he'd made to her and broken.

"Sounds like heaven." Griffin twisted his face.

"Perhaps not, but it was controlled and staid and proper." He ran a hand through his hair as he sank back into his chair. "I was definitely *not* supposed to meet some country chit and get coerced into marrying her."

Griffin let the silence in the room stay for a long moment as he stared at Noah. Noah knew why his best friend did it. He wanted the comment to hang in the air for a moment, to let the emotions Noah felt behind his words build as he waited. Finally, Griffin smiled.

"And you weren't supposed to fall in love with said 'country chit' either, were you?"

Noah sighed, surprised at the relief that filled him when Griffin said the words. Now that *someone* had expressed them, the tension that filled him every time he thought of his feelings for Marion left him.

"No." He gave a hollow laugh. "I was most definitely not supposed to fall in love with her. But I did."

Griffin couldn't cover the shock that leapt to his brown eyes. Noah couldn't really blame him. After years of avoiding love, even professing that it didn't exist, this was a change for him. Even more of a change was being able to admit his feelings.

"I know." Griffin cleared his throat. "It's obvious by every way you behave when she's around. But how long have *you* known?"

Noah shrugged one shoulder as he swirled the liquor in his glass. "I'm not sure. One day I looked at her and I just knew. It was like… like…"

"A thunderbolt."

Noah smiled at his friend. Griffin did understand, more than Noah had ever realized. "Yes."

"Have you told her?"

"No." Noah thought of the night they made love. The way he had held her, the way he'd kissed her. Weren't they ways he'd told her he loved her? "Not in words. I want to do it right."

Griffin shook his head and poured himself a second drink. "The words are important. Women need to hear them. If you feel this way about her, you need to say it."

Noah ran his hand through his hair a second time as he set his drink down on the sideboard between them. "I know. And I will tell her… I will when the time is right."

"When?" Griffin's eyes narrowed and Noah felt him searching his face. He turned away from the scrutiny.

"Soon!"

Instead of reacting to his friend's sudden outburst, Griffin leaned back in his chair with a short laugh of disbelief. "Incredible. After all these years. Incredible."

Noah glared at his friend. "What?"

Griffin leaned his elbows on his knees and met Noah's gaze evenly. "You're afraid."

The statement hit Noah like a punch to the stomach and he reeled away to press his back flat against the cushioned seat.

His first reaction should have been anger to be accused of cowardice, but that wasn't what twisted his gut into knots.

It was recognition that his keen friend spoke the truth.

"I..." he stammered, trying to find the words. "I've never loved anyone before. I've risked my life for cases, but never my heart. I don't know even how to do it."

Griffin's laughing face softened. "You just say how you feel and trust it will set you free. Risking your heart is terrifying, but the alternative is even worse."

"What's the alternative?" he asked with a hard swallow.

Griffin held his gaze once more. "A life without her."

Noah shivered as he stood up. "No, I don't think I could live with that."

His friend nodded. "Then you already know what you must do."

"I know what I must do," Marion muttered as she stumbled up the back staircase toward her room. Her eyes blurred with tears and she came to a halt to lean back against the stairwell.

What an idiot she was! To go downstairs ready to confess to Noah how much she loved him only to hear him telling Griffin how sorry he was that he'd ever become involved with her. That it 'wasn't the way it was supposed to happen'.

All of Noah's reassurance that she would make a good wife, that they could be happy, had been an act on his part. A chivalrous way to ease her worries even while he hid how unhappy he was at the thought of a union with her... what had he called her?

A country chit.

And what had making love to her been? Just another night with a warm body? Or a way to make her believe, yet again, that he cared for her even though he obviously didn't.

Nausea swept over her but she choked back the bile in her throat and continued up the stairs. The hallway was nothing but a blur, but her feet found her room from feel and memory. She twisted the door handle and fell inside. When her body hit her bed she allowed herself to succumb to the wracking tears she'd wanted to shed since she heard Noah proclaim that she wasn't in his plans.

She'd run away so she wouldn't hear more. Run away from his tired voice, from Griffin's agreeing silence. But the pain in her heart she couldn't escape. It kept her in its grip. Unavoidable and inescapable.

"Marion? What in the world?"

She glanced up from her tearstained pillow to see her mother enter from the adjoining door. She stood in the doorway for a brief moment before she rushed to her daughter's side and gathered her into a warm, comforting embrace.

As a little girl, Marion had believed if only her mother had been there to hold her all her pain would have gone away. But she now realized just how wrong she'd been. Even her mother's comfort couldn't wipe away this agony.

"What happened?" her mother asked as she rocked her back and forth like she would a child. "What did he say to you?"

Marion drew in a shuddering breath as she tried to form words through her sobs.

"He said I wasn't in his plan," she hiccuped. "He doesn't love me."

She broke into hard tears again as she pressed her face into her mother's lavender scented shoulder. Ingrid clucked her tongue and Marion could hear the anger in her mother's voice. "Heartless man."

"No." She struggled to sit up. "He is a decent man trying to do the right thing. I'm glad I kn-know." She wiped her eyes with the back of her hand. "Now I can do what I need to do."

"And what is that?" Her mother dug a handkerchief from her pocket and handed it over to Marion. She took it with a wordless smile of thanks.

"I must leave here as soon as I can. You were right. I can't marry a man who doesn't love me. A man who views me as an inconvenience and a duty." She choked on another batch of tears. She had to be strong. "Please, Mama. Will you help me?"

Her mother's face softened. "For years I could do nothing to make your life easier. I'll do anything I can now."

"Then take me away from here. Help me leave with as little upset as possible. Help me hide until Noah's sense of duty has been spent and he's gone back to the life he wanted in the first place. With the *ton*, with a woman of breeding."

She shivered at those words. Of course Noah would find a new woman to marry. She'd seen the predatory looks on the women's faces at the ball when he walked by. Many of them wished to have him as their husband, even more as a lover. Would he choose one of the young women who'd fawned over him? Or would he make things up to Charlotte Ives? Call Marion a dalliance he regretted but that he'd come to his senses?

"Oh!" She struggled to her feet and hurried to the window to look out as she twisted the handkerchief in her hand around and around.

"When do you want to go?"

"Tomorrow." She nodded at her own reflection in the glass. "We'll behave as if nothing is wrong and simply climb into your carriage and ride away. We can enlist Sally's help to prepare us for our journey without rousing the suspicions of the house staff."

She turned to face her mother. Ingrid looked uncertain as. "Are you certain you want to do something so rash as to sneak away?"

Marion nodded. "I have no choice. If I confront Noah,

he'll try to appease me with pretty words and with…" She blushed. "Making a clean break is best for us all."

She could only imagine what Noah would do if she confronted him. He would try to convince her to stay and it would only break her heart even further. She couldn't bear the thought of him lying to her in order to keep her near him, or worse yet, tell her the truth that he could never love her but that he was planning to force her into the marriage regardless.

Her mother pursed her lips. "Very well, my dear. If you feel running is your only chance, I'll help you. I certainly understand wanting to flee. I'll make all the arrangements for our leaving and for a place for you to stay until Lord Woodbury has ceased any search for you."

Marion nodded, but a sudden wave of exhaustion worked through her. Now that the decision had been made, the only thing she wanted to do was collapse on her bed and cry herself to sleep. Alone.

"I should rest if we're to travel tomorrow." She hugged her mother. "Goodnight, Mama."

"Do you want me to stay?"

She shook her head slowly. "No. I need to be by myself for a while."

Her mother nodded slowly as she leaned down to place a kiss on her daughter's forehead. "Marion, Marion. You'll find your happiness someday, my dear. I promise you."

Marion somehow found the ability to nod as she watched her mother slip from the room. As soon as she was gone, she dropped her head into her hands and let out a low sob.

CHAPTER TWENTY-SEVEN

Noah paced across the sitting room floor and checked the small clock on the wall once more. It was two in the afternoon, and he was waiting for Marion's arrival. Each time the pendulum swung his anxiety grew.

In all the years of spying, all the times he'd nearly been caught, he'd never felt such a sickness in the pit of his stomach. But telling a woman he loved her, a simple task in theory, made him weak. If it hadn't been so painful he would have laughed at how far he'd fallen in such a short time.

The door creaked open and Noah spun around, but his expression fell when he saw it was only his mother, sister and Griffin who came to greet him. It was all he could do to control the twist of disappointment from coming to his face.

"Good afternoon." He crossed the room to kiss his mother's and Audrey's cheek and shake Griffin's hand.

"Well, you look suitably awful," Griffin teased in a low voice. "How very romantic she'll find your bloodshot eyes."

Noah turned away with a glare. "Will Marion and her mother be joining us soon?"

He did his best to ignore Griffin's chuckle as he took his seat beside Audrey. His sister reached up and absently wound her hand through her husband's. Noah winced with jealousy. He hoped he would soon enough be able to show his feelings for Marion with the same ease. Until then, his sister and brother-in-law's happiness was only a reminder of what he risked to lose.

"Did you not receive my message?" Tabitha asked as she motioned for the maid to pour tea for their party.

"No. I was out running a few errands."

He'd gone to pick up the ring he'd had designed for Marion. He planned to go down on one knee and propose to her properly. Much the same way he had planned to propose to Charlotte, but with real emotion and passion behind the words he would say.

"She and her mother went out this morning to visit and shop." Tabitha cocked her head. "In fact, I'm a bit surprised they haven't returned as of yet. I thought certain they'd be home for luncheon, but they've yet to arrive or send word."

Noah's heart leapt with concern, even though rationally he knew he had nothing to worry about. "She's sent no explanation for her tardiness? That doesn't seem like Marion."

Audrey shook her head with a laugh. "You worry too much. She had a wonderful debut last night and it's likely she and her mother met with people who desired to increase their acquaintance. It's often difficult to tear oneself away from the matrons of the *ton*. Even more difficult to do it without offending them."

Noah was surprised that the worry he felt was growing. He'd come to trust his instincts over the years and now stood up with a frown.

"Was there anything out of the ordinary when she departed?"

Audrey drew back at his intense stare. "Noah, what on earth has come over you?"

"Please don't argue. Answer the question," he managed through clenched teeth.

His sister shook her head. "She seemed fine. A bit sad, but there is bound to be a modicum of let-down after such an exciting night."

Noah interrupted her before she was finished speaking.

"She seemed upset, and you did nothing to inquire after the reasons?"

"Noah!" Griffin said as his face grew red. "I would adjust your tone. There's no need to attack my wife."

"Really, Noah," Tabitha agreed. "You're getting so upset over nothing."

Audrey stared at him with the eyes of a former spy and he could tell his sister realized he was truly worried, not simply acting the over-protective fiancé.

"I'd never let her leave this house upset without trying to find the cause." Her voice was soft, but her eyes never left his. "I did speak to her but she revealed nothing. Why this concern?"

"A feeling," Noah answered as he moved toward the door.

Audrey hurried to her own feet and followed him. "A feeling…?"

Noah nodded. "I want to see her room."

Now Tabitha and Griffin were both close behind the siblings.

"Noah!" Tabitha cried in outrage. "That would be entirely inappropriate. You cannot go barging into the young woman's room."

He ignored his mother's pleas and began to climb the stairs two at a time. Something was wrong. Something had happened. Marion wouldn't leave the house in upset and simply not return without an explanation. It wasn't in her nature.

"Noah!" Audrey caught up to him in hurried strides and blocked his way with her body. "Your feelings are generally correct on these subjects, but Mama is right. You can't go searching through her room. I'll go. You wait in the foyer."

Noah hesitated, but saw the wisdom his sister's advice. With a frown, he nodded and turned back to the main floor. At the bottom of the stairs, Griffin and Tabitha stared at him with a mixture of shock and worry.

"I don't understand you, Noah," his mother said as he stepped off the last stair. "Causing all this uproar over a shopping excursion."

"You're right, Mother." He put an arm around her while he continued to watch up at the staircase where his sister had vanished. "I've probably lost all my instincts over the years and am panicking over nothing. If that's the case, I'll apologize wholeheartedly to everyone involved. But if not…"

He trailed off as his sister came hurrying down the stairs. Her face was pale and she clutched a note in her hand. Instantly Noah knew.

Marion was gone.

Marion gripped the seat edge as the carriage rocked along the bumpy road out of London. They'd almost escaped the city, leaving the plush houses and crowded neighborhoods behind as the countryside became greener and wider. The hour since they left the Berenger mansion that morning had dragged by, for Marion knew each moment took her further and further from the man she loved.

She winced, but didn't cry. She'd run out of tears and didn't intend to weep anymore. She hadn't when she watched Noah leave the house after his enlightening conversation with Griffin Berenger. She hadn't when she wrote the note to explain her departure. She hadn't even when she said her last goodbyes to Tabitha and Audrey, though it had been difficult. Audrey had even seemed to sense her pain, though Marion had withheld the cause from her.

In a few hours Noah would discover she was missing. She wanted to put as much distance between them as possible during that time. He would certainly make some chase, but if he couldn't find her right away, she hoped he'd just give up.

Or did she?

"You seem tired, my dear." Her mother guided Marion's head to her comfortable shoulder.

Sally looked up from her sewing. "You should have eaten before we departed, Miss."

Marion shook her head. "No. I couldn't have had a thing and if I'd gotten ill Audrey and Tabitha never would have allowed our pretended visits."

Ingrid shook her head. "Perhaps being forced to stay would have been the best thing for you."

Marion straightened with a gasp of shock. "You were the one who said I shouldn't marry a man who didn't love me. I thought you agreed with my decision."

She took a sidelong glance at her maid. Normally she wouldn't have said anything so personal in front of a servant, but Sally was different.

"I did." Ingrid patted her hand. "But seeing you so miserable makes me question whether or not I let my own unhappiness in my marriage to your father cloud my judgment."

"I would have been just as wretched staying," Marion reasoned. "Only then I would have been unhappy and married."

Her mother raised both eyebrows. "We'll see. If Noah comes after you, then we'll be certain you're important to him."

"This isn't a test, Mama." Marion sighed. "I'm doing it to set us both free. I only hope we can put enough distance between us that he doesn't find us. The last thing I want is some pathetic scene where I blubber and he tries to convince me I'm important to him."

Ingrid winced at Marion's harsh self-judgment but didn't argue. For a long time the two women simply sat lost in reverie.

She was so lost in emotional turmoil that it took her a moment to realize the carriage had stopped. With a frown, she pulled back the window curtain and looked around. Outside, two horses grazed by the roadside and she heard male voices. Had Noah found her so soon?

Her heart leapt with joy at the thought before she could control the happy emotions that swelled inside her. With a scowl she folded her arms and pushed them back. She didn't *want* Noah to find her.

"Who is that?" Sally broke the silence as she, too, pulled back the curtain. Her face fell. "Oh miss, there's two of them…"

"I would suggest you get down from there, sir."

Marion froze and her eyes trailed first to her mother, then to the carriage door. Her father's voice. That was her father's voice.

"Walter," her mother gasped.

Marion didn't pause to think, but leapt to the carriage door and pulled back against it with all her might to keep anyone from entering. Her mother's vehicle wasn't fancy enough to have a lock.

"Stay quiet," she whispered to the other two frightened women. "Perhaps it isn't him."

"Marion, open this door!"

She shut her eyes. It was him.

The door lurched under her grip as her father tugged and pulled at the handle. She braced her feet against the floorboards though ultimately her struggle was futile. It wasn't as if her father would give up and leave. Not if he'd tracked her all the way to London. He wanted something. He wanted her.

"Go away!" She pulled even harder.

"I'll rip the door out of your hands!"

True to his threat, Marion felt the handle slipping from her grip as her much more powerful father yanked. She careened backward across the carriage floor as it popped open.

She struggled to sit up as her father's sneering face blocked the light from the sunny day outside. Instinctively, she rose up and moved in front of her mother to protect the other woman.

"You aren't wanted here, Papa." She hoped her voice didn't reflect the fear she felt. The last thing she wanted was for her father to sense her weakness.

"I didn't ask." He smiled maliciously at her, but then his eyes went to her mother and he paled.

At first Marion thought he was having a romantic reaction to seeing the woman he'd once been married to, but when she looked closer she could see it wasn't love or desire in his eyes, but something even more powerful.

It was hate.

She gasped and edged closer to her mother.

"Walter." Ingrid's voice trembled from behind her as her hand gripped Marion's shoulder.

"I heard Woodbury found you," her father hissed. "I couldn't believe it was true." His eyes strayed to Sally, who was crouching in the corner of the vehicle. "And *you*. Mr. Lucas would probably like to take your insubordination out of your scrawny backside. I think I'll give him the opportunity."

Marion flinched. Was Josiah Lucas there, too? Sally had said there were two men. Nausea washed over her as she remembered the older man's desire to have her. Perhaps being ruined by Noah wouldn't be enough to keep him from taking her.

"Is Lucas here?" she asked.

Her father sneered. "No, but I can send for him quick enough to collect his wayward serving bitch."

Sally whimpered and Marion's ire was raised to a point past reason. "What do you want? Why did you follow me?"

Walter glanced back at her. "Why do you think? I won't *give* you away to some man when I can sell you."

"You can't sell what has already been taken!" she snapped, casting a glance at her mother. How humiliating to have to discuss her tarnished virtue like this. "Lucas won't reduce your debt now."

He grinned. "You think not? We've already talked about a new way to pay my vowels. Now that Woodbury doesn't want you, there's no reason I can't take you back."

Marion turned her face away in disgust and utter terror. She'd never realized just how desperate her father was. Her only chance was to make him think Noah would be coming for her. Perhaps he'd leave them be, for he feared Noah.

"On the contrary, Papa. Noah can't get enough of me. We're heading back to Woodbury to prepare for the wedding. He had to attend to some business in London, but he'll be following shortly." She arched an eyebrow with what she hoped was the cool sophistication Tabitha Jordan had so much of. "I assure you, if he finds me missing, he'll be very displeased."

Her father began to laugh. "You little liar. Just like your mother." His tone turned to a hiss of hatred as he turned on his estranged wife. "Did you teach her to be a whore, as well?"

"Papa!"

"Go ahead, Ingrid. Why don't you tell your daughter the truth since we're having this little intimate family moment." He shook his fist. "Tell her what a wanton you are. Tell her what kind of blood she has running through her veins."

"That's enough." Ingrid sat up straighter and looked at Marion's father with a dignity more befitting one of a higher class. "You and I had an agreement, and I expect you to keep your end of it."

"What agreement?" Marion shook her head in confusion.

Her father ignored her question. "Why should I keep up my end of it? You haven't. You revealed yourself to her. That wasn't the bargain we struck."

"What bargain are you talking about?" Marion repeated looking from one parent to another. Their eyes were locked in silent combat.

"Walter, don't." Her mother's voice was low and pleading, but it didn't stop her father's smile or his reply.

"Your mother loved another man." Her father's dark eyes narrowed as he glanced over Marion's head at his wife.

"She lay with him after we were married and voila." His rage turned back on her. "*You.*"

Marion reeled back until she found she was pressed against the carriage seat with nowhere to go. No way to escape her father's words. Even the outside gave no release, for the carriage had started moving again and was racing along at a healthy clip.

"You're lying." She looked up at her mother with pleading eyes. "Tell me he's lying."

Tears began to slip down her mother's cheeks and gave Marion all the answer she needed.

"I'm sorry, my love. It's true. Your father…" She shut her eyes and corrected herself. "Walter knew the courts would assume you were his flesh and blood. He agreed to keep you from being called a bastard if I would stay in the marriage and keep getting money from my family. But when that ended, he used those same laws against me to keep me from you forever."

Sally gasped, but Marion hardly heard the sound over the rushing of her own blood in her ears.

"Oh, God."

A wave of nausea washed over her and she thanked her stars she hadn't eaten. The things she was hearing were just too much, but they explained everything in her life. Why her father had been so cold to her. Why he'd hated her mother. Why she'd never felt a strong connection to him.

"Why didn't you tell me the truth?"

Her question was posed to both parents. Her mother had the chance when she arrived in London. And her father could have told her when she came of age and been rid of her forever. Instead he'd kept her in indentured servitude and nearly sold her virtue to a lecher and a murder suspect.

"Why would I tell you?" Her father laughed humorlessly. "You were a commodity. And after everything I'd been through, I had a right to make something from your existence."

"By nearly selling me to a man who may have killed his first wife?" Marion burst out with a rage she hadn't realized existed in her.

Walter's eyebrows furrowed. "What are you talking about, girl?"

"Georgina Ross. Her fall wasn't an accident."

She gave a glance to Sally but the girl was strangely silent and stared at the floorboards. Why didn't she speak? Why didn't she tell Walter Hawthorne exactly the kind of man he had bargained with?

"Of course it wasn't. Lucas didn't kill her though. She killed herself." Walter shrugged. "Not that it makes much difference now. He won't have you as a wife, though perhaps he'd still like a night with you."

Marion's heart sank as she spun to face her friend. The maid's eyes were answer enough that her accusations, too, had been a lie. Again she'd been betrayed. First her parents, now this woman who'd professed to be her friend. Noah had warned her Sally might only be using her interest to further her own desires, and he'd been right. The maid had used Noah's investigation just to get away from Josiah Lucas.

"Sally?"

"I'm sorry, miss," Sally said through tears. "I tried to tell Georgina not to do it, but she didn't listen. And after she killed herself, Mr. Lucas refused to let me leave."

"And so you used my fears and Noah's investigation as a way to escape?" Marion shook her head in shock. "You allowed me to remain in that house, knowing that I was in danger from Lucas's desires and all along you had information that would have ended our hunt for answers all the sooner."

"I'm sorry."

"I could have been raped!" Marion said in a near-scream that revealed more of her tangled emotions than was wise considering her father was taking her captive against her will. She needed all her self-control to escape.

She refused to look directly at anyone in the carriage. It

was just too humiliating.

"Why are you here now Papa, Walter, whoever you are? What do you want from me?"

Walter caught her chin and forced her face up painfully so she looked him in the eye. "I want payback for all I went through. If I can't earn back what I spent for your upkeep by your marriage, then I'll earn it while you lie on your back. Mr. Lucas has associations with men who will be more than happy that you're already a whore."

Marion tensed. He was talking about selling her into prostitution. Her body began to tremble uncontrollably at the thought.

"And as for you…" He glared at Ingrid. "You must face some punishment, too."

Marion shivered as she stared at the man who'd raised her. The man who was now a stranger to her in every sense of the word. They were all in terrible danger.

And Noah had no idea where they were or how to find them.

CHAPTER TWENTY-EIGHT

"Don't you dare leave this house without thinking through a plan!"

Audrey hurried across the foyer to block Noah's exit. Her eyes flashed and he could see there would be no arguing with her.

She was correct anyway.

"What would you have me do? Stand here and scratch my head while the woman I love goes running off to God knows where for God knows what reason?" He held up the note Marion had left and shook it over his head. "This gives me no clues, it only says she doesn't want me trapped into anything I don't want."

Audrey's eyes softened. "I knew you loved her."

He shook his head in exasperation. "Of course I love her. But that doesn't do me any good unless I find her and tell her."

"Where would she go?" Tabitha asked as she stroked her chin. "Her mother is with her, so they may head south first."

"Yes, but Marion might avoid Dover all together if she doesn't want Noah to find her," Griffin added with a shrug. "She could go north just to throw you off the trail."

"Very helpful, Grif, thank you," Noah spat.

His friend sighed heavily. "Perhaps *now* would be a

good time to trade in on those years you two spent with the War Department."

Audrey and Noah locked eyes. Yes, Golding would help. He rushed for the door and was surprised that when he reached for the doorknob there was a sharp knock. He drew back and stared at his family for a moment.

"Well answer it." Griffin laughed. "You all look as though you don't know how a door works."

Noah did as he'd been ordered and turned the knob. Charlotte Ives stood on the stoop with a maid behind her. She glanced down at her fingernails and didn't yet see that Noah, himself, had answered.

"Lady Charlotte Ives to see Lord Woodbury. I'm told he's here," she said with a yawn designed to make it look as though she couldn't care less.

"Charlotte?"

Her eyes darted to his face and a blush colored her pale cheeks. "Lord Woodbury." She paused and cocked her head. "Have you taken a position as a butler here?"

Normally Noah would have taken a moment to appreciate Charlotte's unusual stab at humor, but today he had more pressing concerns. "No, I was on my way out."

"I'm glad I caught you then." She motioned her head toward the foyer in a subtle reminder that he hadn't invited her in. "I need to speak to you on a matter of utmost importance."

Noah sighed in exasperation, but stepped back to allow her entry. Charlotte drew back at the crowd of Jordans assembled in the foyer, but didn't comment.

"G-good morning." She cocked her head at Noah with question in her eyes.

"Charlotte." Audrey smiled tightly. "Would you care for some tea?"

Noah's eyes grew wide. He had no time to share tea with the woman he'd once been planning to marry. He needed every moment if he was going to catch up with the woman he would marry even if it meant dragging her to Gretna Green kicking and screaming.

"Charlotte, I realize we have much to discuss," he said before the situation could get more out of hand. "But I'm afraid I'm on my way to a very important appointment. Please feel free to stay for tea with my family." He turned and stalked back to the door, opened it a second time and prepared to hurry from the house.

"Isn't the safety of your new fiancée important enough to stay five minutes and hear me?"

He froze at Charlotte's soft voice and turned back. She stood with a hand on each hip and looked at him with a face half-accusatory and half-understanding.

"Explain yourself." He shut the door behind him as he came back into the foyer.

"This isn't something to discuss in the entryway in front of servants." She turned her back to him.

"Of course, how rude of us." Tabitha motioned to the breakfast room with one sweeping gesture. "Come in."

Charlotte smiled at Tabitha and the crowd moved inside. Noah shut the door behind them and immediately turned to his former paramour.

"What do you have to say about Marion? Time is of the essence, so please, don't punish me by dragging out what you have to say."

Charlotte raised a brow at his angry words and plopped into a chair by the fire. She stared up at him for a moment, then whispered, "You're in love with her. I didn't think you capable, but…" She shook her head as if she hadn't meant to say the words out loud. "I had a visitor yesterday evening. I thought nothing of it and decided to forget it even happened, but I pondered it all night. I cannot let what he said slip by. I had to tell you."

"Who?" Noah took the seat beside her. For the first time since they'd begun their closer acquaintance, she actually met his eyes.

"He told me his name was Walter Hawthorne."

The blood drained from Noah's face. "Marion's father."

"Yes. He said he had a proposition I might find interesting." Her eyes narrowed. "I should have thrown him out right then, but he told me it was a way to get even with you for the humiliation you caused me."

Noah's heart clenched, not only out of fear for what Hawthorne had planned for Marion, but for the fact he had caused Charlotte pain, yet she still came to him and told him the truth.

"What did he say?"

"He told me if I'd help him get Marion away from you, he would help me find my way back to you." A small smile crossed her lips. "I promptly told him I didn't want any man who would leave me and told him to get out of the house. I even called one of my larger footmen to escort him."

Noah rose to his feet. His hands trembled at his sides and his head throbbed. He had no idea if Marion had left his sister's house of her own accord or not, but he did know she was in great danger. Her father would surely hear she wasn't under his protection anymore and make chase. If the beating Hawthorne had given Marion was any indication, the consequences for Marion and her mother could be devastating.

"Thank you for telling me, Charlotte." He smiled down at her. "I know this couldn't have been easy for you."

She stood, too and returned his smile. "Noah."

It was the first time she'd ever said his Christian name and Noah leaned back in surprise.

"Find her and be happy."

"Thank you." He turned to his sister. "Audrey, contact Golding and start a search for Marion."

"Where are you going?" Audrey and Griffin followed him into the hallway.

"To find her. But if her father has her I may need help." He nodded to his sister.

"Then take Griffin. I can handle Golding and you may need another set of hands if you encounter trouble." She turned to her husband. "Be careful."

Noah turned away as the two shared a heated kiss. The last thing he needed was a reminder of what he could lose if he couldn't find Marion, or if he found her too late.

"Foster!" Griffin called out as he released his wife. "Foster, have the carriage brought around for my wife and bring me my pistol."

The Great Northern road out of London seemed to wind through city streets and bustling roads forever, even though Noah and Griffin rode horses which were easy to maneuver around carriages and crowds. Noah could only pray he'd chosen correctly and would stumble across Marion and her mother before something happened to them.

What had made Marion run? It was the one thing he still couldn't answer. Could her father have found her and threatened her? Her note had left him no clues, no secret message between the lines. He had to believe she'd indeed intended to leave him of her own free will.

But why? Why had she left the very day he was to declare his feelings for her? She'd seemed happy enough in the Berenger house, and had even kissed him goodnight after the ball. Were those the actions of a woman preparing to flee?

Something else had to have happened between the time they'd separated after the ball and that morning when she left. As soon as he found her, he would discover what that something was.

"What's that up ahead?"

Griffin's question startled Noah from his thoughts, and he cursed himself for letting his mind wander.

"Where?"

He scanned the area around them. They had finally departed the last of the city and were now in the outskirts where there were few people. There was a tree beside the road, an old oak with a trunk as thick around as two or three large men standing side by side. At first Noah saw nothing out of the ordinary, but then he noticed a man's foot sticking out from behind the tree as if he'd passed out.

"There, a man…"

"I see him." Noah guided his horse around the tree, then skidded Phantom to a hard halt and hopped off the creature. He grimaced when the men trying to help parted and he saw who it was lying on the ground: Ingrid Hawthorne's driver, and he had a large gash across his forehead. His arms were tied behind his back and he was unconscious.

"Wake up." Noah shook the man. Even though he was injured, and normally Noah would have let him wake on his own accord, this time he couldn't. "You, wake up."

The man's eyes slowly fluttered open, and with Noah's help he struggled to a sitting position that allowed Griffin to untie his hands. "Oh, my head."

"What happened?" Noah asked through clenched teeth.

"Lord Woodbury." The young man's eyes cleared with recognition. "Oh, I'm glad to see you, sir."

"What happened to Miss Marion and her mother?" he repeated, unwilling to participate in any pleasantries.

"Two men, sir. They stopped us as we passed by. One was Mr. Hawthorne and the other a burly chap I didn't catch the name of." The young man rubbed his wrists where he'd been tied. "I tried to stop them, but they cracked me over the head and that's all I remember."

"When?" Griffin asked as Noah bounded to his feet and ran a hand through his hair.

"I'm not sure how long I was out, sir." The boy checked the sun through the shade of the tree. "An hour, perhaps two?"

Noah cursed. A two-hour lead could put the three of them anywhere. "Did Hawthorne say anything about where he was taking them?"

"I'm sorry, sir." The boy got to his feet, but immediately teetered to the side. He barely caught himself on the tree trunk with one arm and looked very green.

"Griffin, take the boy back into the city. Make sure he's treated for his injury and get word to Golding about which road to follow."

He swung up on Phantom in one smooth motion and turned him back down the road.

"And where will you go?" Griffin asked.

He shrugged. "To find Marion. We can't leave the driver here, and he'll only slow us down if he rides with you in his condition. If you hurry, you'll catch my trail in a few hours."

Griffin opened his mouth as if to protest, but then took one more glance at the boy who was now vomiting on the other side of the tree. He looked at Noah with a grim nod.

"Be careful. Hawthorne is a desperate man. I'll send the cavalry as soon as I can get word to Audrey."

Noah lifted his hand to wave as he galloped off down the road. His heart throbbed and his mind raced. Marion was in terrible danger. If he couldn't find her soon, he had no idea what her so-called father would do. Or where he would take her. With a shiver at the thought, Noah dug his heels hard into Phantom and doubled his time toward the woman he loved.

CHAPTER TWENTY-NINE

Marion glared at her father, but her angry stare only served to amuse him. It had been almost two hours since he had abducted the three women and Walter had the upper hand in every way. Noah would have a difficult time tracking them, if he came at all. Despite her bluff, Marion knew he might read her letter, be relieved she'd set him free, and never come.

She choked back a sob at the thought and looked out the window. She was trying desperately to identify the scenery around them just in case she could manage an escape. Of course her father, no, the man she'd always *thought* was her father, had never taken her out much. She couldn't have said where they were even if she had a map and compass to aid her.

Even if she *could* figure it out, he never took his eyes off her and her mother. The women hadn't had the opportunity to speak at all, let alone plot an escape. She'd have to depend on herself to save them all.

"I need to relieve myself," she said loudly, crossing her arms and glaring at her father as if daring him to refuse her.

"You'll have to wait. We aren't stopping for at least a few more hours. We need to get distance between London and us in case that driver of Ingrid's wakes up."

Walter sneered at her mother and she mother shivered and looked away.

Marion tried to block an image of the strapping young

man who'd been their driver unconscious at the side of the road. "Fine. I'll just have to do it right here then. It will punish you as much as it does me."

Walter glared at her for a moment. She could see he was weighing whether or not he wanted to take the chance she was lying. Finally, he reached back and thumped on the wall three times. The carriage began a slow stop. A surge of triumph made Marion smile to herself. Once she was out of the vehicle, she was halfway to freedom.

"If you're lying to me." Walter leaned closer and put his face in hers. "If you try anything, your mother will suffer for it."

Marion glanced from her father to her mother for a moment. She was inclined to believe him. Although he'd beaten her weeks ago, Marion didn't believe he'd kill her. After all, he had raised her even though she wasn't his own flesh and blood. But he hated her mother, had hated her for years. If he had the opportunity to harm Ingrid, Marion had no doubt he'd take it.

Still, she and her mother were in just as much danger if they didn't fight. It was a risk they'd have to take.

The carriage door opened and the three women filed out. For the first time, Marion caught a glimpse of her father's accomplice. He was a burly man, but he didn't look too bright to her. Her mother and Sally might be able to take care of him if they worked together.

She saddled up to her mother while her father spoke to the man for a moment. "When I go to the bushes, have Sally distract the other man, then you hit him over the head with…" She looked around her. "With that big stick over there. Hit him as hard as you can. If he falls but tries to get back up, hit him again."

Her mother's eyes grew wide and for a moment Marion feared she'd refuse. But then a steel came into the gentle brown and she nodded. "I'll pretend he's your father."

Marion laughed despite herself and moved back away.

"Are you going to go then?" Her father asked, motioning for her to lead. "I'll follow at a respectable distance to be certain you don't try anything tricky."

Marion winked at her mother, then strode by her father with her head held high and headed toward some brush far in the distance. She wanted to be sure her father had to run a long way if he decided to go back to help his cohort.

She bustled about behind the bushes so he'd think she was taking care of her needs, all the while listening in the distance for some indication that Sally and her mother had done their part. She peeked around the hedges just in time to see the driver hit the ground. Unfortunately, her father saw the same thing at the same moment.

He started to stride back toward the carriage. "Hey!"

Marion ran out from behind the bushes and threw herself across her father's back while she wrapped her arms around his thick neck.

"Let go of me!" he bellowed as he began to twist and try to get hold of her. She kicked him in the back of his knee and he howled in pain, but responded by hitting her across the side of her head. She winced. Thank goodness he hadn't had a clear shot.

"You let us go and I'll let you go," she yelled back at him as she continued to hit and kick at him. She sighed with relief as Sally and her mother ran up to aid her. The relief was short-lived, though, as her father flipped her over his shoulder and to the ground. The air left her lungs and she gasped for air.

"You're going to be sorry you did that, girlie." He grabbed her hair and yanked her to her feet.

Marion grasped at her roots as the sting rushed through her scalp, but was surprised that suddenly he released her. When she turned, it was to see her mother sitting on her former husband's chest, pummeling him with her small fists.

"You may have gotten away with that with me, but not with my daughter," her mother screamed as she continued to beat at Walter Hawthorne.

He was too stunned to fight back for a moment, but when one of her mother's fists came in contact with his bulbous nose, it snapped him from his shock and he cried out.

Marion flung herself across his body so he couldn't swing at her or her mother and barked up at Sally, "Get some rope and help me tie him up."

Sally stared at the two women in shock, but then nodded mutely and ran over to the carriage.

"This is it, Walter." Beneath her, the man she'd known as her father struggled and let loose with a long string of curses that burned her ears. "You don't own me and you don't own her." Marion met her mother's eyes and the two women smiled. "And you never will."

Noah pushed his horse faster than the poor beast had ever run. But Phantom seemed to sense his master's urgency and continue on without so much as a whimper. It had been at least an hour he'd been riding and trying to track the carriage in the muddy roadway. An impossible task considering the road was moderately traveled. His frustration had grown until it reached a fever pitch.

He looked up from his quick glance at tracks and maneuvered Phantom around a bend. There, not one hundred yards ahead of him, was the carriage he'd been so desperately looking for.

"Marion!" he called out as he forced his horse even harder.

A woman ran to the side of the road at his call and to his relief he saw it was his fiancée. She appeared uninjured from the rapidly shrinking distance.

"Noah!" she cried out in relief.

He pulled the horse up short and swung off to catch her in his arms. Damning propriety, he brought his mouth down on hers and kissed her as hard and as deeply as he could. He felt her body relax against him almost instantly as she returned his kiss with the sweet fervor of a person who'd been through hell and now found themselves home.

Finally, he reluctantly pulled away and gave her the gentlest of shakes. "What did you think you were doing sneaking away like that?"

Marion paled as she regained her composure. She pulled from his embrace and nodded her head in the direction of the carriage. Near the wheel, two squirming men were tied. One was Walter Hawthorne.

"You son of a bitch!" Noah crossed the distance between them in a heartbeat. "I ought to kill you right here for kidnapping her. Your own daughter, man!"

Marion grabbed his arm to keep him from swinging against the defenseless man. "I need to tell you the truth. He didn't kidnap me. Well he did, but not until *after* I'd left you." She paused and turned her head away. "And he isn't my father."

Noah flinched. The pain in Marion's eyes and the guilt in Ingrid's told him what she said was all too true. It made him ache to see her in such agony.

"What?"

She sighed. "It's a long story. It seems everyone in my life has lied to me, including Sally."

Noah wheeled back. "I don't understand."

"Georgina Ross killed herself," she said with a sigh. "Sally knew all along, but used my fears to endear herself to me in the hopes I would help her escape Lucas's employ."

Noah stared at Marion with a shocked expression. She couldn't help a wry smile. "You told me making friends with the servants could help us. It's just too bad we didn't resolve this sooner so we could have avoided this mess. Your plans wouldn't have been ruined if she had."

She let him digest her last comment. It was a low blow, but seeing him again, feeling him kiss her when she knew she was nothing but an inconvenience to him, hurt her. And in her hurt, she lashed out.

"What do you mean, my plans?" he asked with a shake of his head. "I don't understand."

"I know you don't understand." She turned on her heel and walked toward her father. "No one understands and everyone is sorry. Well..."

She was about to go on a tirade, but to her surprise, her father caught her wrist with his suddenly untied hand. He dragged her across his chest as he slowly rose to his feet. The cold bite of steel touched her throat. She realized in horror that he was armed. She was a fool! She hadn't even thought to check him for a knife or pistol.

"Hawthorne," Noah yelled. She saw the wary fury in his eyes as he analyzed the situation they now found themselves in.

"You're going to let me go or I'll kill her and I promise it will hurt." Her father backed toward the carriage horse. "Ingrid, come untie this stallion."

Marion's mother looked to Noah with wide, questioning eyes. They grew even wider when he nodded. She scurried forward and began to clumsily unhitch the animal.

Noah looked at Marion with an unwavering, soothing stare. "You can go, Hawthorne. Leave the girl."

Her father laughed. "I don't trust you, Noah Jordan. I'll take her down the road with me a few miles and leave her for you to find. But don't you try anything or what you discover won't be worth having. I can see you've gone daft for the girl, so I trust you wouldn't want her injured."

A muscle in Noah's jaw twitched, but it was the only outward indication he gave of his fury. Marion was amazed at his self-control. Her heart was beating like butterflies wings and she trembled in her father's tight grip. She looked to the man she loved with pleading eyes.

"Put that knife down."

A new voice came from the road and Marion looked to

see Griffin with his gun trained on her father. Her heart leapt. As much as she despised the man right now, she didn't want him shot. Or for her to be in the crossfire.

"Put that away," Hawthorne warned as he dragged Marion closer to him. He shook the knife and she felt it dig into her flesh. "Put it away."

She looked again at Noah and saw something in his eyes. Walter was distracted and he was moving ever closer to the older man.

Swallowing back her fear, Marion moved her arm forward and brought her elbow back into her captor's chest with all the force in her body. Noah let out a guttural cry as Walter briefly loosened his hold on Marion and put an elbow into his temple. The man dropped immediately.

"Tie him up again." Noah panted as Griffin lowered his pistol. He turned to Marion. "The first thing I teach you when we get married is how to tie better knots."

Marion almost laughed at his quip but couldn't. Not when he'd mentioned the wedding that would never happen. "I'm not marrying you."

Noah's eyes widened. "You think not? I just chased you from London!"

"Don't make jokes." She turned and was dismayed to see both her mother and Sally watching the pair with interest. "Are you both unhurt?"

Noah watched as Marion crossed over to embrace her mother and say a few words to Sally. She'd been through an ordeal. A terrible one considering she'd apparently found out that Walter Hawthorne wasn't truly her father and that Sally had lied to her. But if she thought she could avoid his questions and his love, she was dead wrong.

"Come on." He strode forward and grabbed her arm. She pulled back, but he hauled her away nonetheless. "Griffin, get the ladies into the carriage and take them home. Marion and I will follow in a short while."

Griffin's eyebrows knitted together. "Noah, are you

certain..."

"Go!"

He swung up onto the horse, taking Marion with him and settling her in front of him in the saddle before he thundered off down the road and away from prying eyes.

"Where are we going?" Marion asked as she tried not to let her body touch Noah's. Each time it did, heat seeped through her gown and made her very aware that she wanted him. Despite the fact that she was about to tell him she would never marry him even if he dragged her off like a barbarian.

"Somewhere to talk," was his grim reply, then he snaked his hand around to rest on her belly.

Marion sucked in her breath through her teeth. Closing her eyes, she said a silent prayer that she wouldn't melt with his touch. "We aren't going back to London?"

"No." He pulled her toward him a fraction so her back pressed against his broad chest. "We aren't. We're going," he paused and pointed toward a secluded spot along the river. "There."

He pulled the horse up and helped her down. She didn't fight him when he took her arm and led her down to the river's edge. Soft heather was the perfect seat, and she sat down in it and stared up at him.

"I already told you I won't marry you." She refused to break their gaze, even as he sunk to his knees beside her and touched her face.

"Then tell me why." The anger and teasing were gone from his voice, replaced by genuine confusion.

She shook her head. "You don't want this."

"We had that discussion weeks ago." He clenched his jaw. "You didn't want this, I didn't want this. And then we grew closer. What changed to make you run away so suddenly?"

He brushed his knuckles over the curve of her cheek and the line of her jaw. Awareness crackled through her like an electric shock.

"Nothing." She swallowed hard. "Nothing. I just realized it was folly."

"Don't lie." He smiled as he leaned up and brushed his lips against her hair. "It doesn't suit you."

Her lower lip trembled and she turned her face so he wouldn't see how much it hurt her to have him touch her. "I heard you talking to Griffin last night. I heard you say that a country chit wasn't in your plans. I know you don't want to marry me, and I don't want you if you'll only grow to resent me after you're bored with my body."

Noah froze in his caresses, and Marion waited for the inevitable denials of what she'd heard. For a long moment he held her gaze, then he leaned forward and kissed her. The touch removed her careful guard and she responded. His tongue probed her mouth, tasting her, testing all the hollows and curves. She couldn't hold back the moan of pleasure at even the simplest of touches.

"I will *never* tire of your body," he reassured her against her ear. "But as much as I also respect your mind, you, my dear are a lousy spy."

She might have bristled at his words if he hadn't slid one hand up to cup her breast. Even through the muslin, her nipple hardened in anticipation of his mouth on her body, of him joining with her.

"I don't know what you mean." She tried to draw back, but he refused to let her.

"You didn't stay to hear the entire conversation."

"I heard enough."

He was lowering her back against the grass, and she somehow couldn't do anything to fight him. In fact, she arched against his chest like a hopeless wanton.

"Did you hear that I love you?" Noah's voice was

suddenly breathless, but it wasn't only from desire. She could hear the anticipation in his words, the need for her to say the same.

But was he telling the truth?

Her breath hitched. "No, I didn't."

He smiled. "Then you didn't hear enough. I love you, Marion Hawthorne. I love you and I cannot wait until you are my wife. In fact, after I ravish you here beside the river." To accentuate his words, he slipped one hand beneath her skirt and began a slow slide up her leg. "I plan to take you to Gretna Green and make you my wife. Before you can convince yourself of any more nonsense and try to run away from me again."

Her eyes blurred with a combination of tears at his confession and desire when his fingertips found her very center. "You love me?"

"With all my heart." He kissed her gently as he slipped one finger inside her.

"But..." She caught her breath as the wall of pleasure began to build in her. It took all her energy to focus on her rebuttals.

"No buts." With his free hand he cupped her chin and forced her to look at him. "Just tell me you love me."

"But..." Her self-control slipped away inch by inch, thrust by thrust.

"Tell me."

"I love you." No sooner had the words been said than she fell over the brink in a wave of pleasure that had her grasping at Noah's shoulders and arching against him. She found herself repeating her declaration over and over again.

Her hands trailed down to Noah's breaches buttons and one by one she wrenched them open. His erection popped out into her hand, hot and hard and ready to fill her. He hiked her skirt up even further and with little fanfare, thrust into her.

Immediately the wave she'd just ridden on crested again and with only a few hard thrusts she came, this time joined by Noah as he gripped her against him and drove his seed deep inside her.

For a long moment, they laid together, their bodies merged as Marion smoothed her palms across his back.

Finally, he withdrew from her and buttoned his pants while she smoothed her wrinkled skirt back down, but she didn't rise up from the grass and neither did he.

"I'm not even Marion Hawthorne any longer," she said with a sigh as she reached up to touch his face. "How do you know if you love me? Marion with no last name, the bastard."

"You'll have a last name." Noah frowned at her. "Mine. And as for being a bastard, no one need ever know about that."

"My father." She shut her eyes with a sigh. "I mean, Walter Hawthorne…"

Noah shook his head. Marion loved him, and in the years to come he'd teach her that she could trust him to take care of her. For now, he'd have to tell her.

"Hawthorne will be taken care of."

Her eyes widened and he understood she took his meaning to be sinister. As much as he'd like to wipe the man away, he wouldn't.

"Griffin has a spice plantation in India that probably could use one more worker. It will be a respectable job in a place where he'll never be able to harm you or your mother again."

"Josiah Lucas-"

He interrupted her again. "I'll make sure he's run out of the shire. I'll take great pleasure in destroying him."

"What about Sally?" Her brown eyes were finally clearing of some of the fear that had been in them before.

"She won't tell." He shrugged. "For all her faults, she seems to truly care for you."

"But she lied." Marion shook her head. "If she'd only told us the truth about Georgina's suicide from the beginning, you wouldn't have pressed your investigation and we wouldn't have been forced to marry."

Noah pursed his lips. "Then I plan to not only keep her on, but give her a raise in pay. If she's the reason we found each other, then bravo to her."

Though he could have stayed in the heather for days and simply made love to Marion, the afternoon was growing late and they had a long way to travel. Reluctantly, he drew himself up to stand and helped her.

"Marion." He took her hand and raised it to her lips. "I'll make everything right for you. I promise you with all my heart."

She smiled and the love they shared seemed to glow between them, as bright and warm as the sun above. "If I have you, everything will be right."

He swung her up on the horse and followed behind. After giving her a light kiss, he turned the mount northward and into a gallop.

"Noah!" Marion leaned back against him with a laugh. "Has making love deprived you of your sense of direction? We're still heading away from London."

Marion could feel him grinning even if she couldn't see it. "I told you. We're going to Gretna Green to give you that last name."

She tried to pivot, but couldn't without falling off the mount. "You must be daft! The gossip… the rumors…"

He laughed and gently turned her face to kiss her on the lips. "The rumor will be that your husband is completely besotted and couldn't wait to have you all to himself. And that, my love, will be the truth."

Marion laughed and settled back against him with a contented sigh. Somehow, despite all the trial and pain of the day's events, now that she was in Noah's arms, she was safe and happy. And as long as she was with him, she knew it would be so for the rest of her life.

Also in the Jordans Series

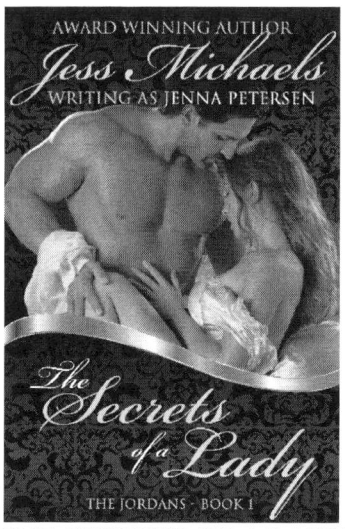

THE SECRETS OF A LADY
(THE JORDANS BOOK 1)

THE DESIRES OF A COUNTESS
(THE JORDANS BOOK 3)

Other Books by Jess Michaels

THE LADIES BOOK OF PLEASURES
A Matter of Sin
A Moment of Passion (Coming in 2014)
A Measure of Deceit (Coming in 2014)

THE PLEASURE WARS SERIES
Taken By the Duke
Pleasuring The Lady
Beauty and the Earl
Beautiful Distraction

MISTRESS MATCHMAKER SERIES
An Introduction to Pleasure
For Desire Alone
Her Perfect Match

ALBRIGHT SISTERS SERIES
Everything Forbidden
Something Reckless
Taboo
Nothing Denied

Jess Michaels raffles a FREE Kindle or Amazon gift certificate EVERY month to members of her newsletter, so sign up on her website:
http://www.authorjessmichaels.com/join-the-jess-michaels-newsletter/

Take a Sneak Peek at the final book in the Jordans Series, *The Desires of a Countess* **(November 2011):**

CHAPTER ONE

1816

"If he comes here, I'll run him out myself!"

"Calm down, Ginny."

Virginia Blanchard turned on her heel to stare at her best friend. Harriet Percy smiled back with a serene expression. Ginny frowned. How could her friend not see the problem?

"Did you just tell me to calm down?" She motioned wildly to the letter Harriet held in her hand. "After *this*?"

Her friend nodded. "You have no idea what this-this-" She glanced back down at the missive. "Simon Webber is like. He may not be the ogre you believe he is."

"He's a Blanchard!" Ginny snapped as if that explained everything. In her mind it did.

Her friend rose to her feet and returned the letter with a wry smile. "Actually, he's a Webber."

Ginny paused to shake her head, but most of the heat was gone from her voice and from her emotions. The fear was taking over, and that was much worse. She was so tired of being afraid. In the last few months, she'd thought her fears were gone for good, but now they returned with vengeance.

"Simon Webber's mother was raised a Blanchard," she whispered. "Which makes him my husband's cousin. If I've learned anything from the past four years in this family, it's that all those people are fiends."

Harriet's face softened with pity and Ginny winced. She didn't want that. Not even from her best friend.

"Jack is one of 'those people'."

Ginny sank into a chair by the fire. Was it too early for

a drink? Rubbing a hand across her throbbing temple, she struggled for calm and control.

"My husband is dead. Henry won't be raising Jack, I will. And I'd never raise him to behave like one of that family." Ginny tossed the envelope on the table with a disgusted sigh. "Or a Webber."

Harriet sat in the chair next to hers to place a warm hand on her own. "Don't assume the worst."

"I have no choice, don't you see? This man has been named trustee of Jack's inheritance. He'll have the power on a whim and at will to give or take my son's future until he comes of age and is given the title." She took in a shallow breath and somehow managed to keep weak, useless tears from filling her eyes. "After Henry's death, I swore no one would ever have the authority to do that again." She swallowed and found a bit of strength somewhere inside of her. "Unless I get rid of this man, I'll have failed my child one more time."

Harriet shook her blonde head. "Don't talk like that! No one could do more for a child than you have done for Jack."

Ginny pursed her lips as she dismissed all she'd gone through in the past. She had more pressing problems in the present. "I just hope all I've done won't be for nothing." She ran a hand over her eyes. "It doesn't bode well, though."

"Why?"

She motioned to the dreaded message with one slender finger. "First, the man didn't even bother to write himself. He let Henry's loathsome solicitor do the deed. Mr. Randall probably took enormous pleasure in removing my purse." She grimaced as she thought of thin weasel of a lawyer. "And the letter clearly states that this Webber isn't only the trustee of the estate until Jack comes of age, but he's to have some part in overseeing my son's upbringing, as well."

She jumped back up to pace the room. "Oh, this is so frustrating. At least when Henry was alive, I knew what I was dealing with."

"A bastard," Harriet interjected with heat.

Ginny smiled at her friend's loyalty. "But this Webber

could be far worse. He's an unknown enemy."

"Or so you believe."

Ginny couldn't fathom her friend's naivety. Of course, Harriet had never had to reckon with a husband or in-laws like hers. No, Harriet's late husband had been the love of her life.

"Knowing that family as I do, I feel I *must* assume the worst. And so I'll have to do my best to get rid of this man." Ginny glanced up at her best friend. "Will you help me force his retreat to London?"

With a nod, Harriet brushed her hand again. "You know I'd do anything for you. I only wish I could give you back some of the happiness you deserve."

Ginny dipped her head to shield Harriet from seeing the effect of her words. Happiness was a luxury she could ill afford. "Getting rid of this man will be the closest I can come to happiness."

Her friend's grip on her hand tightened. "Well, perhaps once you've done that, we can concentrate on finding you a new love. A new husband, even. Or at least someone to take away the loneliness that has haunted you for so long."

With her friend's words, every nerve in Ginny's body crackled. Just the thought of another husband made her sick with anxiety. Another man's hands on her, not with tenderness, but violence. The clumsy taking in the bedroom. The tears.

No. Those were things she'd left behind when Henry had mercifully left the earth. She never intended to revisit them again.

"Let's just concentrate on one thing at a time, shall we?" she asked with a shiver. "And right now all my attention has to be on Simon Webber. If he thinks he can waltz in here and take what rightfully belongs to my son, he's in for a nasty surprise."

Printed in Great Britain
by Amazon